Pamela Jooste was born in Cape Town, where she still lives. Her first novel, *Dance with a Poor Man's Daughter*, won the Commonwealth Best First Book Award for the African Region and the Sanlam Literary Award, and the Book Data South African Booksellers' Choice Award. Her second novel, *Frieda and Min*, was equally well received and both are also published by Black Swan.

Dance with a Poor Man's Daughter:

'Both moving and funny . . . A brave and memorable debut' *Observer*

'Tough, smart and vulnerable . . . emblematic of an entire people' *Independent*

'Highly readable, sensitive and intensely moving . . . A fine achievement' *Mail and Guardian, South Africa*

Frieda and Min:

'Perceptive and sensitive and extremely funny' Isobel Shepherd-Smith, *The Times*

'One of the new breed of women writers in South Africa who are telling our story with such power and talent' *Cape Times*

'She has created something rare; an uplifting book about life under apartheid' *The Economist*

Also by Pamela Jooste

DANCE WITH A POOR MAN'S DAUGHTER
FRIEDA AND MIN

and published by Black Swan

LIKE WATER IN WILD PLACES

Pamela Jooste

LIKE WATER IN WILD PLACES
A BLACK SWAN BOOK : 0 552 99867 2

Originally published in Great Britain by Doubleday,
a division of Transworld Publishers

PRINTING HISTORY
Doubleday edition published 2000
Black Swan edition published 2001

1 3 5 7 9 10 8 6 4 2

Set in 11/13pt Melior by
Kestrel Data, Exeter, Devon.

Black Swan Books are published by Transworld Publishers,
61–63 Uxbridge Road, London W5 5SA,
a division of The Random House Group Ltd,
in Australia by Random House Australia (Pty) Ltd,
20 Alfred Street, Milsons Point, Sydney, NSW 2061, Australia,
in New Zealand by Random House New Zealand Ltd,
18 Poland Road, Glenfield, Auckland 10, New Zealand
and in South Africa by Random House (Pty) Ltd,
Endulini, 5a Jubilee Road, Parktown 2193, South Africa.

Printed and bound in Great Britain by
Clays Ltd, St Ives plc.

For TGJ

The day we die
a soft breeze will wipe out
our footprints in the sand.
When the wind dies down,
who will tell the timelessness,
that once we walked this way
in the dawn of time?

(from a Bushman song)

THE CRY OF THE ELAND

In the Beginning

In the beginning is Tum Tum Boro the mother goddess, pregnant with all living things, animals and people.

On her right is Xwa Esa Xhe Guba who is Man with his hunting bag on his back.

Beside him are the future generations of men and women ready to go out and at their side fire and the trees of the future that will provide them with fuel and all that they need to sustain them and they and Tum Tum Boro and Xwa Esa Xhe Guba were made by the Creator who has no name and lives in the sun.

Tum Tum Boro's fingers stretch out into the cosmos, the universe in which are the moon and the stars and the two suns, the cold sun of winter and the fiery sun of the hot season.

Except for the accident we might all have stayed in that wonderful place but one day Tum Tum Boro fell from the sky and split in two and all living things came out of her and she died and became the earth and remained our mother and we are all still part of her, so when our time comes and we are called we have to return.

She is in the sand that trickles our time away and the trees and veld grasses and the animals that roam free; she is in the birds that fly and the lizards and snakes that slither.

She is in ourselves and we are in her.

CONRAD

Heiseb the Honey Taker

When I was twelve years old, my father sent for an old Bushman tracker and gave him a job which was to be my 'boy' and teach me the ways of the bush.

'It isn't enough to be able to shoot and shoot straight,' my father said. 'If you want to be a hunter you must be able to read the bush.'

The old 'baster' stood in front of my father and listened while he explained what it was I had to be taught.

He said from now on, for the rest of the season, the bushman would be my 'boy' and answer to me. I was the 'little master' to him and he was Bastiaan to me. He had some other name but they called him Bastiaan because it was at least a halfway civilized white man's name. So that was the name I used.

Bastiaan's face was withered and wizened as an old water course. He had gleaming baby gums and a permanent toothless smile. No-one knew where he came from or how old he was. They said although he'd worked around white people from time to time, from the look of him he was almost certainly pure Bushman.

My father and his friends were happy to get on with men's business of hunting and in our own way, which was different, Bastiaan and I were happy too. I wanted to please my father and as far as Bastiaan was concerned his was not difficult work. I was keen to learn and although my father had a name in the district for being tougher than nails and harder than a rock, if you kept on the right side of him he paid well. It was, on the face of it, a good arrangement.

But my father and his friends were white men and already halfway on their journey. They had gone too far and were in too deep for anything to change them. For them it was too late. There was no possibility of turning back but I was a boy when they gave me to Bastiaan and there were many things I did not know.

Bushmen are not like other men. They have powers other men don't have and they use these powers to travel to worlds more marvellous than this one and have seen things more wonderful than we can ever see.

This was not what Bastiaan told me but somewhere inside myself I knew it and wondered at it and in that great silence that is the bush I pondered on it. I wondered what the full extent of Bastiaan's powers might be and it came to me that perhaps, among his many powers, Bastiaan might have the ability to read the future.

I can't say where this idea came from. It didn't come from Bastiaan. If it were true, he would never have boasted of it because bush people are not like us. They are modest and don't vaunt such gifts as are bestowed on them. There may be a song or a story about a great hunter or painter or music-maker but a man will never make mention of his own talents himself.

But as I was his master and he my 'boy' and had to do as I said, I asked Bastiaan about himself. I said it had come to me that he could see the future and if this was indeed so and he could tell what mine was going to be, I should like very much to know it.

He evaded the question which didn't surprise me. Bush people rarely speak directly. They're fond of riddles and their greatest pleasure is to see an answer elude the listener and prove difficult or even impossible to find.

I knew this. I knew patience was needed to come to the end of a riddle and patience is not a gift given to the young but I asked my question anyway and Bastiaan listened.

He considered what I said for what seemed a long time and at the end of all his consideration, he gave no direct answer. He indicated that he thought the question a grave one which was why he could not answer in a moment. He would, he said, have to go away and consider the matter further.

It wasn't enough for me.

I said I would give him a full jar of Virginia sweet wine and a pouch of Boxer tobacco and he thought about this too and showed with a flash of gum that he understood the notion of my pressing gifts on him.

I was trying to hoodwink him and he knew it.

All I offered had already been promised by my father whose power in such matters far exceeded my own. My father had already said that if, at the end of the season, he was satisfied Bastiaan had taught me well, a full jar of Virginia sweet wine and a pouch of tobacco would be his.

I tried to brazen things out. I said I would double my father's offer. If Bastiaan did as I asked, he would have two jars of Virginia sweet wine and two pouches of Boxer.

'You can trust me to keep my word,' I said. 'I'm my father's son and my word's as good as his.'

But Bastiaan declined. If a man tries deceit once he is not a man to be trusted and will almost certainly try again and Bastiaan knew this.

So I tried a new tack. I said if he would tell and tell to my satisfaction, to the gifts my father had already promised I would add a preserving jar filled brimful with honey. Brown honey on the comb. Town honey, not taken in the proper way, but very fine all the same and trickling with sweetness.

I said if Bastiaan had not already heard it from little Meraai, the kitchen girl, I would bring the honey out and show it to him so he could see it with his own eyes.

It was our way when we left the farm to leave behind, aside from wages, small gifts for the farm people which would only be given if they'd stayed sober and worked well and were found in every way to have rendered satisfactory service. Of all these gifts sweet wine and tobacco were the most favoured.

'They'll drink like lords the minute we leave,' my father said. 'No boss to put them in their place and every one of them the King of Kaffirland for the night. Or at least until the wine runs out.'

'Oom' Faan the bookworm, who worked at the university, saw it differently. He didn't believe in wine and brought honey instead and the bush people knew him from past seasons and knew he would bring it.

'I'll give you honey if you tell me,' I told Bastiaan. 'But watch out. If you don't do as I say I may not be in such a good mood and so free with my gifts and perhaps my father will feel the same.'

Bastiaan stood small before me, his skin creased and folded into the soft deep baby courses of old age. He wore an apron of springbok skin flashed white in the front and rust red at the sides. His shoulder blades poked out sharp through the woody skin of his back. At his neck, elbows and knees, the skin pouched into what looked like lappings of well worn leather.

I knew that in return for knowing all of my life what I offered was not a very remarkable gift but it was all I had. My father would not have allowed two jugs of wine or a double ration of tobacco to be given to any single tracker, no matter how well he'd performed, but I knew I could wheedle an extra jar of honey out of 'Oom' Faan and that was the best I could do.

I was young. I thought the temptation of honey would be irresistible to Bastiaan. I expected him to wait a while for the sake of face and then succumb to my offer but I was wrong. He said he would not make up his mind at that very minute. He would not agree, nor would he refuse, and I didn't like it.

I called him ungrateful. I asked him if white people had not always been good to him. Didn't he work the hunt every year and get paid money for it? He was old. Not everyone would take the risk of going out into the bush with such an old man.

I asked why he thought he'd been given such a simple job this time. Was looking after a boy in his first season a job becoming to a seasoned and venerated hunter such as Bastiaan claimed to be? I was, after all, a boy still so green in the ways of the bush I hadn't even made my first kill.

The things I said shamed me even as I said them. The minute they came out of my mouth I felt very bad because nothing I said was true. Bastiaan was all the things people said he was and many other things beside and I spoke in anger as a boy accustomed to having his way, and anger and truth are not always good companions.

I suggested to him that perhaps it was because he was too old and no longer strong enough to go with the huntsmen or sufficiently clear-eyed to see those things he had always been depended upon to see, that he had been left behind.

That too was a lie. He was, of all of them, the only one who was truly at one with the bush and they knew it. He could read the land as other men who have the secrets of reading read books and in return the land opened its secrets to him and sang out to him the stories it kept from the ears of strangers.

When he went with the hunt, it was Bastiaan who told which animals were about and which way they were headed. He could say the size of a herd to the last one and never get it wrong.

When the hunt was on and the huntsmen anxious for the kill he was the one who could place an ostrich-feather wand in the ground and do it in such a position as to divert alarmed stampeding animals straight into the path of the huntsmen.

He could show birds' nests and where to find water. He could point out where other men had been before and how long ago.

It was he who had taught me about honey in the first place and showed me never to try and smoke bees out and said it was because the mother of bees was also the wife of the god Goa!na, who did not like the burning-out of bees, or too much greed in regard to their honey.

Bastiaan revered the bee who he said was everything we ought to be ourselves. Patient, industrious, diligent and selfless.

He told me Goa!na had the power to turn himself into honey and poison men who tried to take his treasures by burning and told me the story of Heiseb, who had once tried to trick the bees and take more than his fair share of their hive.

He did this by returning to the bees two or three times a day, each time pretending to be a different person and the bees were sorry for him and shared their honey and gave him as much as he asked for, which was as much as anyone could want but his greed overtook him and he gave himself away by singing a little song about his success.

Angered by his trickery the bees took their revenge and stung him until his skin and hair were gone and only his brains, sorely exposed, remained and Heiseb, in great pain, ran from the place.

To take bush honey, which is wild in flavour and luminous to look at, you must wait for the summons of the little brown honey-guide and he will lead you to the hive by fluttering around and calling till you follow and when the hive is found and the honey taken with a scoop made from a buck's shoulder blade, the honey-guide must be rewarded by being given his share.

This is the proper way. But town honey is sweet too and Bushmen love sweetness.

I asked again if Bastiaan would promise to think about what I'd asked and he said he would and we did not speak of it again until the night before the last day when the farm 'boys' were packing up and my father and his party were getting ready to leave.

The way it is with the farewell gifts is this.

We do not deal directly with our labourers. These gifts are not handed over man to man. Gift-giving is the job of the 'boss boy'. My father, the Master on whose land the hunt takes place, tells him who should be rewarded and in what way and the 'boss boy' allocates the gifts and will do exactly as he's told and every man will get his fair share, because next year the white men will be back and if it was not done as they said, they would know about it and there would be trouble.

Bush people are not like the people who belong to the farms. They appear when the hunters arrive and are attached to no-one. They own nothing they are not prepared to offer up or share and no-one has any responsibility for them. When the hunt is over they don't stay on the farm. They return to the bush, to their own people and sometimes they come back again the following year and sometimes they don't.

In that way they are like water mirages which glimmer silver on the horizon and deceive us, so we don't know what it is we see with our eyes and what is seen only in the mirror of our imagination.

I didn't know if I would see Bastiaan again once we'd parted. That was up to him.

He was no longer young. He'd told me it was in his mind one day to make a place of thorns to keep the jackals out and sit down there, with his body to the ground and close his eyes and be one with the ground and let his spirit go on its way on its own spirit's journey, which he felt in his heart it was yearning for.

I asked when that exact moment would be. He said he couldn't say. It's white men who believe in time. As far as bush people are concerned time is not an important thing or a thing at all and certainly not something a man should try and take into his reckoning.

Death, like life, is a matter of the moment and he would know the moment when it came.

The hunt was over. Leave had been taken and our goodbyes said and we would depart the next day but even at that late moment nothing had been resolved on the matter of the honey and my offer of a bargain in return for the gift of my future.

Bastiaan had not spoken. So I was the one who raised the matter again.

At first he kept his eyes cast to the ground. Then he looked directly at me and for a long time, daring me, I thought, to look away and when I didn't he asked if I believed he could do this thing I asked, and I said I did.

As for himself, he said, he did not believe he had so much magic in him and he showed by raising his empty hands and with a shake of his upraised head that I had asked too much and for something that was not his to give but you have to be careful with bush people.

If I'd learned anything that season it was that bush people are like the honey-guide. They call to you and lead you to the place but still you will not see. Your eyes will see only what they are able to see and that will be very little indeed. It is the same with what the bush people tell you.

For the answers you must look for the unseen, and listen for what is left unsaid.

'I think you will not come back next season,' I said. 'I think you will take what my father gives you and go back to your own people and I will never see you again.'

I did think so but when the thought came it grieved me because although I was only a boy, when I came to know Bastiaan something inside me had already been broken by the things I had seen in that other life I had, for the moment, left behind, to which I would return.

I was looking for solace and found it in him. I found it in his silence and the two of us companions together in the greater silence of the bush.

With him before me as my guide, I had entered a strange landscape and we had been content as men in harmony are and what we shared together was sweeter to me than any honey could ever be.

But I didn't tell him this.

I was young and unversed and didn't know how to put into words these things that were in my heart.

For a long time we stood in silence, I waiting for him to further the matter and he waiting for me.

'I would like to take my final leave of you,' I said. 'I will wait for you tomorrow, very early, before the others are out of their beds. I will come out and away from the house and wait for you there.'

During our time together this had been our way. I would get up in the pre-dawn before anyone else was about and go out to look for Bastiaan and he would be there waiting for me.

Before I had eyes to see, I wouldn't always see him at first and I would be impatient because I was master and he was my 'boy' who my father had given me but in time I learnt to wait and he would let me wait and when he was ready he would detach himself from his chosen place and let me see him.

I'd learnt since then. I'd learnt how to look for him and now when my eyes adjusted I could see him squatting on his haunches, turned in on himself for warmth, as much a part of the land as the bushes and scrub and the small trees.

It is very cold in the veld in winter. The water troughs where the farm animals come to drink freeze over and frost gnaws at the grass.

The air is cold and clear and moves heavy against you and inside it is a drift like the tides of the sea and all the world is above you and you are like a sea creature held fast on some strange ocean floor.

Even when you no longer move the current pulls at

you and it's better to hunch down and make yourself small and turn in upon yourself and be still.

Then it's natural to raise your eyes to look for the coming sun and consider the world above and watch the disappearing stars which are the closing eyes of the night, which will one by one be snuffed out until only the Morning Star, the Great Star of Wonder, remains.

All the stars are huntsmen but of all the stars in the sky the Morning Star is the only one who knows both the power of night and the vision of light. The Morning Star is the only star who hunts in majesty, alone.

In this way we wait before dawn for that moment of perfect darkness when such matters as I wished to know from Bastiaan might safely be discussed.

I'd become interested in the stars that season and Bastiaan knew it. He'd seen me with the 'Oubaas', the old master, my 'Oom' Faan, looking up at the sky and asked me what it was I saw there.

For himself, when he walked under the high dome of heaven, he knew the stars for what they were and they were the eyes of widows' dead husbands peering down at them to watch out for their virtue and welfare.

My uncle was teaching me differently. I told Bastiaan this and he showed a wedge of pink gum so I'd know the story of the widows was a joke and funny to him because no-one owns either the stars or their stories. Everyone has their own story for everything and the stars might be anything they chose and the stories about them as many as there were stars themselves.

I waited that cold morning not knowing if Bastiaan would come, because the day was our last and not like other days. He'd been paid for his services and his obligation to me was ended but that is a white man's way of thinking and I waited all the same.

I looked out, hoping he was there and he was there but I couldn't see him, even though I'd become quite good at it, because it was too dark.

I knew what Bastiaan would say if I told him.

'If you wish to see in the dark you must become the cat,' he would say. 'Become the cat and ask him if he will do you a service and favour you with his powers, so you can see what he sees. Then, to see in the dark will be nothing at all but the easiest thing in the world.'

But I could see nothing.

I waited, as I always did, and when he was ready Bastiaan detached himself from the dark and showed himself and squatted beside me looking outward, so what was said between us, good or bad, would go from our mouths and disappear into the night and stay there and never stand between us.

Bastiaan said he had seen my 'Oom' Faan and myself and he turned his face to the sky to show what it was he'd seen. He asked if, after such a great deal of looking at the stars, I had not found there the thing it was I was looking for, even though he knew I had not.

I became impatient. I told him this was not the way white men look at things. I said, if I'd already found what I was looking for, I would not have done him the honour of seeking his counsel in the first place.

I understood what my uncle taught me and knew now something of the comings and goings of the stars. What I wanted was something more.

Bastiaan asked me then, with my first season being over and I not having been allowed to kill anything yet, if I still wanted to become a hunter.

I did. Which was something we both knew but as it

seemed all he wished to say, I refused to dignify the obvious with an answer and said nothing and we sat for a while longer on the cold ocean floor, held in a ring of darkness beyond which lay the other worlds, the domains of the double-headed serpent, which I did not know, where Bastiaan could not take me.

Then suddenly Bastiaan stood up and turned towards me and in the first early tint of the morning light he jigged a little dance.

Bushmen like to dance.

They will dance for rain and healing. They will dance for the dying moon to show how they mourn her passing, so she will not die and leave them utterly but come back in due time and reveal herself to them again in her full silvered glory, to show their path so they can walk in the night.

They will dance barefaced or in animal masks, by firelight or with their faces turned to the rising sun which is the place their god lives. Sometimes men will dance and sometimes women.

They will dance animals, reedbuck and gemsbok and eland but the dance is a private and magical thing. They will not usually dance in front of the eyeless ones who do not know what it is they are seeing.

I knew little but I knew enough to see that Bastiaan on his spindle legs with his bare splayed feet so gnarled and knobbled and punished by his land, was dancing the eland and the eland is the most powerful and mysterious of all the antelope and he danced this for me. So what I wanted might happen and I would be a hunter.

Then he stopped dancing and knelt in front of me, brown and moon-faced with the baby-eyes of great age and I crouched before him, a book as yet unwritten, and we spoke face to face so that what was said between us would be caught between us and stay between us for ever.

From his mouth to my ears he told me that the man with the heart of a hunter is blessed and also cursed because once he has killed, his heart will always hunger for the hunt and until he smells blood and understands its power and can bridle it, he will never know peace.

It was not what I expected. It was mysterious to me and unsatisfying. I didn't understand and would have pressed him for more but I knew it would be no use. He had stopped dancing and stood quite still and I knew by his stillness and the way he held himself that he had given all he was willing to give.

I knew what my father would say.

'A load of bollocks and you're a damn fool for having asked such a stupid thing in the first place, from a sly little bugger of a Bushman. He'll think you're simple-minded and have a good laugh the minute your back's turned.'

I didn't think so, but I'd learnt some things that season and one of them was that there were more things in the world than my father knew and many things he didn't understand and sometimes there were things he didn't need to know at all.

The matter of Bastiaan remained and the matter of my promise of the honey too.

My father, pleased, although he said so only by way of a slap on the shoulder, told the head 'boy' to see that Bastiaan got the promised wine and tobacco as well as his pay.

The honey was not his concern. 'Oom' Faan was in charge of honey and would have given it anyway as he did every year, by way of a treat.

When I saw him, before the matter of honey or

anything else could be discussed he said: 'You were out early this morning. I heard you leave.'

'Walking,' I said but I didn't look at him and he went on, in his easy way, as if I hadn't spoken.

'You mustn't believe everything these people tell you,' he said. 'Sometimes they like to have their little joke and if it's at our expense, they like it so much the better. I suppose you can't really blame them for that.'

I agreed. I said he was right. What he said was almost certainly true but that wasn't what I thought in my heart.

There's no such thing as parting or length of time. Bush people know this. When they dance they slide through time and it's lighter than air and cool as the water hidden in the deep places under the sand and it doesn't hinder them at all.

All things are possible. It was possible Bastiaan would stand with the others and wait for the 'boss boy' to give him his gifts but I would be gone. I would not be there to see it and if I didn't see it and even if I did, perhaps it had happened or perhaps it had never happened at all.

It was possible he would stand there hungering, with the taste of uneaten honey already in his mouth. That was not for me to know.

'What do you say?' 'Oom' Faan said. 'The old man. Shall we leave a jar of honey for him?'

I knew then what it was Bastiaan had taught me. If I said no, he would know I'd learnt nothing because I didn't believe in him and had no faith and in that case he would go and I would never see him again.

If I gave the honey, I believed Bastiaan would return the next season and would teach me again and because I was hungry to learn, I did not say no.

'Leave it,' I said and it was done.

Bastiaan had kept his part of the bargain. In his own way, which was not mine, he'd given me my future just as I'd asked but I didn't yet know enough. I could not understand what it was he was trying to tell me. Only time could teach me that.

Angel Kisses

No-one waits more eagerly for someone to come than Conrad waiting for his sister.

'It isn't proper, the way you go on with the boy,' Jack says to Sylvia.

Jack is his father. Sylvia his mother. He calls them Mamma and Pappa. Mamma has talked to him about the new baby. She's told him he must be a good boy and accept whoever it is God chooses to send them.

Pappa has his heart set on a boy. Mamma says she doesn't mind if it's not a boy and no matter what Pappa says and all the talk about a new baby brother, he mustn't mind either.

He doesn't mind. It's already decided. He's waiting for his sister and knows she will come.

Pappa has already chosen a name. The new boy will be called Christian Bosman.

'This baby's not his business,' Pappa says and it's Conrad he means when he says it. 'He's far too interested and he's only a child. These things have nothing to do with him. I don't like the way you let him touch you.'

But Jack isn't always there and Sylvia wants her son to love his sister.

'Give me your hands,' she says and Conrad raises his hands flat-palmed, the way he does to Pappa before supper, to show they're clean and his mother takes him by the wrists and draws him to her and when he's close, standing in front of her, she puts his hands flat-palmed against the balloon of her stomach and the pushed-out lump of her belly button which is, he knows, the place where the baby's growing.

'Just wait,' his mother says and he waits and after a few moments he feels his sister float towards him pushing out, reaching for him between the watery barrier that divides them.

'Can you feel it?' his mother says and he nods and waits to feel it again.

His swimming sister seeking him out is the newest and best game and he'll stand where he is and play for as long as he's allowed, until his mother says it's enough for the moment and she's tired but there are other times.

In the mornings after his father's left his mother lets him climb into her big bed and lie down next to her so he can play some more.

She calls him a silly thing and holds him close and lets him slide the side of his face and his ear against her belly and it's like listening to all of the ocean which is trapped inside the spotted darning shell the maid keeps in the mending box.

His sister swims up and down towards him and away and then back again, kicking and retreating, then coming back so he can feel her and he lies in the scented dark of his mother's big bed and loves his new sister, who wants so badly to come into the world and be with him.

* * *

When she does come it's not how anyone thought it would be. His father is disappointed because it's not a boy and it's a boy he's been waiting for.

It had all been decided. When the boy came the world would be ready, polished with sunlight and shining, all its flags bright and flying, waiting to greet him. Except he doesn't come.

Beeky arriving late, pulled from a Caesarean section, covered with slime and blood, screeching in protest comes instead and Conrad is the only one who's ready. He's the only one who's truly happy.

He's taken to see the new baby and because he's small and his mother so high up in a bed, a nurse crackling white starch bends down and holds the baby down to him so he can get a clear view of his new sister for himself.

What he sees is a small face, crinkled even smaller with crossness poking out from inside a pink blanket and a head that seems no bigger than an upside-down teacup, with a soft gold-red cosy of downy baby-hair furring across it.

The nurse opens up the blanket so he can have a better look and he looks at the squirming, tiny-tongued baby for as long as they let him.

'She's to be called Beatrice Marie,' his mother says. 'It's for your great-granny. For Pappa's grand-mother.'

He would like to greet her with her name but it's too much for him. It slides away.

'Beeky?' he says.

He holds out his hand towards his old friend and there's no skin or water between them now, only his hand touching the blanket and his sister pulsing baby life underneath it and Beeky has her name.

Beeky isn't perfect and his father doesn't like it. Beeky has a mark on her and no Hartmann has ever had such a mark before. His father says it must come from his mother's side of the family and be some other not very nice secret she's kept from him.

'It's nothing,' his mother says. 'Such a small thing.'

She pulls the blanket up quickly and the baby's small shoulder disappears but she doesn't do it quickly enough and so he sees. The mark is on her shoulder. A red-purple mark like a small blot of blood that somehow trickled out instead of staying inside.

'It's ugly,' says his father.

'It's very small,' his mother says. 'It'll wear off. These things do.'

There's something he wants to ask but he doesn't want to ask his mother. He waits until he can ask the starch nurse who showed him his sister in the first place and he only asks when he's sure no-one else can hear them.

'Is it sore?' he says, pointing to his sister's arm.

'That little mark?' the nurse says. 'It's not sore at all. It's an angel kiss, that's all. Before your little sister left heaven the angels kissed her goodbye.'

He isn't sure. His father doesn't like too much lipstick. He says only bad women paint themselves up and angels aren't bad, so he doesn't think they wear lipstick at all and he says so.

'I don't know about that,' the nurse says. 'After all, when you think about it, we know so little about angels and a touch of lipstick never did anyone any harm.'

His father says the baby's scrawny and ugly. He's never seen a child like it. They've never had a redhead in the family before. He doesn't know why they should suddenly have one now.

As for the blemish, red and ugly like a burn, one look is enough to show it isn't going away like his mother said it would. It isn't going anywhere. It's there to stay and it gets more livid by the day.

A bad-luck sign, the nurse aides say. The mark of a child pulled into the world who doesn't want to be there at all.

None of it matters to Conrad. He loves his sister. He thinks her tufty red hair is the most beautiful thing he's ever seen. It's the colour of the copper cents he gets for being a good boy. It's the gold of his mother's ring. It's the rusty red colour of the small fallow deer that graze on the Lion's rump above their house.

'Such a funny little thing,' people say. 'I wonder where she comes from.'

They peer into her pram at her tiny head and the flame around it which is her hair and wonder why she looks so much like herself and not like any Hartmann who has ever come before and his father doesn't like it.

'Babies change,' their mother says but Beeky doesn't.

Every day his father comes to see her and takes a good long look and every day she looks more like herself and less like anyone else and his father likes it less and less.

The hartebeest is red because he ate the red comb of the young bees. The eland is dark because he ate dark wasp honey. The different colours of the springbok are there because they ate the little white bees and their red cells together.

Beeky is red because that's the way she was sent into the world and there's nothing anyone can do about it.

Conrad loves his sister's hartebeest hair and her funny fish eyes. He loves the livid birthmark on her shoulder. No-one has a mark like Beeky. There can be no mixed-up babies here. Beeky has her mark so there can never be any possibility of mistake and he will always be able to find his sister anywhere.

'Bloody ugly,' his father says. 'Put something on her that will cover it up.'

'It's such a small thing,' says his mother.

Something has gone wrong. His father doesn't like his mother any more. He can hear it in his voice and Beeky is to blame.

She's not what his father expected and he can see him looking hard at her and knows he's wishing her away. It makes him feel sad and sorry too. Nobody wants to be sent away but no-one wants to be in a place where they're not wanted either.

He goes to her pram and puts his hand on her and wishes she will stay and she pushes at the air with her fists and no-one knows what she's thinking.

'Tell that child to shut up whining,' his father says. 'Must it bloody shriek all the time? You're its mother. Shut it up or take it away somewhere where it doesn't get on everyone's nerves.'

Beeky is growing bigger and getting stronger and becoming more like herself and less like anyone expected every day.

His father's temper's getting worse and he's taking it out on everyone. His mother says there's nothing to be done about it, except be as good as he possibly can and the only good times are the times his father's not there.

When his father's away, Light prances in through the window like a welcome guest. Laughter and Good Humour creep out of the corners where they've been hiding and come right into the room where the three of them are and he and his mother and sister step into another life, which has always been there impatiently waiting for them and they're happy.

The Old Madam

There's a ghost in their house. A great-granny Hartmann ghost from a long time ago who gave Beeky her name. The servants have seen her. They call her the Old Madam and she rests in cool corners on the edges of timelessness. That's what's become of her and there isn't very much she can do about it.

'Find something useful to do to pass the time,' her own mother used to say. People talked like that in those days and young girls listened. Now there's no-one left to tell her anything and there's no-one living who can give you ideas how to pass time when time itself has passed.

You can plague the living and in the beginning that was what she did, but she soon grew weary of it.

In life people had some respect. She was a woman who got down to things fast and didn't care to be kept waiting. Now it seems she'll be kept cooling her heels for all eternity and not very much she can do about it.

'The duration' is how she thinks of it. That's what people said about the old war when the Khakis came from England to give them a hiding and take their gold and put them in their place and keep them there once and for all.

The trouble is no-one knew exactly how long 'the duration' would be and what felt like pain then is history now. Only history. Nothing but history. Not always well treated, or properly remembered, repeated any-old-how to suit the occasion; even by one's own descendants which, once she knew them, was more or less what she expected anyway.

These days she's the gutsy old granny who made fools of the British. But nobody says what it cost her.

She's tried to tell them but there's no-one to listen. She's rattled the windows and set the dogs' hair rising. She's splintered glass. She knocked boiling water off the stove and badly scalded a housemaid.

She's keened. She's keened in the night and beaten against the windows and begged to be let out. When she found the smallest of corners she blew through it so hard the oak trees cracked down acorns and they sounded like rifle shots as they fell to the ground, but even so no-one paid any attention.

She made at least one granddaughter look under her bed every night and tell the housemaid to put her bedlegs in dishes of water to keep the *tokoloshe* away, because she thought it was loose in the house and up to no good.

It's an ungrateful granddaughter who doesn't know her own grandmother when she lives in the same house, and she wished boils on the girl and a terrible squint in the left eye and an abiding fear of ghosts from which she never recovered.

But that was a long time ago and there's no-one to care now but the house bats. They squeak upside down in the *solder*, the old attic under the roof, and fly, flapping faster than rockets down the long corridor squealing their sympathy but no-one pays any attention.

It's her husband who's to blame. For trying to turn a Boer girl Colonial into a toadying subject of a fat old Queen.

A failure. Boer backs do not bend easily towards greedy old ladies anxious for gold. No amount of sweet talk or rearrangement of geography is going to change that.

She blames her husband for his Hartmann dark hair and his honey Hartmann promises, taking her away from her own people and bringing her to this house where the sea is so close you can smell it when the wind's in the right direction.

She should have stayed where she was. You can live quite happily without smelling the sea. If there's no sea, dust will do just as well.

When she yearns now, it's her birth farm she yearns for. If she were there she could float free on the heat haze, over rusty patches of mielie land, and drift where she liked over grazing cattle and the soft curls of smoke from farmers' homesteads, set so far apart one need never lay eyes on the others, and 'kaffir' kraals and green dams shining in the sun.

She might have lived and died childless under the blue-white arc of that sky and been tucked into the family graveyard among her own people, in that place where the pink and cerise cosmos flowers in the spring. Perhaps there she could have found some peace.

When she thinks about it she knocks her husband's picture from the sitting-room wall and, when the houseboy puts it up, she knocks it down again and nearly takes the boy's toes with it but it makes no difference.

Even when she dances in the firelight and kicks

coals onto the hearth and spits and sizzles and reaches her smoke arms up through the flue, no-one takes any notice at all of her.

Only the moon understands and the moonlight cold through the windowpanes soothes her and makes her sad.

Man is mortal the moon says and she remembers her sons sliding out of her body and it's them she's thinking about these days and they're long gone.

Now there's nothing to do but peer in at the pram and set the new baby wailing but that doesn't bother her. She's wailed herself and no-one's heard.

'Have you seen my son?' she sighs to the baby. 'Have you seen my boy in that place where you come from? Surely you've seen him? Did he give you no message for me?'

The baby cries louder. It slashes the air with its small fists and spits with its tongue. It would send the Old Madam back where she came from if it could, but quite how to do it is a thing not every newcomer knows.

Sometimes it's learnt and sometimes it isn't, even by people who've stayed a very long time, but a ghost, once she's settled, is not so easily got rid of.

Music of the Night

There's a secret at their house. They all know it but they don't say. His father hits his mother. It's their secret and lives in their house with all the other secrets no-one is allowed to know.

He's not meant to see but sometimes it happens so quickly no-one can stop it and then he can't help seeing even if he doesn't want to.

Afterwards his mother comes looking for him and takes him aside and says: 'You must forget about it. Pretend it never happened and most important of all you must never tell anyone. No-one, word of honour, not ever.'

He nods yes. He'll do anything his mother asks. He'll do anything anyone asks, just as long as the hitting stops.

'You must always watch out for Beeky,' his mother says. 'Promise me.'

He nods yes and says he will.

'You're older than she is and a boy. You must keep your eyes open. Always keep your eyes open and watch out for her. You'll remember that, won't you?

You won't always have me there to remind you. You'll never forget?'

'Yes,' he says.

'Say "always remember, never forget",' and he says it and it's easy.

What is 'always' after all but only as long as a single heartbeat?

His mother is thin, see-through and slight with light hair and slender hands and a way of moving so she can slip in and out of places so fast and light if she didn't leave her scent on the air not even the ghost would be able to smell her. But on the days his father comes looking for her he always finds her no matter how careful she is.

Beeky's the trouble. At least that's what his father says.

'You think I'm a bloody fool? You think the people who know me are bloody fools? You think you can make a fool of me behind my back and no-one will know what your game is?'

He hits her with the flat of his hand.

'You're trash,' he says. 'You're nothing. You were rubbish when I found you and still are. This is my house. Everything you have, you got from me. Even your name. It's my name. I gave it to you. It's my name you trollop around with.'

Between each thing he shouts he hits her hard and while she can still stay on her feet she does but every hit knocks her back a little and when she can't stand any more she falls down and sometimes she bangs against things as she falls but even so, standing or falling, she holds her hands to her face to shield it. At least she manages that.

'Please, Jack,' she says. 'Not my face.'

It makes him angry but he listens all the same. He takes out the anger on her shoulders and the tops of her arms and sometimes her ribs. When it's nearly over and he's panting hard and can feel his strength going, he'll hit her just wherever he can lay his hands and then it's over.

'It's your fault,' he says. 'You can't blame me.'

She isn't blaming anyone. She's where he left her, crouched down and folded in on herself. A folded woman with her hands to her face and her hair hanging down.

'You're a bitch,' he says. 'You're a bitch and a whore who's come into my life and reduced me to this. Jesus Christ, what did I do to deserve it?'

He says she's done a terrible thing and Beeky with her beautiful hair and her angel kiss is the thing. Some other man's thing and nothing to do with him. Their mother has tried to trick him and make him a laughing stock. That's the reason he has to beat her. She can't get off scot-free. Because she's been bad she must be punished. She has to pay for what she's done.

'You understand, don't you?' he says. 'I'd never let you get away with a thing like this. Surely you must have known? Not even you could be so stupid you didn't realize that.'

It's always the same. Sometimes he hits harder than others depending on his mood and if she pulls far enough away and he isn't finished yet he has to kick her.

In the beginning, after it was over, he would beg her to forgive him. He'd say how sorry he was. He didn't know what came over him, he'd say. He'd kneel in front of her, as if he was praying, and say he couldn't live with himself if she didn't forgive him.

But things have changed.

She has no more forgiveness to offer and even if she had, he doesn't want it any more.

* * *

Conrad is nine years old. Beeky is six. They are in the upstairs bathroom lying foot to foot in a warm soap bath playing a loud water game. Their mother is sitting on a wooden chair, like a lady in a picture, soft with steam that sets her hair clouding and curling.

Her sweater sleeves are rolled up for the business of bathing and they are in a waterworld playing at splashing and throwing wet flannels at each other and the smell of soap is everywhere.

Beeky loves water. She's slippery as a fish and her head is under and up and her hair is two cut-out pieces of shiny bronze paper and she spits and spouts water to make him laugh and he's happy. Until his father comes.

'What the hell's this?' he says.

He's standing in the open door. Big in the door in outside clothes with the cold all around him, like people from outside always are.

'What the hell's going on?' he says.

'It's nothing,' his mother says. 'The children are having their bath.'

'Get out,' he says to Conrad.

His mother is on her feet and his father is in the room, big at the side of the bath, and Beeky has her knees up and her shoulders hunched and is pulling back from him and away.

'I said get out,' his father says. 'Didn't you hear me? I'm not saying it twice.'

The side of the bath is slippery and he can't find his feet. He wants to be a good boy and do what his father says but he can't do it fast enough and his father's big hands are under his armpits pulling him free of the water and his bare feet are on the wooden slats of the bath board and he's naked and dripping in front of his father and mother and Beeky is crouching in the bath behind him and then it happens.

His father raises his hand and it seems to be coming slowly towards him. He thinks it's because he has done something bad and he's braced for the blow. Even before it lands he can feel it.

He knows it will be hard and catch him, he thinks, on the side of the head and he will never be able to hold himself braced against it. His father is too strong.

It will knock him off his feet and he'll fall, maybe sideways against the towel cupboard and then onto the plastic tiled floor and he's ready for it, drawing in his breath, feeling his heart pump in readiness and he lifts his eyes to meet his father's, to show he's ready and not a coward but the blow isn't meant for him. It's meant for his mother and it comes flat-handed across the side of her face and knocks her backwards. She goes down flailing. Her arms are like windmills in the air and her side and arm crack hard against the wicker linen basket and she falls sprawling.

'I don't want to see this,' his father says and his voice is soft and gentle and certain.

'I don't want this,' he says. 'I won't have it.'

'You get out of here,' he says to Conrad. 'And you get up.'

She must be sore. His mother has pulled herself up. She's sitting against the linen basket. One arm is wrapped around her body holding the other arm close against her side. Her head is against the plaited wicker of the basket. Her eyes are closed and there's a thin trickle of blood seeping out of her nose running down her face snaking its way to her lip.

'Go to your room,' his father says.

He goes as fast as he can and his father's voice chases after him, looping out to catch him, ready to pull him back. He doesn't want to go back. He wants to pretend he hasn't seen. He wants to run but he can't. He's trying to tell his feet what to do but they won't listen. They won't move fast enough.

'Never again,' his father says. 'This kind of thing doesn't happen again. You keep your bastard away from my son. Do you hear me?'

He can't hear what his mother says. He's beginning to get cold. He doesn't have a towel so he can't dry himself. He can't find his pyjamas and he can't get into bed wet. He can't say his prayers without clothes on or God will be angry. He doesn't know what a bastard is. He doesn't know what he's done and whether what's happening is his fault or whether it isn't.

He thinks his father will kill his mother. He doesn't know what will happen then, except that he and Beeky will be alone with no-one to look after them. He wants his mother to be good and do whatever his father says. He wants her to do anything, so his father doesn't hit her any more. He doesn't want her to die.

In the matter of dying it's the moon we must ask and what he'll tell us is a lesson we should all heed. Which is that of all creatures, seen and unseen, man is the stupidest and the hardest to teach. He's so stupid, even the simplest lesson is beyond him.

Hare was a person once and Moon was his friend. Every night Moon looked for Hare and when he found him, he stroked Hare's fur and told him Moon stories and turned him blinking and silver into a moon creature for the duration of the night and Hare was enchanted, as one can be by Moon, and begged to be allowed to be his friend for ever.

'At least until I die,' Hare said. 'For when that day comes I shall be gone and you will have to find some other creature to be your friend.'

'Don't die,' said Moon. 'There's no need. It really isn't necessary. You see me every night up in the sky where I live and every night in my cycle I brush past Death but he never takes me and he never will. If you allow me, I will teach you how I do this and if you do as I say, you need never die and we can be friends for ever.'

Hare was willing to learn but he had to wait for night for Moon to begin his lessons and before night came Hare's mother died and he cared very much for his mother and grieved for her and while he was grieving, it occurred to him that Moon with his smooth silver stories was playing a trick on him. Hare knew some things too. He knew his mother was dead and would never come back again.

'Just watch me and learn,' Moon said.

'I can't,' said Hare. 'My mother's dead and my heart's broken. I have other things to do than watch you preening about in the night sky and my eyes are too full of tears to see, even if I wanted to.'

Which vexed Moon.

'If you don't watch me how will you ever learn?' Moon said and Hare turned his back on Moon which vexed Moon even more, because you have to be as stupid as Hare not to know that for the small price of being blind in the day, at night Moon can see everywhere.

'Will you learn or will you not?' Moon said.

'I will not,' said Hare. 'There have been Hares in the world for as long as there have been Moons and my Hare mother has taught me all I shall ever need to know. I am a Hare not a Moon and clever as you think you are, there's nothing you can teach me.'

'Then you will be stupid all your life,' Moon said. 'You are a false friend and a stupid Hare and I will have to punish you.'

He was so angry he struck Hare in the face and split his lip and Hare struck him back and scratched as hard as he could and marked Moon's beauty with terrible scratch marks you can see to this day and that was the end of the friendship.

'From now on,' Moon said, 'you will be an animal, doomed to be hunted by men and savaged and eaten by wild dogs and everyone will know who you are by the split of your lip and because you have rejected me, you have lost your chance and men will never again be offered immortality.'

The First Season

They have a farm and every year in winter his father goes there to hunt.

'To get away from women. To have some peace and quiet. To spend some time with people who have something to say for themselves that's actually worth listening to,' he says.

Conrad is twelve years old. Beeky is nine. It's his second year waiting for his father to tell him he can come to the farm and Beeky doesn't want him to go.

'If he tells you to go say you won't,' she says.

'Conrad's getting to be a big boy,' his mother says. 'If Pappa asks him, he'll want to go.'

'No, he won't,' Beeky says. 'Why should he want to go away and kill things, when he could stay here with us instead?'

He thinks this year his father will ask him. He has let him come into the study and look at the guns and hold them and feel the weight of them in his hands.

'You'll have to throw away your popgun if you come along with us,' his father says. 'That's only good for field mice and birds. It won't take you very far where we're going.'

Every year for as long as he can remember he's seen the freezer full of meat his father brings back. He's heard the men's stories. Back and forth they've flown across his head and in their travels some of them have caught fast in his imagination but there's an end to imagining and he can't imagine any more. He wants to go with them, so he can find out for himself what it's like.

'It'll be a great adventure,' his mother says.

'It'll be a waste of time,' says Beeky. 'If you want animals so badly I'll make you some.'

Beeky can draw. She's very good at it. She doesn't copy out of books the way he does. She draws things as she sees them and all the things she's going to draw, all the things she will ever draw, are already inside her, locked in the copper vault of her head.

'You've never seen a lion,' Conrad says.

'That doesn't mean I don't know what a lion looks like,' says Beeky.

She has drawn him a lion and a giraffe and a big elephant and a spotted cat that's meant to be a cheetah and they're sweet-faced child's animals, drawn in crayon, in bright colours.

'It looks like Noah's ark,' he says. 'We'll never see all of these things and anyway, nothing we do see will look like that.'

He knows what to expect. His father's told him. They can bargain on a few buck and although sometimes there are lion, they're killing for sport and for the pot and for making biltong and *boerewors*. Big cats are for trophies. Buck is what they're after this time.

'I know,' Beeky says. 'That's why I made them for you. Now you've seen them, you needn't go away looking for things you're never going to see.'

'I can't tell Pappa that,' he says.

'That's because you only tell Pappa what he wants to hear. You do it so that he won't stop liking you but I don't mind,' she says.

She won't meet his eyes when she says it. She looks down at her drawing and he looks away because he knows what she says is true.

His father says hunting's not for sissy boys.

'If you're going to come along you have to get rid of your mother's apron strings first. Do you understand what I mean?'

He says he does.

'No matter what happens, there's no crying for Mommy,' his father says. 'Out in the bush you can cry for Mommy as much as you like but no Mommy will come, because Mommy will be a long way away.'

He understands that too.

'Good,' his father says. 'I've decided that I'll take you and I'm taking you because I want to see what you're made of. I'm giving you a chance to make me proud of you. I don't want to be disappointed in you. Do you understand?'

'Yes, sir,' he says.

'You'll take whatever comes your way and take it like a man,' his father says. 'And don't expect any favours from me or from any of the other men, because you're not going to get any, and remember one thing. Out at the farm I'm God and what I say is law and while we're out there it's the only law that counts.'

'Yes, sir,' he says.

This, at least, he understands completely.

The farm is called Liefdefontein. Fountain of Love. It stands in the drylands that run close to the border of

Namibia. If you don't have eyes that see, the land looks like nothing. It looks as if its soul has been snatched away from it.

It's flatscape, and sometimes there are small hills and gullies that trap the afternoon shadows and are ice-cold at night. Even in summer, when the rain sings down, the grass clings tight to the ground in small khaki tufts.

Winter, when the frost comes and the ground is bare and the trees pared down, is the time to hunt. Then the game run looking for water and the landscape is pale and clear. The sun is sharp and you can see for a very long way. Even without telescopic sights, all moving things are easier to see and to track and to hunt down.

It's many miles and they go by car, flying along a road that spools out like gunmetal ribbon in front and behind them. On either side, miles and miles of barbed-wire fence marks off the land and pens in the game, barring their natural migration, netting them into the vastness.

'Men's country,' his father says and with every mile that drops away behind them his father begins to change. He sheds skin after skin like a snake.

His small vanities fall away. His voice coarsens. The things that are important to him in town, in that other life, when he takes his seat in the Senate, or works on reports or writes articles for the newspapers, are not important here.

The gleaming shoes, the fine watch, the carefully chosen silk ties aren't needed. Here it's khaki bush clothes and bush boots so old they welcome returning feet with a soft sigh like slippers and high thick socks so the thorns don't scratch you to pieces when you go into thorn country.

'Forget town,' his father says. 'There are lessons a

man has to learn and there's nothing you'll learn in town the bush won't teach you better and harder.'

He has a shotgun, a boy's gun his father gave him and he's anxious to use it but he has to wait for his father to give him the word and when at last it comes there are a group of men standing among the trucks at the bottom of the farmhouse steps. They've only just arrived and no-one has gone out yet and he won't go out until his father thinks he's ready and he's invited.

'Aim at that camelthorn tree over there,' his father says. 'Take a piece of bark off it. Anywhere on the trunk will do.'

He does and the shot goes wild and the recoil kicks him right off his feet so he falls flat on the ground, still clutching the gun pointing to the air above him. It's an expected joke and everyone laughs.

'Let him balance against something,' 'Oom' Faan says.

'Let him learn,' says his father. 'He has to learn.'

To Conrad he says: 'You control the gun, the gun doesn't control you. That's the first lesson. You'll learn.'

He does learn. You fall over a few times and then you know exactly how to plant yourself on the ground and how to brace your body so you can stand firm and every day his father comes to see how well he's doing and no matter how well he does, he's never doing well enough.

'You'll have to do a lot better than that before you can come out with us,' his father says.

Conrad knows how to kill. At the beach house he's fished. He's caught eels from the river and skinned them alive. At the farm he's watched the herdboys straddle a sheep and with a sharp knife, in a quick slice ear to ear, slaughter it for the pot. He's chopped the head off a chicken himself and watched it running crazily headless around the chicken run at the back of the farmhouse but it counts for nothing here. Veld game is different and more skill is required but he's ready and waiting for his father's word.

At their farm they don't take potshots. They shoot to kill, preferably clean with one shot. No-one wants to spend time tracking a wounded animal for as long as it takes until you can bring him down and finish him off, because that's what has to be done and sometimes, if the animal has fight in him and a will to live, it can take many hours or even days.

If you have eyes, everything you need to see is all around you. If you can see it, what is written in the sand is the full drama of all the world acted out right in front of you.

In the first season you are the least and, even with a man you call 'Uncle' out of familiarity and respect, you know your place.

Sometimes one of the men will make a joke and call out something, or offer some remark and you can smile along with the others and make acknowledgement but until you've killed, or until someone younger or lesser than you comes, you have your place and must know how to keep it. Before he's allowed out with the men he has to be a proven shot and someone they can depend on.

'If you don't get it right no-one's going to do the dirty work and clean up after you,' his father says. 'Before you go out, you have to be good and then you have to be better than good.'

In the beginning he stays close to the farmhouse and practises on tins and bottles set up for him by a labourer's boy on a lopsided kraal wall. The boy doesn't like the job. Newcomers are wild shooters and bullets ricochet but he has to do it. He has no choice.

Once the targets are up, he scuttles out of the way on his bare feet and squats, hands over ears, on his haunches until the fusillade is over, the number of hits counted and noted. Then the little master says: 'Set them up again' and it begins all over and he has to keep on doing it, day after day, until the little master can hit a spinning bottle at fifteen metres and bring it down in showering shards and splinters of glass.

In the first season the hunting's good. Kudu and gemsbok, some blesbok and even wildebeest. There's plenty of sport and game to be butchered for biltong and *wors*. There's a fire every night and meat to eat and wash down with beer and with brandy, and the skins and the heads, the offal and the bones, go to the farm people who stay behind in the *kampong*.

They start early, ahead of the late-rising winter sun, when it's still so cold the air stabs at your lungs like daggers and a man's breath vaporizes on the air and all the open water troughs are covered with a layer of ice.

The brandy bottle is handed around, drunk from, wiped clean with the back of the sleeve and passed on.

'God, it's cold. Freezing my bloody balls off. Come on then. Let's get going.'

Engines of the open-back trucks vibrate into life, headlights flicker. Vapour from the panting exhausts rises up. Men sit close together overlapping each other in padded hunting jackets. Guns are secured on a gun rack. Ammunition has been checked and counted. Headlights slice the air. Tracker boys, in thin shirts and bald jerseys, scramble barefoot onto the open truck backs and handbrakes are released and the trucks pull away kicking at the earth, leaving biting tyre tracks in the hard ground.

He's left behind with Bastiaan and the boy who sets the targets up and the farm people, the 'boss boy' and the herdboys and shepherds and the women and old people and children and babies who live in the *kampong*. They stand, sharp-boned, behind the fence, watching the trucks roar away and the air is scented with the smell of damp scrub wood smoking sullenly, refusing to kindle and the surly *kampong* dogs lope a little way after the hunters' trucks and then lope back again.

He likes to shoot but he uses up his allotted rounds very quickly and the day is long. The hunters won't be back until dark and if the hunt is good they'll set up bush camp for a night, or perhaps two or even more.

He must wait for his father to come back before he can shoot again and, once the target shooting is over, the day lies empty in front of him and he shows he's ready for Bastiaan to come but Bastiaan will not come and he shouts as his father would and says he's a lazy little bugger and if he expects to be paid, first the work must be done.

Still Bastiaan won't come and he shakes his fist and shouts and shoos him into life, the way you would shoo a dog and chases him up, so the old man runs and he must run behind him and the first thing he learns is because of the magic in him, the old man can move very fast.

He's disobedient too and enjoys the joke of the boy running behind him and he runs like a hare and stops when he's ready. The boy stops too and the boy is panting and it's the old man who stops to give him time to get his breath back and when he has, it's the old man who turns and lopes into the bush.

He doesn't look back and there's no signal to follow

but the boy follows anyway, breaking branches as he goes, heavy as an elephant moving into the silence with a sound like thunder.

When he comes upon him, the old man is sitting on his haunches on the ground waiting for him and he sits like a man who's been sitting for a long time and is comfortable.

He has his fly whisk in his hand. It's made of giraffe-tail hair and he flicks it from side to side in the air and left, right, left, right and then down again with a rustle to show that he's ready to talk.

All animals were once people like ourselves. If you ask who made us anyone will tell you.

There are two gods. A greater and a lesser.

There were two creations and in the first all animals were people and all were at the mercy of the lesser god as well as the greater, but the lesser god is a trickster as well as a creator and mischievous and malicious and capable of stupid deeds.

The greater god is more powerful. From him comes life and the rising sun and in the second creation he separated man from the animals and gave him the great rule of life, which he denied them.

Old people say, when their time comes and they wonder how they will return to the world, it is Kagga the greater god who chooses the body of the animal which will honour them. It is he who puts the brand of that animal upon them and this is how it happens: the kori bustard fans the giant flames of the eternal fire with his great wings and heats the branding irons used by Kagga to mark those going forth.

First the zebra with his stripes and then the eland, hartebeest, ostrich, gemsbok, giraffe and duiker and all the other animals with their markings and last of all the black-backed jackal and brown hyena which are the least of the animals, and men who wish to be hunters must be marked in the same way.

White men say bush people kill dispassionately these creatures who were once people themselves. It is not so. It is the nature of hunters to kill animals but bush people show respect for the lives they take, never killing more than they can eat, never wasting any part of the animal that falls to their arrows.

He asks Bastiaan how it is that he and his people hunt so well and he gets his answer with a small flash of gum. 'It's because it is ourselves we hunt,' he says. 'Understand that and ask yourself: "What would I do now if I were that animal?" and your animal self will give you the answer.'

And there are other things to be learnt also.

A man may kill for food or self-defence but wanton killing will be punished and accidental killing, of even the smallest creature, should be guarded against for we are the protectors of those creatures we once were ourselves.

His father's friend, his 'Oom' Faan, the bald-headed bookworm, asks what the old 'baster boy', the 'outa' is teaching him.

'Things,' he says.

'Don't let him fill your head with a lot of rubbish,' he says. 'They love their liquor, you know. Our fault probably but once they got the taste for it, they took to it like ducks to water and it gets to them in the end.'

He taps against his bald head with his finger.

'Harmless enough but one foot in this world and one in the next.'

'Oom' Faan is older than the others and has more time for him. He tells him this season or maybe the next will be his last.

'I'm getting past it,' he says. 'I get tired and to be honest, I don't enjoy it as much as I once did.'

Sometimes he leaves the men inside the house drinking and telling their stories and puts on his jacket and shows Conrad to do the same and come outside with him and they sit on the top step of the stoep together looking up at the great dark dome above them and the lacing of stars that covers the night.

'They're not just a random speckling of lights, you know,' his uncle says and he too has gifts to give and he teaches him to read the night.

'If you know how to read the stars you need never be afraid. Wherever in the world you are they'll be there and they'll welcome you. They'll be a beacon to light your way just like it says in the Bible.'

His uncle tells him fear and uncertainty melt away before knowledge. He tells him of Shakespeare and how man is the noblest creature in all creation.

'Because he is a reasoning creature,' he says.

Like an angel, like a god, the paragon of animals.

Scientists say it is not possible to equate human consciousness with animal consciousness. A man cannot get inside the soul of an animal. Such anthropomorphic projection is not possible.

But how can we be sure of this?

The little tracker tells him and shows with his hands that we must respect the lives we take, for the animal soul is no different from our own and when it falls to us to do what must be done, that soul must be delivered from its body without causing undue suffering.

He knows this now and this too is knowledge.

'You're thinking a lot these days,' his uncle says. 'You mustn't worry so much about things. Learning is never easy but it gets better. As you get older, it becomes easier.'

Fear and uncertainty melt away before knowledge. This is what his uncle tells him and it is so and yet it is not so.

The farm does something to his father. When he gets back the old town skin goes back on again and the quarrelling is worse. It's dark and ugly, in the air all around them, in every corner of the house and Conrad lies awake waiting for it, knowing it will come.

The sound of it brings Beeky out of bed into his room. She stands in the doorway in her pyjamas, outlined small and square against the passage light and her face is invisible.

'Tell them to stop,' she says.

As if there's nothing he isn't able to do, if only she asks him to do it; but he has to tell her he can't do this.

The shouting is bad but the muffled noises in the silence are worse. They wait for them together. She in the doorway and he sitting up in bed, with his heart cramping in his chest and his breath stuck in his throat, wondering how long it'll take this time, before it's over.

He'd rather have shouting than the terrible thudding and the silences between them and Beeky feels this too.

He and Beeky are not allowed ever to be in the same bed any more. Not to read books together, not to hear stories at bedtime or play board games or cards to pass the time on winter afternoons.

'Beds are for sleeping in,' his father says. 'Not for playing games.'

He can't go to her bed even to say goodnight to her. He has to stand at the door of her room and wave. He can't go in, just in case his father comes past and finds him.

His father says if he ever finds them together it isn't God who'll punish them. He'll see to it himself. He'll give each of them a hiding they'll never forget and they'll be sorry for it for the rest of their lives.

It never used to be important. Once they used to share. Not for the whole night, but at bedtime his mother would open the covers of Beeky's bed and he'd climb in and his mother would read to them both and then he'd climb out again, and they'd all say goodnight to each other.

Goodnight, sleep tight, sweet dreams, see you in the morning and they'd blow each other kisses and then he'd leave her with her toys and her night light.

He's too old for that now.

'You have your own room and she has hers,' his father says. 'She stays in her place and you stay in yours. You hear what I say?'

He knows what his father says but the terrible thudding is happening again and the sound of something like a chair falling over and his sister wants him now and he wants her close to him.

'Come here,' he says.

He moves to one side and pulls the covers open.

'Jump in quickly. We'll make a Christmas bed.'

At Christmas, at the beach house when they were small and there were friends and cousins all together and not enough places for everyone to sleep, the youngest children bundle together and make a Christmas bed and it's lovely to lie all tangled up in the summer dark guessing who'll get what for Christmas and listening to the grown-ups and the clink of men's glasses outside on the veranda and the women in the kitchen rattling cups down from the shelf and putting out biscuits and cakes.

He lies in the dark with Beeky next to him. He can feel her heart beating through her soft, bird-bone ribs, right through her body. He moves his hands free and puts them over her ears so all she can hear is her own blood flowing with a soft whisper like the sea and all she can feel is him and how safe she is with him.

When the silence with the terrible thuds inside it ends and the shouting comes again it doesn't touch them and they lie warm and safe together in their Christmas boat bed.

Today the girl is painting blue pictures. Blue as bruises. Ultramarine and cobalt, Winsor blue, indigo and azure. Purple as blood and mauve for half-mourning. A blue mountain and a white house, blue faces and tears and bright blue slashes that run across the page going nowhere and in the middle a terrible cry of red.

The Old Madam has found a new place. In a gabled armoire in a small bedroom at the back of the house. A neglected room, closed up because of the rising damp. The room of an indigent relative taken reluctantly into service a long time ago. No longer remembered. Long since gone.

A river runs under the house. Its source is two eyes in the high rock. They have a snake god to guard them and they never close. They see everything and the river comes down as it always has and takes the form of its god and snakes its way along its old path under the house, stroking at the house's foundations, creeping up through the walls, swelling the bricks so the paint blisters and big pieces of plaster detach themselves and fall to the ground.

That's the revenge of the lord of the river on houses that stand in his way.

The room smells of water oozing through clay. It groans with the swelling of bricks. There's a trickle of slime down a wall and a furious ceaseless drip that refuses to be pacified.

It's a storeroom now, with unused furniture stacked up willy-nilly. A Regency pram, the old hip bath she used once upon a time when she still had a body to care for.

There's a gramophone and the skull of the last hippopotamus in the Berg River which was shot by her husband two days before he died, and dust everywhere. An iron cot and a rocking horse stiff with age and lack of use and a misted mirror disintegrating on the wall.

It's a fine place for ghosts.

The Old Madam has made up her mind. If a house turns discordant, the best thing to do is retreat for a generation or two and the back of the cupboard, in the slimy damp room, is as good a place as any.

Not even the servants go there. They leave her in peace. Which is more than she can say for her own descendants.

'The Old Madam spooks in that room,' the servants say. 'If you go in there your hair will turn white and she'll slam the door behind you so you'll never be able to get out. You'll be trapped there for ever and she'll fly out from the cupboard and hit you till you bleed.'

Well, not exactly, but servants are easy to scare. The creak of an unoiled hinge, a quick hard blow of icy death air. A door slamming. A mirror detached from the wall with a nice splintering crash to the ground and they're up and running and gone for ever.

'Lazy buggers,' the current master says. 'Got to watch them like hawks. Cook up any story to get out of doing their work properly.'

'They're frightened,' says his wife.

'I'll give them frightened,' her husband says. 'Back of the hand frightened is what they need to worry about. Not a pack of old wives' stories about ghosts. You tell them, it's the living they need to be worried about. The dead can look after themselves.'

In such a house it's better to roll up into a small ball and lie dormant among the lingering smell of naphtha and dust and wait for the wink of an eye it will take while the generation passes away and the lord of the river does his best to pull the house down.

Scratch, scratch goes the girl. Her head is sparking fire. Her elbow swings backwards and forwards radiating light and the scratch is stick charcoal on paper and the Old Madam's room is filling up with the fire-head's things. Paper and little tins of paint. Bright coloured jars of water and dirty pieces of rag and pens and pencils and crayon everywhere.

She can smell the girl coming.

They all have their own smell. The mother eddies past on roses and fear. You have to be quick to catch her. She's so soundless she's almost more ghost than person herself.

The boy smells of salt and the outside world. The man is anger and saltpetre and the sudden rich smell of dark earth being opened with the quick turn of a spade.

The girl has a smell all her own. The red-hair smell of musk and sweet peas and the sweet drift of cat underneath and gardenia and old coals and old hurts coming from the mark on her arm, which glows in the half-dark with wistfulness.

She comes and goes and a swift light puff of air and the Old Madam is buzzed awake and the cupboard door stands open to catch her up quick and she bends to her work, pinned in the streaks of its mirror, and the Old Madam can watch everything she does and she doesn't seem to notice at all.

Flowers and faces, a cat and a bird. A gecko

sleeping on a stone. A lemon tree glowing with lemons. Clouds and the sun and the stars and the moon. Whole worlds grow from her fingers, spinning out like a spider's web, weaving themselves into being.

She cares nothing about the Old Madam or the ghost or the servants' stories and the Old Madam shimmers close and blows light on her hair and she swipes her away with a scrape of her hand. So the Old Madam adds a little ice wind to the blow, grave wind, colder and ranker than anything anyone here can know and it doesn't make any difference at all. The girl doesn't even turn around, the way people do when they know they're not alone.

'A goose walking over my grave,' they say and they say it with a shudder.

Which is nonsense. Geese don't walk on graves. They pick their way hot-step past them and keep their beaks up and their heads to the wind. The disturbed dead can be very troublesome, even the silliest goose knows that, but Beeky the fire-head doesn't seem to.

JEROME

The Night the Lyceum Burnt Down

The night the Lyceum burnt down the chief projectionist at the Alhambra took a chance and ran the evening show alone. He sent his assistant round to tell Jerome's father it was all over.

Jerome was there when the news came. He was sitting at the kitchen table having supper with his dad and his mum and his Aunty Doris who lives in the flat across the way from theirs.

'If I know the Lyceum, it must have been rats and fleas and cockroaches first,' Doris says. 'And after that every man for himself and women and children to shift for themselves.'

But his father isn't in the mood for laughing. He puts his face in his hands, right there at the kitchen table, and cries. He cries the way a man does when a close relative dies. That's what the Lyceum meant to him.

When he pulled himself together he asked Jerome's mother for his coat and hat and went off on the bus to Salt River, to see for himself and pay his last respects and he got there so quickly that when he arrived what was left of the old place was still smouldering.

There are bits and pieces still left in one piece. Not much. Nothing worth taking but what's left and is up for grabs, he takes. Out of sentiment's sake, he says. He can't bring himself to leave anything for the insurance people. He's never had the idea that insurance people have any real feeling for bioscope, so why should they have the things that are left.

People may call bioscope 'cinema' these days and very grand it sounds too; but he isn't one of them. He was born a bioscope person and he'll die one and it's bioscope people who know what bioscope's all about and in his book that gives them rights.

He gets a friend with a lorry, gives him a couple of bob and brings just whatever there is to be scavenged back to their place and Jerome watches while he does it.

'Helped himself to it,' Doris says. 'Place wasn't even burned down yet and he was there for the pickings, out to grab just whatever he could before it was even cold.'

'Makes no odds,' says his mum. 'He had no choice. It was that or the insurance people.'

It isn't much. Just six old bioscope seats made of red velvet, all joined together with brass flip-top ashtrays on the back.

Jerome is standing at the top of the steps outside Highcliffe Flats where they live when the lorry arrives. He watches his dad and his dad's friend carry the chairs in and you can smell the fire on them and they're still wet with hose water.

'They'll dry out,' his dad says. 'They'll be good as new. You see if they aren't.'

'What are we supposed to do with them?' his mum

wants to know. 'I'm not running a storage yard, you know.'

'I wouldn't worry about that if I was you,' Doris says. 'You know what he's like. They won't be around for long. He'll flog them. Mark my words.'

'No, he won't,' says his mum. 'He'll expect me to find a place for them here. I can see it in his face.'

It's all in the newspaper the next day. His mum likes her newspaper and although they know all about it already, first-hand from his dad, she reads it out to him anyway.

'If it wasn't in the newspaper she wouldn't believe it really happened,' Doris says. 'Not even though your dad saw it with his own eyes and half what's left of the place is sitting in your front room.'

No-one else cares what the newspaper has to say about anything at all but his mother sticks to her guns.

'I like to keep up with the times,' she says and it isn't every day 'the times' happen in a person's own house, so this once no-one can begrudge her.

'Just listen to this,' she says. 'It says here that the fire brigade had their hands full and they did their best, but even so they couldn't save the old place.'

Doris says it's because it was built on the cheap in the first place and it's a miracle it hadn't fallen down all by itself years ago. Never mind those buckets of sand all over the place, in a place full of people where there's hardly a face without a burning cigarette stuck in the middle of it, if they'd asked her, she could have told them it was a fire just waiting to happen.

'They say it's a write-off,' his mum says and puts the paper down. 'Come have a look at the picture, lovey,' she says to Jerome. 'It's a shame it's gone really, it wasn't such a bad place for the kind of place it was, but it's a sight to see just the same.'

It is a sight to see. Firemen with their helmets hanging back off their heads holding onto their hoses for dear life as if the hoses were wild things with a life all their own and smoke billowing out of the old turrets at the top of the building and flames everywhere.

The picture's nice but he can look at the picture anytime. It isn't the picture that worries him. He asks his mum if it doesn't say anything anywhere about the chairs.

'What chairs?' she says.

She gives him a know-nothing face with a blank look on it and a raise of her eyebrows and a little wink just between him and her.

Before, once upon a time, he would have said 'the chairs in our front room' because that was the truth but that doesn't go down, so he doesn't do it any more.

'What chairs?' and a wink is his mum's idea of a joke. It means if anyone should ask, even him, even though the chairs are right there in the room next door, they've never heard of them, they wouldn't know a thing called a bioscope seat even if they fell over it in the road and they don't know anything about it at all.

Jerome is afraid because the seats have been stolen from Mr Immelman, his father's boss who owns all the bioscopes in town and a whole lot of other things too and he thinks what Doris says may be right. Which is that money has clout and people like Mr Immelman who have it, don't take kindly to being relieved of it without so much as their say-so.

Jerome thinks the insurance company will find out what his dad's done and tell Mr Immelman on him. He thinks Mr Immelman will be furious at being done down and send the police and the police will come to the door and take them all away to jail.

It's too much for him. He can't get it out of his mind. A picture of the police arriving and his mum and dad and him and maybe even Doris, for being an accessory, being dragged away, plays like a bioscope show in his head and keeps him awake at night.

He can hear the bang on the door and his dad saying how he didn't do it and the bioscope chairs, large as life in their front room, showing him up for the liar he is.

He can see the smirk on the policemen's faces and hear the click of the handcuffs and he knows for sure, no matter what happens to him and Doris, his mum will be one of the ones taken off, because of her keeping stolen goods in her front room and never reporting it.

'This nonsense of Kenny's has finished the child's nerves off,' Doris says. 'A child has its own way of looking at things. Once an idea is stuck in its head there's nothing in the world that will shift it.'

It gets so bad Jerome doesn't want to go out at all and every time there's a knock at the door, even if it's only Doris, he nearly jumps out of his skin.

'He's your child, Bet,' his dad says. 'You speak to him.'

And she does.

'Don't be such a bloody little fool,' she says. 'No-one's coming to take anyone away. You see too much bioscope. That's the trouble. It puts ideas in your head.'

He loves the pictures. Sometimes he'll go to a different film every day because of his father being in the trade and him getting in free.

He likes war films and gangsters and science

fiction, but horror films are his favourite. He can watch a horror film seven or eight times, until he knows exactly when the most scary parts are coming. Then he'll stop looking at the screen and look at the people around him instead, waiting for them to put their hands over their eyes and scream and hang onto each other and nearly jump out of their seats with fright.

People are funny when they're frightened. It's funnier than any comedy you'd ever see. It's so funny it makes you want to laugh out loud, except you can't because then you'd give yourself away and you'd be the one everyone was looking at, instead of the other way around.

In bioscope, in cops and robbers before the picture ends, the police always catch the crooks. There's a big bang on the door and they're out there, standing on the doorstep with their badge in one hand to show who they are and handcuffs in the other, ready to take you away and put you behind bars.

'But they have to catch you at it first, don't they lovey?' his mother says.

It was only a bioscope but things were different after the Lyceum burnt down.

It was after that it began and it began in a small way, on the day he went to Mr Osram's shop to fetch his mother's newspaper and stole a Chappie's bubble-gum. He got caught and Mr Osram handed the shop over to his wife and brought him home right up the front steps to his own front door and handed him over to his mum.

'You better sort it out,' he says. 'Otherwise you're going to have a proper little crook on your hands.'

When his mum told his dad what happened, his dad didn't like it.

'Bloody nerve he's got,' his dad says. 'Damn coolie talking about a white kid like that.'

'Your dad's right,' his mum says. 'You should have tried bigger. If you're going to be insulted by a bloody curry-muncher you should have made it worth your while. It shouldn't be about a few cents of bubble-gum.'

He didn't go back to Osram's after that. He switched to Nick's instead, but Nick had eyes everywhere so that didn't last very long. Then he went two blocks further, to Pombo the Portuguese and after that there were always sweets in his room and comics too. Just whenever he wanted them.

'He's pinching the stuff,' Doris says. 'You don't have to be on *Test the Team* to work that out.'

'So what?' says his mum. 'It's nothing anyone will miss. All the kids do it and if you ask me, it's the kind of thing that'll probably make him a rich man one day. Kenny's honest. Straight as a die, no matter what you think. Hasn't got him very far. Not like some other people I can name.'

The 'other people' she means is Manny Immelman, who people say burnt the Lyceum down for the insurance money.

Doris says his mum can dress it up anyway she likes, no matter who Manny Immelman is and what he owns, if he did what people say he did, it's still common-or-garden thieving.

'Am I saying it's not?' his mum says. 'All I'm saying is at least it's thieving big-time and if he can pull it off and walk away a richer man and his wife walks down Adderley Street with a fur coat on her back, I say good luck to him.'

That's the trouble at their house. His mum feels hard done by. If Mrs Immelman wanted to change places and move in at Highcliffe House she wouldn't have to ask twice. His mum would say, 'Yes, don't mind if I do,' and have the fur coat off Mrs Immelman's back so fast she wouldn't even have time to change her mind.

Jerome, busy with sweets and comics and a plastic model of an armoured car he's putting together piece by tiny piece, doesn't say anything. He doesn't like it when the subject of people taking things that don't belong to them comes up and Doris snaps her eyes on him.

'It's an ill wind,' she says.

She's looking right at him, sitting out of the way with a newspaper spread for tidiness and the print plan for his model laid out neat across the top corner of it.

'You hear what I say, Jerome?' Doris says.

'Yes, Aunty Doris,' he says and, over his shoulder, he gives her his beautiful, angel smile.

One thing you can say about Jerome. He may be everything Doris thinks about him and worse but you have to admit he's a beautiful-looking boy. Everyone says so.

Jerome doesn't think about it much but if you asked him, he'd have said he didn't expect to amount to much in life. His mum says life works in mysterious ways and you can never tell how it'll all turn out in the end so they may as well look on the bright side, which his dad says is 'stuffing ideas in his head'.

'He's got plenty of ideas already,' is Doris's opinion. 'Wouldn't do him any harm to listen to a few down-to-earth facts for a change. It doesn't matter what you say, Bet. He'll find out soon enough that life and bioscope are two different things.'

He's in 'Special' class in school and that's a joke all by itself, because no matter how his mum tries to dress it up 'Special' doesn't mean what she makes it out to mean.

He isn't 'special' because he's God's own gift. He's 'special' because he can't get his reading right and so he can't write properly.

'He reads the newspaper,' his mum says.

'He looks at the comics,' says Doris.

'We read the newspaper together, don't we lovey?' says his mum, and his dad and Doris give each other a look and his dad's the one who speaks.

'You read him pieces out of the newspaper, Bet, and you can do it as much as you like,' his dad says. 'Until he can read for himself and I'm not talking about just a word here and there it's no bloody good to him.'

'A railway porter,' is Doris's opinion. 'That's about as far as he'll go.'

'No son of mine,' says his mum. 'Not with his looks. With his looks he could be a film star. Gregory Peck doesn't make his money out of being able to read the newspaper and nor does Paul Newman. You don't need book-learning for that.'

'If we lived in America,' says Doris. 'Not here. Here it's a different story.'

CONRAD

The Second Season

In Conrad's second season it's warmer during the day than it should be. The humidity is high. The grass is sighing and the animals are silent and elusive. They have sought out what shade they can. It's hazy and the whole world is quiet.

They've seen the rain snake, a puff adder, the green and yellow colours of the rainbow slithering across their path and away.

Bastiaan comes close to him and says there will be a storm and it will rain.

'From a clear sky,' the others say. 'Bloody nonsense. We should have shot the bloody thing. If we see rain today I'm a horse's arse. Wrong time of year for it in this bloody part of the country.'

The sky is light and clear as an unrippled pond and Conrad says nothing but he believes Bastiaan. If he says the storm will come bringing rain with it, then it will come and it is as Bastiaan says and the lightning comes, whirling with a sullen rumble of thunder drumming against a bruising sky, and he's afraid of lightning.

He can feel it coming. The clouds that appear ahead of it are high as mountains, stained with grey and purple as mountains are and as majestic.

They flash and flicker. They ride above the earth with a terrible clashing sound like cymbals and Conrad knows little but when the storm comes he knows how it will be. It will be the rain bull, a He-Rain and not the She-Rain that falls gently and blesses the earth.

Dead men ride with the He-Rain. This is why people fear it. These men come out of the ground and gallop with the rain and what we call rain are their Rain-legs riding over us and they hold the rain in their power, with thongs like horses' reins, and they ride the rain free and powerful like this because they own it.

He knows about Lightning; that it is a simple thing and not a thing to be afraid of. He knows because Bastiaan told him.

Lightning is sent by Rain to carry off girls; and Lightning can follow their scent and find them wherever they are. This is why women keep themselves hidden when the feel of rain is in the air; because they don't want Lightning to take them.

Clouds are the hair of the people already taken. Their hair flies up into the air and becomes black rain clouds and before the rain, the clouds come back as a reminder, so women can hide themselves in good time and learn from what has gone before and be safe.

If a shower catches them in the open they must find a place where Lightning has already been, because he will never go back again. Places where people have already been taken are the safest, because they are the most sacred. Lightning knows this and would never be so foolish as to return.

The girls are not taken for no good reason. Being so small and beautiful they're turned into stars, which are small fragments of lightning, and they lend their beauty to the night sky but wherever beauty goes envy comes in its wake.

Rain became envious. He loved the stars so much he wished for some for himself and even though water and fire can never be one, Lightning agreed and because the stars were already so many, those that could be spared became water lilies instead, the Wives of the Water, the flowers that grow in pools. This is the fate of women. Everyone knows this. Lightning is not the business of men, but there is too much of his father in him and he cannot in his heart believe and so he's afraid.

Rain is a giant leopard and its eyes flash lightning and thunder roars from its throat.

Rain is the story of Elephant and his wife, the beautiful Antbear girl, who begged so hard for his secret and could not make him tell. For his secret was the secret of Water which was Rain's gift to him and he wanted to keep it all to himself, but one day he came home from the waterhole and his wife saw mud caked on his legs and demanded to know what it was he was keeping from her. Still he refused to tell. So, as we are all the children of !Goa, she called for her brothers, the little black birds called 'the children of rain', and told them what Elephant was up to and how he had kept secrets from her and they killed him.

To bring Rain, to set the earth right, you must first charm a water animal and attach a rope to its nose and the rope must be sturdy and long because it must extend as far across the land as you wish rain to fall.

You must call sorcerers and tell them to bring with them tortoiseshell boxes filled with the bitter leaves of buchu to seduce with its wonderful fragrance and the boxes should be ornamented with strings hanging down and if Rain comes it will come bearing gifts not only of water but of mopane and monkey orange.

It will kiss the leaves of the Shepherd's tree and coax red syringa and donkey berries, brandy bush and Kalahari sand raisins out of the earth, for being as Rain is, is not an easy matter, and the work is much harder than it looks.

When the rain comes it catches them unprepared; in the middle of nowhere with nothing to do but look for open places to crouch low on the ground. Those that can, pull ground sheets from the truck over themselves for protection and wait for the rain to hit.

'Jesus Christ,' someone says.

There is nothing else to say. They are not Bushmen or Basters but they are men after all and in some things all men are the same, even if they don't know it, and all men, young or old, have lessons to learn and they all learn from the same teacher and that day they know once again that they are small and few and God is mighty and should not be angered.

Conrad cries. He feels it coming and he doesn't know where it's coming from but he can't stop himself. The ground under them seems to shake with the hammering of the thunder. The sky boils and there's a terrible stillness and then a wind like a thousand horses' hooves pounding and everything around them shivers and shudders and there's no shelter for miles.

He's crying out of fear and frailty and awe and the foolishness of his own vanity, imagining that a boy only in his second season could even begin to know the enormity and greatness that is the world.

He's crying with such a terrible sound that it makes the other men look at him and then look quickly away. He's crying in a way that brings his father to him, tall in front of him, angrier than he's ever seen him, angry with an anger reserved for men which is very different from the anger to do with women or boys. He's angry, enormous, his face red with shame.

'What are you?' his father asks and the rain is still gathering its forces, not yet at its full strength, although it soon will be.

'Are you a baby?' his father says. 'Are you a girl? Are you peeing in your pants because of a little bit of thunder and lightning? What is this thing you are? Tell me. Because you're certainly not a man.'

It's too much for him and there's nothing he can do. It's as if something has leapt inside him and taken him over. Something that has him in its grip and shakes and cavorts inside him and he can't stop crying and then his father hits him flat-handed, hard across the face, with a sound like a rifle crack and with such force that he's slammed to the ground and lies there for a few moments with all the wind knocked out of him.

'Get up,' his father says.

He has cracked his head hard and his nose is streaming blood. He can taste it in his mouth, in the back of his throat and they can all see him, crouched like an animal, with his hand against his wet aching cheekbone.

'Get up,' his father says.

'For God's sake, Jack,' says 'Oom' Faan. 'It's enough. Leave it. He's only a boy.'

But his father has the dark burning thing in him and he cannot leave it. He has been shamed by his own son, in front of his own people and even if he had the will to, his devils have him now and he cannot leave it even if he wanted to.

'Get up,' he says.

He bends down and grabs the boy by the elbow and pulls him up, until he's standing, hurting, sobbing with fright in front of him with his arm across his eyes to hide his shame.

'Come with me,' he says.

'Forget it, Jack,' one of the others says but they know him and know they speak into the wind and nothing they can say will change anything and the thing must take its course.

He has the boy by the arm and he moves away dragging the boy behind him and the boy is crying against the wind and the world boils around them and the thunder cracks in their ears and he pulls the boy to a solitary tree.

A thorn tree, a pain tree, its branches bent double from the stab of a porcupine quill in the days when it was young.

'Climb it,' his father says.

'I can't, Pa,' says the boy.

'Climb,' says his father. 'If a baboon can climb, so can you.'

Conrad's arms are like lead. He lifts one up and then the other and pulls himself up waist high onto the lowest branch and with a side swing turns around and sits where he is.

'Higher,' his father says.

It has begun to rain now. Grey stripes of water that hack at the ground and the branches of the tree.

'Higher,' his father shouts. 'Right up to the top.'

He is near the top and there's nowhere else to go and there's a cleft to wedge his body into and the tree sways and bends with the force of the coming gale and his body is wrenched with fear and with knowing, in some place inside himself, that when the He-Rain comes trees are the most dangerous place to be.

'You stay there, boy,' his father says. 'You stay there and you don't move. You don't move, until I tell you you can come down.'

From a distance away, where they crouch small-figured, they can all see him, the other men. The 'basters', the trackers, the lowliest servants. They can see him lodged in his tree, crying in the wind and the rain like a girl, while the thunder shakes and the lightning darts around the sky and the burden of his shame is unbearable.

It's what the yoke ox must feel, he thinks, with the yoke heavy around his neck, immovable, to be endured, to be suffered, no matter how great the pain.

These men know him now. They know him for what he is and they'll always remember. Even when he's an old man and they're even older, they'll never forget and his humiliation is complete.

It's quiet when he comes down and his father is himself again.

The ground is wet. Slippery with mud and there's slipping and sliding and laughter and men with rain-slick hair and faces whipped red by the wind who look very strange to him. As if they're ants, rolling around inside a cowhide drum they think is the world.

Their jokes and relief and laughter reverberate inside and around, moving a little distance and bouncing off the sides like echoes that vanish away and are of no importance in the great silence which is outside, but his father is pleased.

'I sent a baboon up a tree,' he says. 'But I got back a man.'

He puts his arm around the boy's shoulders and offers him brandy.

'To put some fire in your belly,' he says and the boy drinks but he doesn't like it. He feels no fire. All he feels is a burning emptiness.

'Take it,' 'Oom' Faan says. 'It will burn the cold and the pain away.'

He's covered in livid scratches from his climb and they sting like viper bites and later his father takes him aside, away from the others, and talks to him.

'I do it for your own good,' he says. 'We all come into this world afraid. It's God's plan. It's His test for us. You stand in church on Sunday. You know what God wants from us. Those who learn to conquer fear and stand up and be counted as men, He makes great.'

The brandy, which his stomach didn't like, swims into his head.

'Don't waste your time being afraid of God's messengers,' his father says. 'What's thunder? A child banging a drum. What's lightning? Fireworks. Forget about such things. Be afraid of God. Your life is in His hands. He can protect you or He can take your life from you. That's all there is. That's all you need to worry about.'

That night, the last night, it's quiet and clear again. He sits alone on the top step of the stoep and reads the stars. He thinks how sensible his father's God is to light heaven with them and then draw the darkness over Himself to shield Himself from men and find peace.

There's meat cooking and the air is full of the smell of it. The men are around the fire and there's laughter and electric light spilling out of the farmhouse windows and although he no longer needs a teacher, 'Oom' Faan comes and sits next to him. Just sitting. For a long time. Until he's ready to speak.

'I've decided,' he says. 'We spoke of it last year. This

year I've decided. This will be my last season. I'm getting too old for it. I've had enough.'

'Oom' Faan likes a pipe. At home Aunt Sara won't let him smoke in the house. Here no-one minds and he can smoke where he likes but old habits die hard. He's used to being sent outside to smoke. Now this is the way he prefers it.

I'll miss it, the boy thinks. The pipe-tapping, the pipe-filling, the striking up and the long draws. The smell of tobacco and firesmoke and 'Oom' Faan's bald head and his quiet way of speaking and the way he's different from the others.

'This business of manhood,' 'Oom' Faan says. 'It comes to different people in different ways. I've seen it. I know what it is.'

He sits where he is and looks out at the night and the bush as deep and dark and unknowable as the sea and he's not afraid. He feels nothing.

'Now I've made up my mind,' his uncle says. 'There's something I want to give you.'

He wants to give Conrad his rifle. He says he won't be needing it again. It is a 375 Holland and Holland, a beautiful gun and good for this kind of territory.

'Your father's got his eye on it,' he says. 'He likes a good gun but I want you to have it. It'll make me proud to give it to you. It needs a man worthy of it. A man who knows how to treat it with respect.'

Conrad thinks his uncle would like to reach out his hand and touch him. He wouldn't mind if he did but he knows he won't. So they sit beside each other for a while longer and the smoke from 'Oom' Faan's pipe curves up in a slow, predictable way and scents the air.

'I know you, Conrad,' he says. 'You mustn't worry about it too much. Your father is the kind of man he is. You'll be the kind of man you'll be. That's how it is.'

He isn't sure.

He isn't sure if he's in his father but sometimes he fears his father is in him and will be too strong for him and it makes him afraid.

When he goes home again it is bad but it is different and their mother has changed.

'If I should leave you,' she says, 'you must always watch out for each other.'

'Where are you going?' says Beeky.

'Nowhere,' their mother says. 'I didn't say I was going anywhere. I'm just supposing.'

Conrad doesn't like 'supposing'. It's a game Beeky and his mother play. He could play too, if he wanted, but he's too old for games. He never liked these kind of games anyway and 'supposing' is his least favourite.

Supposing we lived in a house of our own with roses round the door and the afternoon sun knocking at our windows and a green grove of *naartjies* and sweet and bitter orange trees covered with blossom.

Suppose we had crystal muscatel grapes and freckled hanepoort and strawberries planted in between and there were just the three of us and there was no winter and we could eat as much as we liked of them just whenever we liked. I think we'd be happy then.

Suppose we lived in a fisherman's house with white walls and a thatch roof and swam in the waves and the rocks gave us mussels and perlemoen and fat *alikreukel* fast asleep in their shells and fish every day for our supper and fires of driftwood to cook them on. Supposing we did. Just we three. I think we'd be happy then.

‘That’s what Mamma means,’ Beeky says. ‘It’s only a game. We play it sometimes to cheer ourselves up.’

‘I don’t like it,’ Conrad says. ‘I think it’s silly. I don’t think we should play it any more.’

JEROME

The Almond Hedge

Special Class are going to some rich person's house for a picnic and Jerome doesn't want to go.

'You should go and have a look at it, lovey,' his mum says. 'It's in the news and you know about it. You know who those people are. I've read to you about them out of the newspaper.'

At first it was touch and go if they'd be allowed to go at all. Suddenly the place was so special it was almost more special than they were. All because the Forestry Department were clearing up and found some bones there and it turned out they were the bones of some kid who'd died.

'It's an exceptional find,' Miss Belcher says. 'The experts from the university think these are the bones of a Bushman child and there's a story there somewhere. They're working on it at the moment, trying to piece it together.'

As if it mattered.

'The child may have got caught in the hedge,' she says. 'Bushmen are very small people. A Bushman child could easily have crawled into the hedge to look for something and then not been able to get out. He could have got stuck there.'

Like a rat in a trap.

'That's what the hedge was for,' Miss Belcher says. 'The early settlers, the first people who came to this country, planted that hedge to keep Bushmen away from their settlement.'

'Why?' Jerome wants to know.

'To protect their possessions,' Miss Belcher says.

What she won't say, because teachers can't, is that if the whites hadn't done something to stop them, the little buggers would probably have helped themselves to everything they could lay their hands on.

'Well, they didn't do such a bad job then, did they Miss?' he says.

The hedge is still standing. Even now, with all their book-learning, they haven't enough brains between them to get it out. Which shows whoever put the hedge there in the first place meant it to stay and while they were at it they did a good job.

That much he can work out for himself.

The hedge is an ugly thing, deep-rooted, impossible to get out and it too has its story which is not told often now.

There was a Bushman once and his wife who lived in that place and they were blessed with a child. A boy. Which was a cause for much celebration, because the great sorrow of bush people is that the Great god gives them so few children and such children that come are gifts and precious.

This was a fine child and he grew strong and he danced and played *djani*, which is a game of reed and sinews and guineafowl feathers which can be flicked with a stick and spun high into the air and caught when they fall and flicked up again, which everyone knows is how Light was carried into the world in the first place.

His father taught him to make string from leaf fibre and how to use it to snare birds and how to bait a trap with an insect and sweet gum which is always a small bird's undoing.

When the boy was born his mother adorned herself for joy. She put on bracelets and pendants and asked her sisters to put bright beads and feathers in her hair. She tied strings of rattles to her ankles and the rattles were cocoons where moths had slept and flown free as butterflies and the small chips of stone and ostrich shell sang together, embracing each other, making music for the boy, who was a gift to them all.

Then one day when he was grown the boy wandered too far and didn't come back and they feared for him. They searched day and night and their name people searched with them, as if for their own child, for the loss of one is the loss of all and the stars know it.

They searched in the places he knew. They searched in the places beyond his knowing but the boy could not be found.

There was a terrible sadness and talk of lions and the brown hyena and the shaman danced and he danced through the mountain and into the rock.

When he returned he threw himself to the ground and blood poured from his nose and he told them he'd seen many wonderful places and things such as other men only dream of, but he had not seen the boy.

He said what they feared. That the boy, because of his beauty and promise, had been taken by the //gauwasi to be their husband in the other world, in the eastern sky where they live.

When she heard it, the mother's heart cracked open and she put away her beads and her anklets. She plucked the feathers from her hair and lay down to die and she had already begun the journey when she was called back by the sound of her husband's drum beating.

She raised herself up and asked what he was doing and he told her to stand up and come out from their hut and see for herself what it was he'd done.

He'd built a high fire which could be seen all around, that much she could see for herself. The promise she could not see, for it was given in words, and this is what he said.

He said he would sit all night by the fire beating his drum so the boy might hear and find his way back to his father's home fire and his mother's hut.

His wife sat beside him and together they gazed into the fire and no-one can know the depth of a mother's grief which is deeper than any river and runs with a stronger current which is the current of birth-blood.

But the Bush-father knew it, and knowing it and not wanting it to take his wife along on its course, he put a question to her and the question was this.

As time is nothing but the coming and going of the sun and the moon and the stars, perhaps his wife would sit beside him and wait with him. So she would be there, ready with her pendants and anklets and the beads and feathers for her hair when their son was restored to them, in whichever world at whichever moment that great thing happened.

She looked into the fire which was her hope and when she'd thought about it for a long time, she turned to her husband and said she would do it.

Jerome gets on the bus with the others and he's quicker than they are and smarter too. The first thing he does is find a seat at the back where he's out of the teachers' way.

Not seen, not heard. That's the best way.

The teachers have their hands full with the smaller ones who are nearly out of their minds with excitement about the bus and going on an outing and doing something different for a change.

He isn't interested in them. He has something in his pocket which is far more interesting than they could ever be. Something new. A two-bladed knife he took from the general shop down the main road.

It's big for a pocket knife because the blades inside it are so long. He measured them and the longest blade was almost twenty centimetres. He showed the knife to Ronny Lombard who lives in the flats just down the road from them.

'You want to watch out,' Ronny says. 'You could do some damage with that.'

That's what he thought too and that's as much as Ronny Lombard knows even though he's got his Standard Eight certificate and his apprentice's papers.

The knife is fine as far as knives go but when he first got it the blades were so blunt you could just about cut an apple in half with it. But he fixed that. He sharpened them so they shone like razor blades and were just as sharp. Now, if you drop a sheet of paper on the blade it will shave it in two. Or just about.

The blades are bright silver the way he's sharpened them and their points are dagger points. If you press a point to your skin, just the very lightest touch, a small bubble of blood will pop out.

He won't do it on the bus, in case someone catches him, but when he's alone he likes to take the knife out and flick the blades free just to look at them.

When they get there it isn't as bad as he thought it would be.

The house has big gates like big houses do in films and when they get to them the bus driver has to stop and hoot.

A coon boy in uniform comes out from a small guardhouse and shows to wait and they wait. The bus engine chugs while they wait and the coon boy goes back to the guardhouse to phone up to the big house and while he's away it's Miss Belcher's turn to chirp up and throw in her tuppence ha'penny worth.

'Look children,' she says. 'If you look behind the gate you can see the wild almond hedge.'

'Why is it important, Miss?' some bright spark says.

'Because it's a piece of history,' Miss Belcher says and she doesn't say any more.

History is for her to know and them to find out. History is something that doesn't concern them, because of them being so stupid and she's said all she has to say on the matter.

Then the coon comes back and calls to another coon and there are Dobermanns behind the gates, not doing anything, just pacing up and down and coming up and pushing their heads against the gates so they can look out and Jerome sees them looking and he looks back.

He feels the weight of the knife in his pocket and although they're there to keep you in your place he feels nothing for the dogs. One slit of the throat and they're dead. So his knife has changed some things and that's one of them.

They're all out of the bus and walking in pairs up a path that's about as wide as the National Road and all you see is trees and you get the idea that if you keep on walking you'll end up in Johannesburg.

He likes making a nuisance of himself with Miss

Chevalier because she's young and always rises to the bait and her tits are bigger than Jayne Mansfield's.

Miss Chevalier is oohing and aahing so you'd think she's just landed in heaven and every single thing is the most wonderful thing she's ever seen.

You'd swear she'd never seen a flower or a tree in her life before. It's 'Look children' this and 'Look children' that.

'Miss Chevalier, Miss,' he says. He shoots his hand up just like she said they must. 'Where do I go to take a piss, Miss?' he says.

'Piss, Miss' is funny. One or two of the bigger boys snicker and he gives his nice smile because there's nothing in this world Miss Big Tits can do about it.

You can be as 'special' as you like but you'd have to be very 'special' if you never had to pee and an absolute bloody fool to ask to leave the room when there's nothing around you but trees and bushes and all that other rubbish she keeps going on about.

'If you'd like to go to the toilet, Jerome, that's what you should say.'

'I'd like to go to the toilet, Miss,' he says and, even though it isn't funny, the way he says it is good for another snicker.

'We're allowed the use of a toilet, Jerome,' Big Tits says. 'When we get up to the house the housekeeper will show us where it is.'

'I don't think I can wait, Miss,' he says.

'If you really can't wait you'll just have to excuse yourself and go behind a bush,' she says.

She knows he doesn't want the toilet. All he's trying to do is get a rise out of her. He can see it from the red spots on her cheeks and the way her eyes go hard.

'I can't, Miss,' he says. 'I don't think it's just a pee. I need a lav.'

It's very funny, even some of the girls are giggling.

He's got her rattled, he can see that. She must be counting the days till the School Inspector comes and signs the papers that say they don't have any say-so over him any more, because when he's sixteen years old, it's time for him to leave.

As if they'd care. They'll probably throw a party.

'Then we'll just have to walk a little faster,' Miss Chevalier says in her schoolteacher way. 'The house is just up ahead.'

He couldn't care. He's had his fun. He may get on her tits but he can live without her just as much as she can live without him.

He wouldn't have her on a plate, even if she was offered to him, because she's a cow and she'll be a cow all her life. She'll stay where she is for ever, preaching at one wave of simpletons after another.

It won't be like that for him. Once he's out, something will turn up for him just like his mum's always saying it will and when it does, he'll grab at it and go on to better things.

He's already made up his mind about that.

The lav joke was OK. It gave him an excuse to get away and he thinks he wouldn't mind seeing the hedge up close. It isn't far and you couldn't miss it, even if you tried.

He thinks what he'll do is use his knife and cut through a piece just for the hell of it but when you get right up close you can see what old Belcher said is true.

They call it a hedge but it's like no other hedge he's ever seen. It's more like a tangle of small thick trees all knotted together. You'd really have to hack like hell to make any headway and even then, it would be slow going and a waste of time.

You'd never think a stupid plant could cause so

much trouble. Now he's seen it he doesn't know why they bother with the Dobermanns. They don't need dogs. All by itself the house is like a prison.

A stream runs next to it and there's a bridge and trees and a dark gleam of water and another smaller house and steps going down from it to a swimming pool so deep and brown it's almost black and it looks weird, like a mirror.

Banks of flowers are reflected in it as if they're painted on water and he can just imagine some poor fool thinking it's hard ground with flowers growing on it and stepping onto it and falling in the water and getting a water snake or a river eel up his jack for his trouble.

The small house by the pool is open but there's no-one there. There's a sun umbrella outside and tea things set out on a table under it. A jug of juice and glasses and ice in the juice jug and a plate of biscuits. Pink and blue and green, kids' iced biscuits, with zoo animals iced on them in different colours.

Someone has been swimming.

There's a towel thrown over the chair and a wet bum mark on the green seat cushion and a watch lying on the table next to the tea things.

It's a girl's watch with a gold face and a gold link strap like a bracelet. It's lying on the table next to the full jug of juice and the uneaten biscuits and the clean glasses no-one could even be bothered to touch and the second hand of the watch is fanning the dial and he picks it up and holds it in his hand and looks at it.

Bentley, fifteen jewels. It's written small on the face. What kind of jewels he wonders? If you opened up the back you could probably find out. Maybe you could even dig them out and these are rich people so they could probably be diamonds or real rubies but even if they were they'd be so small it wouldn't be worth the trouble.

It isn't a thing he'd really want, but leaving it lying where it is looks like an invitation to him. So he picks it up and puts it in his pocket and it's all so easy he doesn't even bother to look over his shoulder like he usually does, just to make sure the coast's clear.

He doesn't even think about it. The last thing he thinks is that when he turns around, there'll be a girl standing right behind him watching and he knows she must be the juice and biscuits girl and it wouldn't even be worth asking how he knows. You can just see it.

She's wearing white shorts and a white bikini top. She's got light skin and very bright hair and small freckles on her nose and on her shoulder is a blood-red mark and it's got a funny shape. Like when no-one was looking a cowboy in a film took a cow iron and heated it up and burned her with it, instead of the cow.

He's cross with himself for being caught. He hasn't been caught for a long time. He's been too smart for that. He hasn't been caught since Mr Osram caught him with a Chappie's bubblegum.

'You're a bit old to be one of the picnic children,' the girl says.

She's looking at him as if she's expecting him to say something, except she's wrong. He isn't planning to say anything. What he's planning to do is play dumb and stare her down.

All he has to do is stand where he is and keep looking right at her, as if he's the boss and she's the one who's the charity case brought in by a bus to eat stale fish paste and old polony sandwiches.

Most people mind someone looking at them the way he's looking at her. After a few seconds they get frightened and look away, but she doesn't. She looks right back.

'Are you deaf?' she says. 'Can't you speak? We heard "special" children were coming. You don't look like a child to me and you certainly don't look special.'

It's funny about her. She doesn't talk down to him the way other strangers do, so he knows as long as he plays dumb, he's safe. He can see in her face she knows he's not as stupid as people make out, which, in a way, makes them equal. So he can be himself if he likes because she knows who he is anyway.

'Daft,' he says. 'When they say "special" they mean daft. Just in case they didn't tell you.'

' "Special" means "special",' she says. 'And you still don't look special and you don't look daft either. You look as if you're out looking for trouble.'

The watch is in his pocket. The knife is in his pocket. His hand is at his side and when he stares harder, she stares right back.

'Can I have my watch back, please?' she says.

He doesn't want it. It's a piece of junk and he never really wanted it anyway. So he doesn't even bother to lie or pretend.

He takes it out and she holds out her hand and he puts the watch in it and even when she's got it she doesn't put it back on her wrist. She just holds it in her hand and stands where she is, not moving an inch.

'Are you planning to be a thief when you leave school?' she says.

'Haven't got the brains for it,' he says.

'Haven't you?' she says. 'I'm not so sure. I don't think you're stupid. I think you just pretend you are because it suits you.'

'Shows how smart you are, then,' he says. 'Because you must be the only one who thinks so and there's no-one else who'd believe you.'

He'd think by now she'd have realized about him and be shouting for help, or at least be trying to get away from him, running for her life but she isn't.

She walks right up to him and grabs hold of his hand and pulls it up and out towards her and he's at least a head taller than she is and older but she's strong for a girl. She pulls hard on his hand and turns it palm upward and slaps the watch down into it.

'You have it,' she says. 'You wanted it. It's yours.'

'I don't want it,' he says.

'Oh, yes, you do,' she says. 'You wanted it badly enough to steal it. Now I give it to you. I'd rather you had it than stole it. Take it. It's yours.'

He knows what his mum would say.

'She gave it to you, didn't she, lovey? She meant you to have it and you're not such a fool as to look a gift horse in the mouth.'

He feels stupid. He should smash the watch or smash her to put her in her place. He could do it, because he's older than she is and bigger and stronger.

He could take out his knife which would be the last thing she expected and frighten her stupid with it and he wants to but when it gets right down to it he can't.

In bioscope, in your dreams, when something like this happens, the other person is so scared you can do anything you like with them. They're on their knees and crying and begging for mercy. They're saying they'll do anything you like, anything you ask, just as long as you spare them.

In real life it's not so easy.

He thinks she must be crazy. She can scream if she wants to. No-one will come but she could scream anyway, except she's not going to and she's right not to because he's not going to do anything and he can see just by looking at her that she knows it.

CONRAD

A Small Box

Bush people disappear. They dance through cracks and faults in the rock. They go through tunnels to the spirit world and when they come out at the other side there's light and lands of forests, lakes and rivers and strange cities bright as day, lit by a sun that has disappeared from the ordinary world above.

'I don't think that's possible,' his mother says.

'I think it is,' says Conrad. 'You have to know how to do it. That's all.'

Then he's sorry he said it. He doesn't want to give his mother ideas. He doesn't want to lose her.

Once, when things were bad, she tried to go.

'And where do you think you'll go to?' his father says. 'What good are you to anyone? What are you but a responsibility and a burden and where do you think the next bloody fool's going to come from who's willing to take that on?'

She's wearing a blue dress and a cardigan. She has on her house shoes, the old pair she wears when she walks in the garden, not the ones she wears to town. Her mouth is a red slash.

'I don't care where I go,' she says. 'Away from here.'

'I see,' he says. 'Is here not good enough for you any more?'

'Please, Jack . . .' she says.

'Is this the thanks I get for pulling you out of the gutter and giving you a name worth having? For putting a roof over your head and food in your mouth? You stand there, with my keys in your hand, and tell me you're going. You've got cheek. I'll give you that much.'

'Just let me go,' she says.

'Am I stopping you?' he says. 'You know what I think the best sight in the world would be? The sight of your back going out of that door for the last time. If only I could live to see that I'd be a happy man. Believe me, I'd throw a party.'

'I want her to go,' Beeky says.

The door that closes the front room off from the rest of the house is open and they are out of their beds standing at the bottom of the passage. He behind Beeky. Not touching. Not breathing. Listening.

'He hates me,' Beeky says, soft and hot so only he can hear. 'I don't care. I hate him right back. I want her to go.'

If she goes they'll be alone. He doesn't want to be alone. He can't take care of Beeky. He can't take care of himself and he's afraid.

He's choking for lack of breath and wanting it to stop. If he breathes now he thinks it will be a sob and his father will hear him and come down the passage looking for him to punish him.

'She won't go without us,' he says. 'She'd never leave us.'

Beeky is braver than he is.

'What are you afraid of?' she says. 'Whatever

happens you won't be alone. You'll still have me. You'll always have me.'

'I say she won't go,' he says.

Even to himself he sounds like a boy whistling in the dark.

'I say she will,' says his sister. 'I say she will because I know it. I feel it. I know she's going and I want her to go.'

The girl is the one who knows. She hears Death tapping at the door but she won't go down to let her in. It's the Old Madam who must bestir herself to greet her old friend.

She floats up damply through the discord and the girl is where she always is, rich with the smell of redhead, slashing away at her drawing with her back turned away from the world. As if that will help. As if it could change anything.

It's a terrible thing that's happened.

They can hear it in the servants' voices. The head 'boy' from the garden is right inside the house. He's in the kitchen on the clean tile floor in his broken-lace garden boots.

He's not standing, face down, hat in hand, in the doorway, waiting for his food like he usually does and he's not quiet. He has a lot to say for himself. He's showing with his hands and shaking his head to show that it's terrible and words are coming out of his mouth in an upside-down stream, so cook and maid have to tell him to slow down and go one word at a time so they can understand and when they do understand, maid throws her hands over her mouth and cook goes running for the master.

His father goes out to the garage with the 'boy', his father in front and the 'boy' behind. The garden 'boys' are there ahead of them standing in front of the open garage door in their blue overalls and they stand aside when his father comes, walking fast in his white shirtsleeves, kicking up bits of gravel with his gleaming brown shoes.

No-one sends for him or Beeky. No-one tells them anything.

It's late afternoon. A rich, warm, late summer day. They know such days. Such days are friends. They've lived more than a thousand days exactly like this one and they may live a thousand more, but a day exactly like this will never come again.

The doctor comes. They know his car. Their mother calls it the measles and mumps car and their father opens the door himself. There's no talk and they aren't sick and their mother is nowhere around and no-one offers any tea. His father and the doctor go out to the garage together and they're there for a long time and they must have sent for 'Oom' Faan.

He comes driving fast and there's no need to send a maid to the study to call his father and say there's a visitor, because 'Oom' Faan stops his car at the garage and jumps out and bangs the car door closed behind him and doesn't even come into the house.

Beeky comes from the Old Madam's room which is her place now. Conrad says Pappa's busy in the garage and they mustn't bother him. No-one's called for them to come down or sent up their supper and they must stay where they are until someone sends for them.

Conrad's sure someone will and he says so. He says it won't be very long before someone remembers them, but it is and the police arrive, then the ambulance and when someone does come to tell them what it's all about, it's 'Oom' Faan.

'You must do your best to understand,' he says. 'It was an accident. No-one expected it. No-one could have done anything to stop it happening. It's important you understand that.'

They're sitting at the dining-room table. Their father isn't there. There's a tray on the table and a coffee pot and used cups and an ashtray with 'Oom' Faan's pipe in it and traces of his tobacco smell in the air.

There's the sweet-sour smell of men at the end of a hard day and there's not enough light in the room because the housemaid has forgotten to turn on the standard lamps and there's no-one there to check up on her.

'She wasn't herself,' 'Oom' Faan says. 'I think her mind was on other things. Women are like that. I'm sure she didn't know what she was doing. You can't switch on a car and leave it with the engine running if the garage door is closed. She couldn't have known that. It wasn't her place to know.'

Why doesn't he look at them?

He taps his pipe and pats at his jacket pocket looking for matches and it takes him a long time to find any. He makes a great show of flaring a match and sucking at his pipe while it rekindles.

'It was a terrible accident,' he says.

He doesn't know what to say but Beeky does.

'I want to see her,' she says and you can see it's not something 'Oom' Faan expects to hear.

'You can't,' he says and Beeky wants to know why not.

'Isn't she here any more?' she says. 'Have they taken her away? Is that what the policemen came for? To take her away? Why should they? She hasn't done anything wrong.'

'Your mother's dead, Beeky,' 'Oom' Faan says. 'There's been an accident in the garage and she made a mistake and she died. It's not a nice thing. I can't think of a nice way to tell you.'

'I want to see her,' Beeky says.

'There's nothing to see,' says 'Oom' Faan. 'The ambulance has come and taken her away.'

'Where to?' Beeky says.

She's in her school skirt and shirt and black lace-up shoes and grey socks. Her face is white and tired and perched on top of her neck as if it doesn't belong there and her whole body is stiff with not being wanted and wanting to know.

'I could have gone with her,' she says. 'If she was in an ambulance, we could have asked the ambulance men and I could have gone too.'

'You wouldn't have been able to,' Conrad says. '"Oom" Faan says no.'

'All I wanted is to be with Mamma,' Beeky says and he doesn't know what to say and neither does 'Oom' Faan and his heart is like lead in his chest.

He's allowed to go to his father's study and sit down in a chair opposite his. It's never been like this before. It's the place 'Oom' Faan sits when he comes for a talk.

His father won't sit down. He leans against the desk resting the base of his spine against hard mahogany. Light shines behind him onto his hair which is neat and it gleams and every hair is in its proper place where it always is, kept there with brilliantine.

Behind the light, shy in its shadow, are the bookshelves and the wall of old pictures and beyond that the high sash window and the pin oaks outside etched against the dark.

'You need to know this, Conrad,' his father says. 'You're old enough. I speak to you as if you're a man.'

'Yes, sir,' Conrad says and his father isn't looking at him and he isn't listening and he goes on as if no-one has spoken.

'Things don't always turn out the way we want them to,' his father says. 'Sometimes, things go wrong and we can't do anything to stop them. We couldn't stop them even if we wanted to because they've got nothing to do with us. What we have to do is wipe up the bloody mess.'

He thinks his father might be drunk. There's a tray of drinks on the side table. Port and a decanter of brandy which his father likes and a syphon of soda and a glass half-full.

'Your mother's dead. She took her own life,' he says. 'It's no good dressing it up or lying or talking a lot of horse-shit about it. She's bloody dead and that's the end of the story.'

He understands. His father can see he does.

'No-one's to blame,' his father says and he moves a little, leaning forward, and the light dances behind him. 'Not you. Not me. Not anyone. Do you understand what I'm saying?'

'It's a disgrace,' his father says. 'What your mother did is a disgraceful thing. A thing to be deeply ashamed of and you must be ashamed and while you're being ashamed, you can blame her because this is what she's done to you.'

He doesn't think so. What he thinks is what he knows. Which is that his mother's spirit has been taken and the spirit is not at all the same thing as life itself and any spirit can be taken at any time and we have no choice in the matter.

Life will lie in a body and will not leave it until it is fetched and it's the living dead who dwell in the eastern sky and are the servants of Goa!na who fetch it. They draw it out from the head and with it the heart and the blood and all this they take to Goa!na and he hangs it on a branch over the eternal fire and out of the smoke from the heart and blood and what was once life he calls for //gauwa, the spirit who will have eternal life and live with him for ever.

All this is known but, even so, it is not wise to speak too often of the //gauwasi and draw attention to yourself because the //gauwasi may do as they please. When Goa!na is busy with other things and not concerned with the comings and goings of his servants the //gauwasi can be mischievous as their human selves once were and cause trouble among the living and even spirit them away if they wish.

If they want a partner in the spirit world they can come down and take a beautiful woman or a brave hunter to keep for ever as their own. This is what happens when someone we want to keep with us is taken and we say we do not know the reason why.

He thinks his mother is like the Wives of the Water and so beautiful and good that someone has come to fetch her, to make her a star or a lily or one of the lightning fragments that dance for joy on the water on the clear cold nights when Moon has her back turned.

He sits still in his place and listens to all his father says and thinks his father doesn't know everything. There are things he knows now which his father cannot even dream of.

All of heaven is a cloth spun out of invisible, unbreakable blue thread and in the Tsodila Hills a single thread touches the earth and this is the way the //gauwasi come back to the world to do errands for Goa!na or make their own mischief and they come armed with miniature bows and small darts to shoot at people and their shots may be felt but not seen and those who've been shot eventually die and are taken out of this world to live with the spirits.

This is what he thinks and if he had courage enough and white men's words to say it, this is what he would say although he does not think his father would listen or want to hear the words that would come out of his mouth. So he sits in silence and silence is a large place and lonely.

He's never sat alone with his father in this special room before, with all of his father's family looking down in pictures from the wall.

His father has never spoken to him in this way, which is the way he speaks to other men. The words float around him and some straight past and he wants to do and say the right thing and make his father proud but he doesn't know what the right thing is and his heart is beating fast.

He knows his father. If he does something wrong that will be the end of it. He'll be sent away and treated like a boy again. He will have failed after his father had put his trust in him and his father will never forget.

'What your mother did is the kind of thing people remember. It's something you're going to have to live with from now on. But it's not a thing anyone can ever be proud of.'

He's not big enough for the chair. He's too thin. His legs are too long. The leather is too slippery. He wants to hold onto the sides to stay up straight but he can't. He has to stay up all by himself, or his father will see, and his back hurts with the effort.

'It's not a thing a man would do,' his father says. 'I can tell you that. People call it the coward's way because that's what it is. Men face up to the realities of life. Whatever comes their way, they face up to it and when it's bad, so bad they think they can't take any more, that's when they get even stronger. That's what I've been trying to teach you. You understand, don't you?'

'Yes, Pappa,' he says.

'You're a good boy,' his father says. 'I may not say it

and I may not always know how to show it but I'm proud of you. I want you to know that.'

He has come to a mountain top. His chest aches with effort. His heart is sore, as if someone has taken it out of his body and beaten it with thorn branches and put it back inside him again. The air is icicles cutting their way into his lungs. There's a constriction in his throat as big as a gull's egg and heavy as a boulder, yet inside himself he feels dizzy and light as if he has crossed alone a great ice waste and come out living and breathing on the other side and found his father there to greet him.

'There'll be a funeral of course,' his father says. 'We'll get it over with as quickly and quietly as possible. Faan is seeing to it.'

'Can we see her?' Conrad says.

It's for Beeky he asks. For himself he doesn't want it at all.

He thinks if he looked inside himself for his mother she would be there, but he's afraid to look. If he called her, and asked her to come into his mind, he thinks she would come but he sits in his father's room and is pleased to be there and he doesn't want his mother to see him.

'Why would you want to see her?' his father says.

'I don't know,' he says. 'I just thought . . . I don't really know. To say goodbye I suppose.'

'Death is goodbye,' his father says. 'It's over and she's done a bloody stupid thing and as far as you're concerned she's left you and you'll never see her again.'

Beeky's not going to the funeral.

'It isn't a place for children,' his father says.

Conrad has been sent to tell her and she's sitting cross-legged on the ground in the Old Madam's room, which she likes so much these days, and when he tells her what's been decided she looks at him and says nothing.

'Before you know it, it'll be over and I'll be back,' he says.

'I wanted to see her,' Beeky says. 'To say goodbye. Did you tell him that?'

'Yes,' he says. 'I told him. I asked. I did ask, but it isn't allowed.'

'Is she too terrible to look at?' Beeky says. 'Will it make us sick to see her? Did something terrible happen? Is that why?'

'No,' he says.

'Why then?' she says and he has to say he doesn't know.

She won't look at him. She always looks at him but she won't look at him now. If she looked, he could tell her not to make things difficult. Not to be a baby. That's what he's done before. He's made her feel better by showing he knows how she feels. He's even made her smile. But he doesn't think he can do it this time, because of her not looking at him.

He feels ashamed.

She knows more about everything and everyone than he does but most of all about him. Sometimes he thinks she knows things he doesn't want her to know and he's never kept anything from her but there are things now he'd rather keep to himself.

'They don't think you're old enough to understand properly yet,' he says. 'They think, if you come to the funeral, it'll make you unhappy.'

He bends down to be closer to her and she draws her legs up and pulls away.

'Don't be like this, Beeks,' he says.

He is close, face to face with her, his face to hers with only their life breath between them.

His sister's eyes are shining gates of water and, if he knew how, he would swim into them and through them and out of them and find himself in another world.

'Mamma is with us, Beeky,' he says. 'With you and with me. She'll be right there at that silly funeral and I'll keep her safe inside me, looking out seeing how foolish everyone's being.'

There's water all around them, above and below and it's warm and they float in it and all the world is below them earthbound and caught fast and only they are free and he would never lie to his sister because he loves her too much.

'You have one half of her and I have the other,' he says and their breath holds them together and the warm pulse of life coming out of their bodies.

'I have something,' she says.

She reaches behind her back and gives him a piece of paper folded over, uncreased, and lets it float free and he looks at it.

She's made a drawing with thin fine strokes which came out of her fingers while the Old Madam watched. It's a boy which is him and a girl which is her and from somewhere, some fine threads of their life have trickled onto the page and they look out through the eyes she has drawn and somehow all of their lives to this moment are caught on the page.

'I want Mamma to have it,' Beeky says. 'I want you to put it with her. You can do that, can't you? If I were going, if I was allowed, I'd do it.'

She offers it up and he takes it because he must.

'It's important,' she says. 'I want her to have it to take with her, so she can look at us just whenever she wants. In case she forgets us because you can never be sure, can you? You can never know.'

* * *

His mother goes to her grave in a small box. He thought it would be bigger. It's a warm day and he's wearing grey flannels and collar and tie and a black armband around a navy blue blazer and his shirt collar is choking him.

His father's in a hurry. He's been looking at his watch since the car door closed behind them and the moment came to leave.

As the car draws away Conrad looks out but there's nothing to see but empty windows like dead eyes looking back from the house and Beeky inside, with her face turned away from them and the ugly old Hottentot hedge near the end of the drive and Beeky's parting gift folded once over so it will fit in the inside pocket of his blazer.

'It's not a party,' his father says. 'There's absolutely no reason why she should be there. She wouldn't know what was going on anyway.'

'Oom' Faan has been at their house taking phone calls and making arrangements, speaking in a soft apologetic murmur. Wrapping everything up in the smoky cellophane of shame and there's a terrible feeling slithering around their house and when people look at him, he can see his mother is somehow the cause of it.

'It's a private matter,' 'Oom' Faan says to the telephone. 'A family thing. They ask that people have respect and understand that.'

'Flowers and hymn-singing and crocodile tears,' says his father. 'People didn't have such wonderful things to say about her when she was alive. Now she's dead, given half a chance, they'll turn her into a saint.'

Josias is driving them. Josias, uniformed, behind the wheel. He and his father in the back seat.

He used to be allowed to ride in front with Josias.

His father stopped it when he was six years old and taken to school on his first day as a new boy.

He was already in front, dressed in his new school clothes, with the smell and feel of new all over them and his school shoes, big boy's shoes on his grey-stockinged feet and an embroidered badge on his blazer and his leather satchel not to be let out of his sight, heavy on his lap with his hands folded over it to hold it down in case it decided to go anywhere.

'Get out,' his father says. 'You heard me, get out.'

The door is open and he does as he's told like a dog to its master's voice coming out in a tumble pulling his satchel after him.

'From now on you sit in the back,' his father says. 'Always. Whenever you get taken anywhere, you sit in the back and Josias sits in front, alone, and you let him get on with his job.'

His mother's there. She's wearing a white dress with blue flowers on it and white shoes. She's carrying a white handbag over her arm. She looks nice. She has a red smile and scent and a scarf like a rainbow cloud round her neck.

'I'm so proud of you,' she says. 'I want you to be proud of me too. I don't want to let you down.'

That's what she told him.

'Do what Pappa tells you,' she says.

'You don't like it, do you?' his father says to her. 'You don't think I'm right, only you won't say it out loud. You think what you like but you don't have the guts to say what you think to my face.'

'You must do as you please, Jack,' says his mother. 'I think there may be another way of doing it. But you must do things in your own way, just as you always do.'

'He isn't a little boy any more,' his father says. 'He must know what his place is and learn to keep it.'

* * *

He knows his place now.

He's sitting deep in leather in the back seat next to his father. Josias is driving. The car is humming forward. His father's looking at his watch and his mother, white-frocked, blue-flowered, white-shoed, smelling of scent with her handbag over her arm and a shiny red smile and a scarf like a rainbow cloud around her neck, has entered the past.

He didn't expect the box to be so small. He thought the graveyard would be a different kind of place, soft with trees and flowers, quiet and gentle, marbled and aged with stone-winged angels but it isn't.

It's a municipal graveyard set beside the long industrial section of main road that leads to the poorer suburbs. Behind a straggling grey-green hedge the railway lines run and along them the sudden rumbling shock of trains, screeching through on the suburban line.

It's the middle of the day. On the way, hemmed in with traffic and their own thoughts they go past a sign for the city abattoir and another for the refuse dump. He's aware of such things. He can't help it. He can smell the rich oaty smell of the brewery and inside it, the undertone of hot-hide cattle packed together on their death journey.

He looks out of the window and makes his eyes glaze over. He doesn't want to see any more.

There is one old camphor tree, gnarled and beaten by the wind. Its leaves are dust-coated and it looks tired. When the car rolls through the open gate the tyres crackle on the pebbles of the visitors' car park and he sees the gates are rusted and there's nothing but a loop of bicycle chain to close them.

'Did you expect heavenly choirs and flights of

angels?' his father says. 'That's a lot of hooey you know and I'll tell you something, if there were such things, they wouldn't come out for a suicide.'

They have to leave the car and walk the last part. Josias opens the door for his father and his father is out first and he on the other side. Out into the light and the unexpected noise and the whine of trucks thundering along the main road and the smell of diesel and the feel of the sun striking him hard in the back spreading hot as blood through the heavy barathea of his blazer.

'Oom' Faan is there ahead of them and the funeral car and the men who come with it and the grave ground has been dug open and there's green baize around the edges and canvas strapping for lowering the coffin down.

'At least they're on time and ready to go,' his father says. 'We need to get on with it. I don't want to hang around.'

He can see the box in the back of the funeral car. A black car. Black cars heat up quickly in the sun. Black attracts heat. You can become uncomfortable and feel the heat very quickly if you're left in a black car on a hot day.

'Never leave Rex in the car,' his mother says. 'He's only a puppy and it gets far too hot. The poor thing could die of suffocation. Put on his lead and take him with you.'

He thinks of that now standing between his father and his uncle and of how small the box is and tapered at the base and light to carry. There are four men to lift it from the car but two would have been more than enough. Someone should have told them. They didn't need so many.

It's a good thing for the person who is not here to rest in the ground.

To rest in the ground, crouched down on our haunches with our heads folded to our knees and our bodies ornamented with beads and karosses and fragranced with *sasa* powder, is a good thing. That we may rest turned homeward to the Great god's home in the eastern sky, all that once was ours which we no longer need broken over our grave and left as a mark, so people who pass after will know the place for what it is and keep aside from it and see that it is sacred.

It's the box he minds and its smallness.

His mother's smile, the sound of her voice, her cheek against his. All of his life in her hands. His life winding around hers and hers criss-crossing his, so that there's no way to know where one begins and the other ends and Beeky swimming towards him touching him through the skin of his mother's belly in the rose-scented dark.

It's too small a box to contain so many things.

'Did you do it?' Beeky says.

He says no, he didn't. The drawing is still in his pocket folded flat. His face and his sister's, paper-kissing in pocket-dark.

'Why didn't you do it?' she says.

'I couldn't,' he says. 'There was already too much. It was completely full. There was no room left.'

She doesn't ask what he means and his heart is full and he doesn't explain, not even to her.

She doesn't blame him because she knows he has a reason for everything he does and even when she doesn't know what it is, she never questions him and she loves him just the same.

But he blames himself, because he went with his father and left them both. His sister alone in the big house and their mother in her small grave.

You shouldn't leave the dead. Three moons or longer should pass before you move away. Three moons to be sure. Three moons to say: 'She is our person, whom we love. We do not want to leave and we have not given up hope.'

Three moons and a fire in front of the place she now is and a pointing reed in the ground and the grave, the fire and the reed all pointing to the place where the person, who is now dead, was born.

'She didn't need it, Beeks,' he says. 'She isn't going to forget us.'

But he looks at his sister and thinks of his mother and blames himself for betraying them both and, in this way, their life changes. In this way they move on.

JEROME

A Natural Gift, God-given

Things have gone against Jerome.

Everyone harping on about how he got arrested for breaking and entering. How it got in the newspaper, all their private business for anyone to read and his mum couldn't hold her head up for a week.

'You can't blame him,' she tells Doris. 'If they're looking for someone to blame they should go down to Ronny Lombard's place. He's the one with the bright ideas.'

'I see,' says Doris. 'Pity, when the newspaper was writing it down, they left that bit out. I'm sure the magistrate would have been very interested to hear it.'

'You have your opinion and I have mine,' his mum says. 'And, in this case, mine just happens to be the right one. All I'm saying is, if they're looking for a door to lay the blame at, this isn't the one they should come to.'

Ronny Lombard's a locksmith. He's got his papers to prove it. He's the first real friend Jerome's had. Just for the fun of it, and to pass the time, he taught Jerome all he knows and one thing you can say about Jerome, he's good with his hands and when it comes to something that can get him into trouble, he's a fast learner.

There isn't a car door he can't jemmy open in two minutes flat and if there's something on four wheels and Jerome can get into it, then he can hot-wire it and get it to go.

Ronny and his friends make a joke of it. They say you can put him behind the wheel of any car you care to name. He's like lightning. It looks as if all he has to do is run his hand across the dashboard, give a pull here and there and say 'talk to me baby' and the engine's purring like a kitten and they're on their way.

One of Ronny's friends, a man called Jonker, was in the mines and for his call-up he went to Army engineers. Putting stuff together and making a bang is his idea of a good time and when he feels like getting up to his old tricks again, he has a few old mine contacts who are good for a favour and get him whatever stuff he needs.

'Playing with fire' Ronny calls it but it can be quicker than lock-picking and it's good for breaking and entering and Jerome likes the idea. He's never been so happy in his life.

Jonker says they can all have more fun if they put some explosive into the mix.

'To put a bit of a kick in it,' he says.

It's dangerous, but that's part of the fun too, and Jerome's the one to do the most dangerous job and actually put the kick in and see if it'll work.

They tell him it's a kind of initiation.

'To make you one of us,' Ronny says. 'You want to be one of the boys don't you? If you want to be, you have to do something to show us you're good enough and this is the thing we've chosen for you to do.'

Jerome isn't averse. He doesn't mind if the others

stand back and leave the most dangerous work to him. They think he's a fool, but these days he knows better. He doesn't do it because he's the stupidest and doesn't realize he can do himself an injury. He does it because he's best at it. Much better than anyone else.

He can put together anything they ask and they can be almost wetting themselves because of some of the chances he takes, but he doesn't worry. He knows now what he didn't know before. If you can leave someone in or take someone out and the choice is yours, then there's no doubt right that minute who the boss is and just for a change and absolutely no argument, for the minute, he's the one.

They may not say so out loud, but he knows it and they know it too. That's why he's cold as ice, as if he doesn't have a nerve in his body. Because his brain may be one thing but his hands are something else and once he knows how to do something, his hands remember it and they're rock steady and never let him down.

'Would have been nice if he'd been half so quick with his schoolwork,' Doris says.

She's with them at the magistrate's court, in her church hat and gloves waiting to hear what the magistrate has to say and what he says is Jerome's going down and it's not reform school and time off for good behaviour this time. This time, it's prison and he's for the high jump.

You can look like Robert Redford and smile like an angel. It may have helped in the days he was stealing sweets from the Greek shop. It doesn't carry any weight with the magistrate. Not when he's sitting there with a juvenile record as long as your arm and all the facts of the current case in front of him.

You can tell, just by looking at his face, that he's

seen this kind of thing before and the slit-eye way he looks at Jerome doesn't give anyone the impression that things are going to go well with him.

Visiting days, it's his mum who comes. In her good coat and shoes and something in a brown paper bag for him. She brings doughnuts and sweets and cigarettes, even though she knows he doesn't smoke.

'You trade them for something else,' she says. 'I asked and they're good as money in here. Maybe even better and if you're smart, while you're at it, you can make a few bob on the deal. Not everyone here has someone to bring them cigarettes, so you've got something they want and you make sure they cough up for it.'

She says Dad's fine and Doris and she went round to the Lombards and she said what she had to say to Ronny, about how she knows very well how her boy came to be led astray. She told him to call his mother and father out of their flat and into the hallway so they could hear it too.

'I wouldn't put my foot in their place,' she says. 'Not any more and they were never our type anyway and it wasn't what you might call a friendly visit.'

She says she's brought him something. She fishes around in her handbag and takes out a piece of newspaper and smooths it out flat.

'Here you are,' she says. 'Don't know why we waste our time talking about riff-raff like the Lombards. This is that house you were at that time. The Hartmanns' house. You remember? The wife's dead. It says so in the newspaper. I brought it to show you.

'Don't worry about the writing,' she says. ' "An unfortunate accident". That's what the paper says, but she gassed herself. They won't put that down in black and white, of course, but it's not hard to work out. She got in her car and gassed herself. You can take it from me.'

It's an old picture, because the mother's still in it and the father and a boy and the girl. The same girl with the same look on her face staring right at him from out of the picture as if she knows he's laying his eyes on her and doesn't like it and wonders how he can have such cheek.

His mother says she won't even greet the Lombards these days. If she sees them out on the street, she crosses to the other side and there isn't a person in the neighbourhood who doesn't know how she feels about what they did to her boy and exactly where she stands on the matter.

'Can I keep the picture?' Jerome says.

'Of course you can, lovey,' says his mother. 'It'll help you remember you've been better places than where you are right now and that's the truth. You don't belong here. Never mind what other people say. It's what your mum says that counts and your mum says you're a good boy.'

'The Man with the Golden Touch', they call him here. Because he's good with gadgetry and electrics and willing to learn.

'Doing very nicely down at the electric workshops these days,' his mum tells Doris. 'The people in charge down there know a good thing when they see it. He can do things. You can't take that away from him. It's a gift. That's what it is. It's a natural gift, God-given.'

CONRAD

The Time of the Yellow-eye Dog

By the third season he's ready but he still hasn't killed and the season is bad because the little rains didn't come in time and when they did they came with bad temper and were mean and insufficient.

The game turned their heads towards water and began the long trek. There were kudu here and there but they were ill-fed and lethargic, slow when the hunt began, showing the signs of the season, hardly worth bringing down.

They go out, drive for miles bumping along in the open back of the trucks and the air is cold and piercing. They pass the bottle from mouth to mouth to keep out the cold but there's no game and no pleasure in it and when they get back with nothing to show for their trouble the 'boss boy' comes to the back door to say a dog has gone sheep mad.

He says at first they thought it was a jackal but when they looked more closely they realized it was a dog. A dog that got into a kraal and hamstrung two sheep on one night and another the next and, if the boss will come, he'll see for himself and the sheep will have to be slaughtered.

It happens sometimes. If a dog gets loose in a kraal where sheep are penned together it will go for a sheep, attack it and pull it about by the hindquarter, knobbling it, and rendering it good for nothing by severing its tendons.

'The dog will have to be found and shot,' his father says. 'Today. The sooner the better.'

That is their job. Labourers don't carry guns. If a dog has to be shot, one of them has to do it. It's easy enough but dirty work and no-one likes it.

'Conrad will see to it,' his father says. 'It'll be an old kaffir dog. Ask the "outa" which one it is and where to find it. Make sure you get the right one and take it out with one shot. Don't waste bullets.'

He doesn't like it any more than the others do. There's nothing pleasing about putting down an old kaffir dog but if it's taken to savaging sheep it has to go.

He doesn't like going to the *kampong*. He doesn't like the meanness of the cottages or the way the children stop what they're doing and scatter when they hear his footfall and see him coming, with his gun slung over his shoulder.

He feels like Moses with the Red Sea parting before him and children and chickens, goats and women and old people going behind the old wood house doors that hang loose and skew on their hinges, leaving open fires untended and laundry clinging still wet to bushes and broken pieces of fence; everyone melting away at the sound of a booted boy, not yet fifteen, carrying a rifle.

The 'outa boss boy' is waiting for him and his head's to one side and he's bent like a weathered tree cringing too many years before the wind.

'You know what I've come for,' Conrad says. '*Jy weet*

waarvoor ek gekom het. Where's the dog? Go fetch him for me. Bring him here.'

'I'll fetch him, little master,' he says. 'I know which one it is.'

He doesn't like it. He doesn't like being in the *kampong* or the cur kaffir dog that has to be put down. He doesn't like the wood-fire smell that hangs over the place, or the bits of brick showing through the mud of the house walls, or the bare-bottom, snot-nose children, or the rubbish dump too close to the houses, or the bright bits of plastic caught here, there and everywhere.

His rifle lies in the crook of his arm.

There's a terrible shouting. A boy shouting. A man shouting back, fast furious bursts of shouting from the man, piercing protest from the boy. All of it coming out in an angry babble.

These people speak a language of their own. A mixed-up language of Afrikaans and English from the missionaries' time and Xhosa and Khoi thrown in. A language bastardized, made outcast like themselves.

The 'boss boy' comes out of the labourer's shack pulling a boy eleven, maybe twelve years old behind him. The dog is his dog. He has been sheltering it. The boy is such a stupid boy even the dog is too clever for him. The minute the boy's back is turned the dog finds a way out and that's why he's been able to make two attacks. It's the boy's stupidity and then trying to protect the dog that's the cause of all the trouble and the boy must be held responsible. He is just as guilty as the dog is.

The boy agrees. He says it's his fault, not the dog's. He's failed to tie the dog up properly at night. It's his fault. It won't happen again.

They all know this isn't so. Once a dog goes for a sheep and gets a taste for bringing sheep down, it'll keep on doing it. It'll do it every chance it gets. The sport is too great for it to resist.

'Tell him to fetch the dog,' Conrad says.

'He's hiding it, master,' the 'boss boy' says.

'Tell him to bring it out.'

The 'basters' are their own people. Neither black nor white but some of each and sometimes, in them, you see the small bones and yellowish skin of the Khoi. Sometimes they're tall. Sometimes there's a throwback of pale peppercorn hair or the light eyes of a passing huntsman or trader and it's the white in them we don't like. We see ourselves and we do not like what we see. For this we deride them more than for anything else, because this is the part we know best and are most averse to.

'Tell him he must bring the dog out,' Conrad says. 'He knows what must happen.'

He doesn't like it. The voice coming out of his throat is a man's voice, his own and not his own. It feels strange. He knows what his father would say.

'To be master you must show you are master. There must never be any mistake about it. These people are like children. You must be firm to be kind. No-one gives you respect just because you happen to be there. You have to earn it.'

The 'boss boy' grabs hold of the boy and shakes him. The words shoot out of his mouth in a nervous babble and the boy will not budge and they can't stand there all day and Conrad isn't quite sure what to do next when from a small lean-to that shelters a chopped pile of winter wood the dog barks and gives itself away.

No matter what the boy says, *kampong* dogs are never tied up at night. They aren't guard dogs or sheep dogs, they're not pedigreed to please or trained to be useful. They're just there. They form part of the *kampong* and roam free and no-one notices them any more, or knows what they're there for. If the dog is tied it's only because Conrad is there and they knew he was coming. All it shows is that the boy is guilty. Otherwise the dog would be free and, with night coming, it would lope towards warmth, towards fire the way all creatures do.

'Go and get him,' Conrad says directly to the boy.

He sees now it is the same boy who used to set up tin cans and bottles for him to shoot at in the first season. Like Conrad, he is older. Taller, but he will never be very tall, light-skinned with freckles on his nose and patches of yellow, white man's leavings, in the colour of his eyes.

'Get him,' Conrad says.

He's shouting. He doesn't want to shout. All he wants is for this to be over.

The 'boss boy' babbles with his head swinging frantically from one man-boy to the other, then the 'baster' boy breaks free and runs towards the lean-to and bends down to untie the rope and for a moment he's invisible, crouched down behind the pile of wood, then he stands up and the dog, yellow and mangy, lopes out and Conrad lifts his gun.

'*Hardloop!*' the boy screams at the dog. 'Run! Run!'

It won't make any difference.

The dog stands in front of Conrad and looks at him with dispassionate yellow eyes.

'Run! Run!' the boy shouts and the dog lopes around once and then again and then it lopes away. But it makes no difference at all. If it ran like the wind, Conrad could fell it with one shot. All he has to do is raise the gun, hold the animal in his sights and pull the trigger and the dog will drop dead in its tracks and it will be done. But the dog will not run. He stays where he is and Conrad raises the rifle and shoots it where it stands, a single loud retort, a beautiful shot right in the centre of the head and he puts the gun down and they watch, as the dog buckles down slowly into death and jerks once or twice and twitches into stillness.

That night there's the metallic sound of metal on metal, except it is not twice-over metal at all. It's metal on hard winter ground. It's a spade chipping into cold unyielding veld.

'What's going on?' his father wants to know.

The way of white Africans in the bush is this. A man goes out with a spade and digs a hole in the ground so he can shit in it and then bury his own leavings.

It's a veld habit. A habit from old wars; white against white, white against black. Civilized men are not like animals. They don't leave their droppings lying around so other men can trace them. But they aren't in the bush now. They are in a house and there's modern plumbing.

Someone looks out of a window and says: 'It's a Baster boy burying a dog.'

'Bloody lucky it's only a dog,' says someone else. 'Ground's as hard as bloody concrete.'

'Should have thrown it on the rubbish heap.'

'These people feel nothing. Don't give a damn. Just as well to bury it. You see how they are. Live among their own rubbish. Don't want disease. All we're short of is an outbreak of something.'

'Get rid of the whole bloody lot of them,' someone says. 'Come to think of it, it may not be a bad thing.'

Conrad, warm inside the house, with a tumbler of beer in his hand, can see the boy through the window and across the stoep at the very end of the stretch of house-light just where the shadows begin.

It's far from the *kampong*. A long walk back on bare

feet in the cold and the dark. The boy must know he can be seen.

The dog is lying on the ground wrapped in a piece of sacking. Just the middle of the body is wrapped, like a child in a blanket, its legs and paws sticking out, its slack head visible.

Conrad stands where he is, mirrored in light, a broad-shouldered man-boy looking out and he's thinking what he learned is right. It's the nobility of the hunted that makes the chase worthwhile. There's no pride to be found in taking a dog.

The Devil's Picture

The Old Madam is young again and has two sons, Wilhelm the elder and Jacobus the younger and they are boys full of fire and there's a war coming.

A baptism of blood and fire, the *dominee* says it will be.

The Khakis are coming. There's nothing that can stop them now. 'Oom' Paul the old President has said so himself. Her sister has written from the Transvaal to tell her so.

'I asked him myself,' she says. ' "Well, Madame," he said. "I will tell you. Our Republic is a very pretty girl. England is her lover. The lover has been refused several times and now he is going to kill her." '

'We'll go, Mamma,' her boys say. 'We'll go to the Transvaal and join up this minute and when the Khakis come we'll be ready for them. We'll give them a good hiding and send them packing. We'll do it all and finish the job and be home for Christmas.'

Traitors. Cape Colonists but Boer boys in their heart. All efforts to re-educate a total waste of time. Their mother's seen to that.

* * *

England is a wonderful place and big. So big the sun never sets on it. This is what their teacher tells them. He shows them a map. A map of the world and England is red and not one country at all. It is scattered all over the place but just to make sure you can find it with no trouble, all of it is red, including themselves.

Tap, tap goes their teacher with his wooden pointer and the canvas-backed map suspended from its string shudders and the continents quiver. That is how strong England is.

'This is where we are,' their teacher says. 'Here at the bottom end of Africa coloured red for England so you know where you belong.'

Their mother has other ideas.

'Red,' she says. 'Red's a good colour. Lifeblood, heart's blood. That's what all the red is about. Other lands bleeding to make England rich.

'As for the sun never setting on them. What a presumption. The sun knows nothing of England and knows even less of man marks on a map.'

Which is why in her pictures the fat old Queen has a small, self-satisfied smirk on her face. A thief's smile and a hook for a nose and greedy little eyes turned towards them and plump little hands heavy with rings ready to count all her money and you'd smile too if every day brought more treasure to lay at your feet.

Imagine asking God to save this Queen who everyone knows is only human like the rest of us; which means God will take her when He's good and ready just as He pleases, just as He always does because it doesn't matter what they make her out to be, in that way she's no different from you or from me.

Who would bow down to such a thief of a Queen and answer to God for it, when the time comes, before a throne much greater than any she or anyone else here on earth's ever known?

So they stand at their desks, the two little Hartmanns in their colonists' school and mouth 'God Save the Queen' but don't sing because God will make up His own mind about the old Queen, to be spared or be doomed and He doesn't need any urging from them.

This is what their mother told them.

'You can make words with your mouth and be a traitor in your heart and it's what you know in your heart that counts,' she says. 'And you'll see if anyone even notices.'

As if God can't see their moving lips and hear their silence for Himself and they scratch on their slates all the lies their teacher tells them and outside, beyond the schoolhouse wall, the mountain drowses in the sun and the doves in the schoolyard, which are the doves of their land and know no boundaries, burble a different song.

'About this war that's coming,' their mother says. 'One will go and one will stay. You have land here to take care of and no father and no choice. One will take a gun and slip away north. The other will stay and help keep this place and there'll be work enough for us to do, because we'll fight too but from the inside.'

She's already thought it out and her mind is made up.

'That's how it will be,' she says. 'And there won't be any discussion.'

'Then tell us who'll go and who'll stay?' say her boys, for shooting or spying are pleasing to both. 'Tell us how you'll choose?'

'Go away,' she says. 'Let me think about it. I'm your

mother. I can take my own time. When I've made up my mind I'll let you know.'

Then she sends them away to learn patience.

She thinks about it long and hard and what she thinks is that the Khakis shoot commandos but they have no love for spies either. Which job for which boy? Who goes? Who stays? Not much of a choice.

'Tell us, Mamma,' they say. 'Whichever one of us is to go, has to go soon. The Khakis are on the water and war is coming closer by the minute.'

'I'll think on it a little longer,' she says. 'Khakis only sail on water. They're not gods. They neither walk nor run on it. They'll take as long as you or me or the next man to get here. Now leave me in peace.'

It's her husband's fault. He brought her here in the first place and gave her sons and left her, a stranger among strangers, in the old Queen's colony, far from her heart's longing and the people she loves.

When her sons come to ask her a second time she says she's still busy thinking, and when she's finally made up her mind, they'll be the first to know.

'In the meantime,' she says, 'go and have your picture taken and tell the picture man to do a good job, for whichever goes and whichever stays, whatever happens I would like a picture for my old age to remember you by.'

'We thought the picture man was here to do the devil's work and steal our souls from us with his camera,' the older one says.

He doesn't believe it but it was she who told them and a mother, she tells them often enough, can never be wrong.

'That used to be his job,' she says. 'But things have changed. The devil has handed over to the British now and it isn't only our souls they want. It's our land and our gold and our freedom.'

She tries a trick. She opens the Bible and looks for a sign. She lets the wafer-thin pages fall where they will and leaves it to God to give her direction but, in a clear indication this is none of God's business, no sign comes.

Lift your eyes to the hills is there and Faith, Hope and Charity and the greatest of these is Charity, which were two of her father's favourite texts; I Know that my Redeemer Liveth but she knows that already even though He cannot help her now.

The truth is, she loves her sons equally. She has never had to choose between them in such a way before and she can't do so now and then something extraordinary happens.

As she lies in her bed in that silvery world between sleeping and waking a very elegant lady, beautifully dressed, wonderfully well spoken, with a soft delicious voice and a very pleasant turn of phrase comes to pay her a visit.

She drifts in through the wall and makes a great fuss about closing her parasol which is made of mauve silk and decorated with black lace.

'I'm sorry if the time is inconvenient,' she says. 'But being a woman yourself I'm sure you know that woman's work is never done and I'm afraid, very shortly, I shall be far too busy to make house calls. I shall be very busy indeed.'

The Old Madam is acquainted with Death of course. They met on the day influenza dropped by to take her sons' father but they're natural and nodding acquaintances and she hadn't expected such an intimate visit.

'May I?' says Death and floats to the end of the bed and there she settles herself and she looks very fine in a black gown and gloves, with a rim of purple petticoat peering out from the hem of her dress.

The Old Madam sits up against her pillows and nothing divides them but the counterpaned length of the bed and they might be two old friends glad of a moment of quiet and the chance to whisper news to one another and make a plan or two.

'It's a sad thing,' says Death. 'But I must have one of your sons. Let me say it direct, for I've usually found that between women like us that's the best way.'

To look at these two, one at the top of the bed and one at the bottom, you'd see very little difference but the world isn't what you see with your eyes and there's a very big difference indeed, because Death has no heart and the Old Madam has and her heart tightens inside her when she hears this news.

'So, you see,' says Death, 'you can sleep comfortably now because the choice isn't yours. It makes no difference at all which one you choose. I've done you a favour and showed you the future and there's nothing at all you can do about it.'

It can't be said the Old Madam wakes the next morning with sunlight flooding the room and birds chirping in the trees outside and finds it's all been a dream.

She does wake. There is some sun, but only a little, because it's early in the spring and birdsong is sparse because birds, like people, are loath to rise early when there's no sun to greet them and they aren't sure if the day is going to be pleasant or not.

Was it a dream? She wakes and her heart, in its resting place deep inside her, oblivious to fine days or sunshine or weather fair or foul, continues to be heavy.

A sense of foreboding wakes with her and refuses to

be wished away. There's the very slightest indentation the length of the counterpane away at the bottom of her bed. A ripple in the coverlet, no more, and the softest smell of gardenia in the air.

'Cheer up, Mamma,' her eldest says. 'We couldn't sleep last night. I don't know what was going on in this house, but sleep certainly wasn't here.'

'We got fed up waiting,' says her youngest. 'Time's running out and we want to get on with things.'

'We took out a sovereign and threw it in the air . . .'

'. . . and he called heads and I called tails and he's to go and fight for you and I'm to stay and mind the land and do a bit of spying on the side and that's the way it is and you can have our devil's picture and look at us whenever you like.'

Right in that instant she can't bring herself to look at them at all but she must put her strange visitor to the back of her mind and seem herself again and herself is strong and it's herself who says if that's the way of it, that's the way it will be.

The Heart of the Hunter

In the fourth season his father says it's time and he's ready.

It's a good season. The little rains were kind. There is new, sweet grass. Buck are plentiful. They roam where they please, arrogant, in herds, as they once did.

His father would like a gemsbok or even a wildebeest. A big one. A bull. A fine year for felling a specimen to be proud of, because the first kill is important and can never be repeated.

The trackers know, everyone knows, that Conrad's time has come.

'You keep your minds on the job,' his father tells the trackers.

'We need a nice big bugger,' he says to his friends.

'You take him out clean with a single shot,' is what he says to Conrad. 'If he catches wind or sight of you and makes a bolt, keep cool, keep him in your sights and take him down when the moment's right.'

They're hunting on foot. A wavering line of men fanned out each a little distance from the other but always in sight, moving, certain-footed, easily visible, across the pared-down winter veld with the trackers ahead crouched conch-backed reading the spoor.

The men are agreed. They will see what presents itself and from whatever there is, they'll single out the best and leave it for Conrad to take. There are gemsbok in the vicinity and hartebeest and wildebeest are possible but Bastiaan says it will be an eland.

'You can tell him if he comes up with an eland and it isn't Scotch mist, I'll personally see to it he gets a bloody five-rand note in his hand,' one of the men says.

Bastiaan says it will be so.

It isn't always the man who chooses the animal. Sometimes an animal will honour a man by seeking him out and Bastiaan says an animal is coming, coming towards the little master. It's on its way even as they speak and it will be an eland.

'How can you bloody know that?' his father says.

Bastiaan says he saw it in the smoke and everyone laughs because it is the standard way of not dignifying a question with an answer.

'Saw it in the bottom of a wine bottle more likely,' someone says. 'If we see any eland today you can kiss my arse. How's that for a deal?'

The eland was made by the Greater god and is a creature of life and the rising sun. In his power and beauty, in his strength and fleetness of foot; in the sleekness of his hide, in his aloneness and the wisdom of his ways he allows us to lay our eyes upon him and see, reflected in him, the smallest part of the Greater god's majesty.

The bush people revere him and dance in his honour. They seek his blessing and, when the shamans dance for eland power, he brings his presence to them and stands in the darkness just beyond their vision and you do not need to see with outer sight to know what is in the world around you, and spirit eland and flesh-and-blood eland are nothing but the same thing.

Bastiaan has told many things this season. Many more than usual. He says it will be his last season. His time is coming. The divining tablets show it, but he knows it in his heart. He says the brown hyena is waiting for him and the brown hyena is a death thing and ready to pick at his bones.

Everyone laughs. Drunk talk, they say. Liquor sadness. But Conrad believes him. It has always been as Bastiaan says. The others don't listen with attention the way Conrad does and they forget. Conrad remembers and he believes.

Bastiaan says that although the Eland Bull Dance is a woman's dance, men are permitted to watch and he has seen it with his own eyes and Conrad believes him.

When he asks what makes the women dance and what it is they dance for, Bastiaan shows his gums and shakes his head and spits a little with laughter as if at a great joke and the callowness of a boy who hasn't yet learnt the things women ask for.

'Come on,' Conrad says. 'You can tell me.'

He says for a pouch of town tobacco and a bottle of wine he'll tell the little master and says it's cheap at the price and fills up his pipe and lights it with a hot coal because bush people love to smoke and then, when he's comfortable, he says he'll tell what it is a woman dances for and wherever it is she dances and whatever dance it is she does, her dance never changes and it never will.

She dances and while she dances, with her face away from the fire, so that only the night can hear, she asks that she will be beautiful and bush girls are very beautiful.

They have golden skin not yet darkened by the sun and bead ornaments hang from their hair. They have sloping eyes, like cat's eyes, and above their eyes, rows of scars etched in delicately with the tip of a knife so they arch over the brow and make their eyes seem even wider.

They colour their faces with yellow-green *sasa* over the bridge of the nose and across the cheeks and scent themselves with essence made from the wood of the chambuti and they walk bare-breasted with their heads high and very proud and when they come towards you, they come swishing, in a clink of leg rattles made from ostrich-egg chips.

Bush women dance that they won't be scrawny and thin so when the time comes, they'll bear children and their breasts will be full so they will be able to keep their children with them and feed them and never have to leave them in the trek time with only a ring of thorns around them for a cradle.

They ask that when there's hunger, they won't feel so very hungry and when there's no water, they won't feel so very thirsty.

They ask that they will be peaceful and the She-Rains which give life will never desert them and all will go well with the land.

All this they ask of the eland when they dance because, of all the antelope, the eland has the greatest blessings to give and Conrad walking in his place beside the other men waiting for his first kill wants it to be an eland and, although none of the signs show it will be, his rifle is ready and his heart is beating sure and calm.

Animals have their time to leave just as men do. His father doesn't believe it but Conrad does. He knows that sometimes an animal will seek out a man and come to him and that is a very great sign and this is what Conrad is thinking as he walks.

They are downwind of the animals and have the advantage. The little people are ahead showing the way with signs of their hands and they are behind, because they are big and heavy and their booted feet make the ground tremble and would give them away if they came too close.

His father says it's rubbish but Conrad wishes his eland. He wishes it with all of himself. He wishes it from deep down inside himself. He wishes it with his soul and all of himself is filled up with wishing, so there's no room for anything else and there's nothing else to think about so when the eland comes he's expecting it, although he's the only one who is and it comes suddenly, as if from nowhere, standing on a ridge engraved against the sky and he knows about the eland because Bastiaan has told him but now, when he lifts his eyes, he knows it in his heart.

There is a Bushman, very hungry, hunting for food. He sees a beautiful antelope. He knows if he is to live the antelope must die. His arrow is dressed with beetle larvae dug out from beneath the magic trees with a hard wood stick. When its magic is being sought and being taken all is silence except for the tribute, which is the nasal grunt of the gemsbok out of the Bushman's own throat, his thanks for what he has been given to secure him food that he might continue to live.

The Bushman walks crouched down in silence among the marula trees and the commiphora and before him stands the antelope which must die if he is to eat and in the close presence of death the silence is profound. Even the birds and the wind hold their breath. One twig or leaf snapped underfoot and all would be in vain.

The animal sees him and raises its head.

The deadly arrow is fixed in the bow and is ready to fly and that which once was living must feed another, for that is the order of life and the Bushman stands in the silence and weeps and when he raises his head he sees that the antelope, too, is weeping.

The trackers show with a small sweep of the hand and the men stop where they are and stand still and in the great quiet, the animal flicks its head, as if its fate is of no consequence and its horns make markers on the sky.

Conrad breathes in the clean dry air and smells the earth and dung sweetness of it and the air is light and shines around him and he feels as if he's suspended and floating inside it free.

He feels what the eland must feel, the beating of its heart inside its body, the hot coursing of its blood, the soft air floating in and out of its lungs. Grazing is plentiful, water easy to find and enough for all. The ground is steady under its hooves, sky and veld cup hands around it.

To be a hunter you must be one with the hunted. Yet, even as you rest inside him, you must be prepared to betray him and ready for the kill and before you take his life, you must take his name and the name of the eland is *sa* and in that moment when you are one with him, in your own heart you must call him *ein* which is the same name but different because it is also the name for meat.

His father gives the sign and he raises his rifle and stands firm and holds the eland in his sights and no-one else moves at all and then some other thing wells up inside him and he remembers the 'baster' boy and the cur sheep-killing dog and the boy shouting: 'Run! *Hardloop!* Run!'

There's no time for this now. He cocks the rifle, holds it steady, and at the sound of the lock releasing or perhaps because of the smallest shift in the wind, the eland turns towards him as the dog once did and his finger is light and sure on the trigger and he's quite certain. He's pulled this trigger a hundred times. A hundred times a hundred. He's a good shot. There's no time for hesitation.

Between the hunter and the hunted all is understood and he takes the eland down sure and certain and clean with a single shot to the neck, because if the head is to be kept as a trophy it must be unmarked.

There's no need for a second shot, but he shoots to the heart to be quite certain and it's done.

A bush boy who makes his first kill sits on the skin of the animal when it is freshly taken from its body and still warm with its life and his body is smeared with the animal's fat.

One of the hunters cuts off a hind leg and makes spoors with it around the place where the boy sits on the skin and when it's done the boy gets up and crosses the circle of hoof prints and thereafter he will be charmed and always able to track down the eland.

White people do it differently.

The animal is killed and skinned and gutted by the trackers with their sharp knives and Conrad is marked with the blood of the newly dead animal, wet and sticky on his face. When the liver is taken, it's brought to the men and they cut off a piece of the still warm organ and the boy, now a man and blooded, eats it.

Conrad feels his father's arm around his shoulders.

'Well done,' he says. 'Nice shooting.'

Pats of approval are falling on his back like stones to the body of a martyr.

Bastiaan is on his haunches helping with the butchering. Tonight everyone will eat this animal. Those who have known want and those who have not, for that is the way the hunted serves the hunter and no part of the animal will go to waste. Meat will be handed around and shared and the boy will eat the *vet derm*, the large intestine, roasted on hot coals and handed to him with great ceremony, but the bush people look at it in a different way.

The eland has offered himself to serve the needs of men. We were once as he is and he shows by his sacrifice the gift of the Greater god, which is that we all have it within ourselves to serve the needs of others.

Tonight it is not the hunter the bush people will celebrate. It is the eland, his wisdom and his gift.

Conrad stands to one side, blooded and praised and he has done what has to be done and it is as Bastiaan said it would be and it is different.

Some men say this is a moment of jubilation. Others say it can be a way with a hunter that, once he has killed, he is changed and his heart runs for ever, burning hot, towards blood.

HER BROTHER'S BOOK

BEEKY

A Feather in Her Hair

They are older and Beeky has done what she did and his father can't forgive her and will never forget and, although you can't see it, she has another mark now, worse and more damning that the birth-brand. Not to be talked about. Never to be said out loud. A matter for whispering.

'You're like your bloody mother,' their father says. 'Bad blood runs in that family. I simply refused to see it. Too star-struck to see it. You must have been totally off your head. No sane person would do the kind of thing you did.'

'It's really not so terrible as you're making out,' Conrad says. 'It's different but it's a nice thing really. It's not the end of the world.'

'Isn't it?' his father says and Beeky can feel their father's anger leaving her and turning towards her brother but he has seen things now and she doesn't think he's as afraid as he once would have been.

'It's just Beeks's way,' he says. 'She doesn't mean anything by it.'

'Then she's got a bloody funny way,' says their father.

It's a small thing, suddenly made big, billowing out around them, reverberating through the house. It makes their father snap and snarl. It keeps the servants cowering in the kitchen and Becky is to stay upstairs in her room because his father can't bear to look at her and its aftershock jolts the Old Madam to wakefulness.

She knows the man by now and the way he can be but this time she smells Woman on the air and the red girl's a strong one who looks life in the eye but she's still young. She doesn't know how it is with men.

The smell of rose has cooled. That ripple on the air can only mean one thing and that thing is the coming of change and a New One coming and the New One will have a will of her own. The Old One can feel it.

'Beeks is different, that's all,' Conrad says. 'She does things differently. There's nothing wrong with that.'

'Bloody different,' their father says. 'She's so different people are saying she must be right out of her mind with difference and it's a wonder no-one noticed before.'

It's his voice but it's the New One talking and the man is the way men are when a New One comes and there's nothing the boy or the girl can do about it.

'She didn't do anyone any harm,' Conrad says.

'Not this time,' says his father. 'But after she's pulled a trick like this we have to ask ourselves what her next little stunt is likely to be.'

'I don't think it's like that,' says Conrad. 'I know it isn't.'

'Then you know something no-one else does,' says his father.

* * *

It's the flowers that caused the trouble. Flowers made out of soft-drink tins, with wire coat hangers for stems. The kind of flowers black children from the location make.

Beeky spent hours and days alone in the water room making flowers of her own.

It's not as easy as it looks. You have to find empty tins and cut them open with wire-cutters. When you do that they curl up and you have to flatten them out so you can cut petals.

The colours are important. Coca-Cola red and white, Schweppes yellow tonic, orange Fanta and purple and green granadilla cordial and the sharp metal petals can cut your fingers if you're not careful but Beeky is extremely careful. She cuts as if her life depends on it.

She works in a copper halo of light in the Old Madam's room which is now her own and the Lord of the River flows tranquil beneath, son of the Father of Pools to whom tribute is paid. She cuts and she twines. She puts bright coloured petals together and her wonderful flowers are like no flowers anyone has ever seen.

They have glass marbles for hearts for the gift must come from both of them and the marbles were Conrad's when he was a boy. Bright-eyed puries and waterbabies with little floats of colour caught at the core. Red and yellow and blue and green cat's eyes like her own eyes, the colour of water, of agate, of soapstone and fish-dappled pools by the sea.

A garden grows from her fingers and blooms bright in the dark corners of the Old Madam's room.

'The worst of it,' her father says, 'is they're so bloody awful-looking. Stuck all over the grave. What for?'

'She deserved something,' Beeky says. 'I wanted her to have them.'

'Why now?' her father wants to know. 'It isn't as if it all happened yesterday. We've had plenty of time to put it behind us. Why now? I don't need this now.'

It's the New One who doesn't need this now. The New One's a smart one, with ideas of her own and fine airs and opinions and she prefers the past dead and firmly buried without any flower-splashed graves as reminders.

The man from the council, responsible for graves and their upkeep, has come and gone and his father has spoken to him and the flowers, Beeky's flowers, have been pulled out of their mother's grave and thrown away.

'What on earth possessed you?' his father says. 'Is it your idea of a joke?'

'It isn't as if she came and went and nobody knew what went on between you. Con knew and I knew too and when she died we were sorry and you never were.'

Her father has a way. A quick close-down and open again, as if what he doesn't want to hear has never been said. It's like a quick-smart bat of an eye that tears open a hole in time and they all three go into it and then out of the other side and somewhere in the middle everything Beeky says falls away.

'You've got a funny idea of flowers,' his father says. 'Most people don't think used-up cool-drink tins and flowers are one and the same thing. The place looked like a rubbish tip.'

'It didn't do anyone any harm,' says Conrad.

'It harmed me,' his father says.

Which is to say it harmed Her, the Old Madam knows and she feels Her coming towards them through the timelessness and with her, acquisitiveness and the sharp eucalyptus scent of self-interest.

'Do you think it pleases me to know what kind of

talk an incident like this causes?' his father says. 'Do you think I don't know what people say behind our back?'

'Please, Pappa . . .' Conrad says but his father doesn't want to listen.

'Do you think I like the idea of having a crazy girl in this house, who thinks it's a joke to use rubbish for a grave decoration?'

There are things he wants to say but he doesn't know how to say them out loud so he says them in silence.

In silence he says Beeky's flowers are magic and beautiful. They shine with her love and are like no flowers ever seen before. They are fine and rare and fit to be seen and admired, not only for their beauty in this world, but also in those worlds far beyond where others are watching and see what we can't.

'You mustn't worry about me, Con,' she says. 'I'm glad I did what I did and there's nothing he can do to hurt me.'

'I liked them,' he says.

'I know you did,' she says. 'You always like everything I do. You're the only one who does.'

He's sad beyond words for what happened to his mother and he loves his sister more than anyone, but even that doesn't make him strong enough, and he can't speak against his father.

There have been letters and telephone calls and Beeky watched like a hawk and made to stay in her room and his father not looking at her and refusing to have her name mentioned.

She's to be sent away to finish her schooling. To a Ladies College in the Eastern Cape.

'A school with an excellent reputation,' his father says. 'Where they have some experience with girls who are "different". We'll see what they make of her there.'

He doesn't want her to leave but he has no words to tell her.

'Tell him why you did it,' he says. 'If you explain. If you just explain perhaps he'll understand.'

'He can go to hell,' she says. 'And I hope he fries there.'

He has a gift for her and his gift will speak for him. A special gift, a gift held back, not given till now.

They are out of sight and alone. They sit together, quiet, held fast by their shared life-breath and the heavy weight of farewell.

He opens his parcel to show what he has for her and inside it are two feather ear ornaments brought back from the flatland and a little packet of yellow-green *sasa* powder which is the bush gift of parting.

'Come closer,' he says. 'Close your eyes. Let me show you how to do it.'

The ear ornaments are beautiful. They're made of small ostrich-shell chips, first bitten into rounds, then slid onto pieces of sinew, then the edges of the whole string of them ground smooth with the hand against a rough piece of rock. At the centre of each is a small hole pierced into it with a sharp-pointed stick.

Beeky's ornaments hang down on three small strings. Attached to each is a downy guinea-chick feather freckled with tiny white dots and her brother reaches out and puts them into her hand and then he unfolds the packet of *sasa*.

It's a small amount. Hardly anything at all. Wrapped in a leaf, tied with grass and when he unfolds it the smell is pungent.

He dips his forefinger into it and raises it to her face and the powder is fine-grained like talcum. He makes dark arches over her eyes and down her nose.

Her skin under his fingertip is soft and warm as an apricot.

His finger traces her face in powder curves. The palm of his hand is warm and soft as the cloud veil across the moon. Powder falls on her brows and her lashes. When she opens her eyes they're cat-green lakes floating in a sea of *sasa* and she looks like a queen and the strange smell of *sasa*, halfway between rose and sage, rises up in the air.

'I'm not leaving you,' she says. 'I'm leaving this house and I'm leaving him. Do you think I mind? I'll only mind if you do. So you mustn't. Let me go because I want you to. I'll write, I promise and I'll be happy, you'll see.'

Dear Con [she writes]

It's lovely here. The flowers are real. They grow where they please and no-one seems to mind. Agapanthus, arum lilies, wild strawberries and white blood flowers. I told you I'd be happy.

There are yellowwoods draped with monkey rope that spread their crowns above the forest canopy. There's wild lemon and forest currant and white ironwood and assegai wood and cabbage trees and holy cypress and crimson loeries with green wings and they fly between the branches as if they have all the time in the world and will even hover for a moment or two expecting to be admired.

No-one is the least interested in me here and no-one bothers me at all. I can do exactly as I please. So that's what I do.

I'm happy here, Con. I think a small bit of heaven must have fallen here or perhaps Mamma sent it as a nice surprise. Just imagine how you'd feel if you suddenly found yourself in heaven which suddenly I have, which I'm sure won't please Pappa. All I miss is you but how can I miss you? You're always with me anyway. Beeky.

My heart is singing,
I shall put on my rattles and my headband,
and feathers in my hair
to explain to god how happy I am
that he has helped me and I am content.

The Boy in the Picture

Something must be said about the boy in the picture.

Yesterday's traitor is today's hero. It's all a question of time. Which is a matter those stuck in timelessness might pause to consider as something useful to pass on to those coming after. If only they were given the time.

Time is precious, people say. Even those who have not stood before a firing squad, court-martialled and killed for spying, bound upon that irreversible journey into timelessness.

The old Queen's lip-service subject, the Old Madam's younger son, the one with a traitor's heart that matched his brother's found that out in a hurry. A shower of lead for him. Despatched from this life. So what? If life everlasting is promised and paradise is just around the corner, then life itself is nothing much to lose but young men think it is and he was young.

Gone. Out of our story. To keep company with the rest of them. The unsung, unquiet dead. Rising up, eddying away, unready, out of life cheated and angry.

When viewed against eternal rest the shortcomings

of the old Queen don't seem quite as important as they once did. Nor do the comings and goings of the empiric sun.

No sun where he is. The sun may make up its own mind where it rises, where it sets and being of no consequence to him now, either choice will suit him equally well.

He would like to have lingered a while longer. There are things, not concerning his mother, his country, his bloodlines, irrelevant now, he would like to have done.

A Bible, a psalm book, his boots and a hat. An embroidered handkerchief smelling of rose water which no-one expected and the small piece of thorn from his mother's home farm, the land she was always going on about, given by her, kept by him for remembering.

All that is memory now. Past trials, past griefs, old enmities which are the cause of all the trouble. Past tense. That is all that matters now.

No psalm-singing funeral procession for him. A quick burial outside the churchyard walls. A small mound, a deep-dug grave and he inside it. No flowers, no headstone for a traitor. Too soon, not yet. That will come later. Fulsomely lettered, guiltily ornate. No rosemary for remembrance. No sign that he lived and shot straight, read Homer's *Iliad* and sang 'Oh, Susannah!' in a full-bodied baritone that fell smooth on the ear.

All gone. No need for any of it in that place he's in now. All that's left is the Devil's picture. It's the only image of him that remains. A graven image which more than likely put him on the wrong side of God in the first place and now that will have to go too.

He may not stay there, fixed in his place in the picture, insouciantly smiling, forever young, his arm brushing the arm of his brother, both grinning devil-may-care at the future. Death's grin now. The old Queen will not have it. Off with his head.

It is the custom of the country.

His face will have to be blotted out and his mother must be the one to do it.

The bitterest price she has had to pay but a true Colonist, a genuflector before the Crown, a patriot, will erase all reminders of one who once lived and moved and betrayed and spied and sold secrets, and will do it before others so that all the world can see.

A pot of Indian ink will serve and the lightest press of an ink-damp fingertip. Eyes, nose, mouth, all gone and the fool's smile too. His mother's place at the Colonial table is safe; bought with his blood. Her suspect loyalty is sure, or so it will seem in the records and all he is now is a round black dot in the picture book of history.

Allow me to plead for his mother. Boer woman that she is. A Crown subject, misplaced among strangers, she said so herself. Yearning for her home farm and her people and farmsteads set so far apart one might travel a day or more and be sure no-one but God will show Himself to you.

Let it be set down in her favour, considering she is destined to self-flagellate herself into becoming a guilt-ridden ghost and remain one for a very long time, that the custom of the country is not the custom of the human heart.

It grieves his mother, black-thumbed with betrayal as she is and her heart cracks inside her where no-one can see.

If only he could.

In need of consolation, in that place where he is, anger dances inside him like a dust devil. The old should go first. Then the good. It's right that the good die young. Being assured of a ripe old age would only make them complacent.

Young men shouldn't listen to their mothers. If you asked him now he would say the old Queen is welcome to as much gold as she can decently carry away. When you come to where he is, gold's not much good to you anyway. You find that out in a hurry.

Saints have been discomfited by less although, had he gone the full distance, he would not have been a saint. Or, at least, he does not think so and when he contemplates so many unsaintly young men's pleasures left unsavoured his anger becomes hot as fire and begins to spill out and away to go back to the world to ensnare those coming after.

So anxious is it to return that he has to catch hold of it in the palm of his hand and hold it there to be sure no-one but himself will ever be injured by it.

Because some residue of his mother's wisdom remains and you never know Who may be watching.

So determined is his anger to escape it burns him terribly. His skin sizzles and his palm fries but he keeps his fingers clenched and won't let it go to plague those yet to come and only the very smallest piece escapes his grasp.

All the rest is trapped and it pains him, so he spends every day in anguish but he holds it fast so it can never fly free and that is his gift to those coming after: that, except for one very small piece, his resentment and grief at what has become of him can harm no creature but himself.

In case Anyone should notice but only time and your own point of view can know that.

A Song of Abraham and of Isaac

His father is proud of him because he didn't ask for the Navy.

The Navy is what you ask for if you want to be safe. In the Navy you can sit out your time with nothing worse happening than bad food and seasickness.

His father can pull strings to get Conrad anywhere he wants to go and where he wants to go is the bush.

'Special Services?' the enlistment officer says. 'What makes you want to go out looking for a job like that?'

'I know the bush,' Conrad says.

His life is in the file in the enlistment officer's hands. His name and address. His father's name. His educational particulars. Twenty-one years old with a Bachelor of Science degree asking to go in the first intake of the new year. Most students stay students as long as they can. As long as you study you can ask for military exemption.

If you're called up and refuse to go and have no good reason it's an offence against the state and you can be imprisoned for it but Conrad will never go to prison.

'If you want an elite corps that's what you'll get,' his father says. 'No yellow-bellies in our family. They can say what they like about us but it's us and men like us who made this country what it is today and if there's anyone who can say we never did our duty, I'd like to see him stand up and say it to my face.'

Conrad's height, his weight, the colour of his hair, his level of fitness. Everything is in his file. There are character references. One from a cabinet minister, now retired. One from 'Oom' Faan and another from an uncle on his paternal grandmother's side who sits on the Synod of the Dutch Reformed Church.

You're allowed to specify a unit. The Air Force is preferred and so are the parabats. No-one wants to be in the infantry and the Casspirs aren't popular. You take them if you get assigned but everyone knows tanks are death traps.

'I know the bush, sir,' Conrad says. 'We have a farm near the border. I used to spend my holidays there. I know the people.'

'Is that where you learnt to shoot?'

It says on his form he's a competitive marksman. A Bisley shot. 'Yes, sir,' he says.

'I speak the local language,' Conrad says. 'Or at least enough to get by. It's my country up there. I understand it.'

All this is noted down in the open space for recruitment officer's opinion and recommendation.

'It isn't up to me to decide who goes into Special Services,' the recruitment officer says. 'That's a decision they make after they've seen how you make out in basic training.'

'I know that, sir,' Conrad says. 'But I thought I'd just mention it. Just in case you could put in a word.'

He can make a note in the file. Conrad knows he

can and if he does and someone later on, higher up the line, notices it that could be the first step.

Perhaps. You can never be certain.

'Do you know who goes into Special Services, Mr Hartmann?' the recruitment officer says.

Conrad knows he isn't meant to answer. Officers speak and enlisted men, even aspirant ones, listen. This officer sits, pen poised, in a bright neat office looking up at Conrad. Trying to read him, to teach him, to warn him, making him wait until he's ready to answer his own question.

'Special Services is for men, not boys,' he says. 'It's for grown-up, bush-hardened men. It's not a boy-scout camp out there. I'll give you my opinion, if I may. If you're offered the Navy you should take it.'

They do this sometimes. He knows they do. It's the first test and he's ready for it.

'I can look after myself,' he says.

'You'll need to,' the officer says and scribbles on his documents and stamps them and tells him he can go.

A good candidate, he writes. In the body of the form where Conrad has written Special Services preferred, he underlines it in dark ink. Highly suitable candidate, he writes. He signs his name and the form goes on a separate, smaller pile.

JEROME

The Pig with a Smile on Its Face

Jerome works for the Government these days. That's what his mum tells her friends and she made sure the Lombards heard it.

'Make a change for him to be on the right side of the law,' Doris says. 'Must be a very special department prepared to turn a blind eye to a man with a criminal record.'

'Jerome's paid his dues, you know,' his mum says. 'He didn't get a life sentence although the way you go on you wouldn't think so.'

'I'm only saying,' Doris says.

'Scraping the bottom of the barrel is what you're saying,' his mum says. 'And thank you, Doris, we know what you mean but happily the rest of the world isn't like you.'

'So we can expect to see him in uniform, can we?' Doris says. 'Well, that's good. At least we know we can sleep easy in our beds then, with boys like Jerome out there to watch out for us.'

'I told you,' his mum says. 'It's special. There won't be any uniform. It's too special for that.'

Put that in your pipe and smoke it is the way she says it. He's one of the Spin Street boys now and she's pleased enough about it on the surface but when she first heard she wasn't so happy as she likes to make out.

'I know about Spin Street,' she says. 'A job's a job but I don't like that place. You watch out for yourself there and make sure nothing happens that causes you an injury.'

'Not me, Ma,' he says. 'Don't you worry about that. I can look out for myself.'

No-one talks much about Spin Street but everyone knows it. From the outside it looks the same as anywhere else. Nine storeys, square windows and a courtyard in the middle. Two entrances, one front and one in the side street round the corner. Wooden swing doors with shiny brass door handles.

Nothing to see from the outside but it's a bad-luck building, people say. It's a police place and if you have to go past it, you go past as quick as you can, without looking.

Bad things happen there. People who go in for questioning never speak about it afterwards.

Sometimes people who go in for questioning never have the chance to because they never come out again.

He slipped on a piece of soap, fell from a window, a loose wire, was found hanging by his tie, we have no record, death self-inflicted, people have been known to kill themselves you know, she died.

'What really happens at Spin Street?' his mum says. 'Now you're there I suppose you must know.'

'Nothing, Ma,' he says.

Some of them at Spin Street talk a lot but not him.

He keeps his mouth shut and gets on with his job.

The less you know the better and he isn't interested anyway.

He does what he does. Does his 'tricks', makes his 'toys'. That's what they call it. He doesn't mind that either. They can call it anything they like. He'll listen to anything they say but all he really wants to hear from them is how they're going to use his stuff and how much time he's got before it's needed.

He isn't interested in details. Electrical circuitry is still his big thing and he knows a lot more about it now.

You need nimble fingers for electrics and he's as good at it as anyone can be and all he wants to do is be given a job then just left to get on with it.

The pig business wasn't his idea. The first he knew about it was when the head arrived. Neat and nice in a cardboard box that used to contain photocopy paper.

They sent old Skulpie to fetch it fresh from the abattoir and he brought it back sitting next to him in its box on the front seat of one of the plain clothes' Cortinas. There was newspaper underneath and pushed down the sides to keep it in its place.

Whoever had packed it had put too much balled and crumpled newspaper underneath so the rim of the crown and two pointed pig ears stick out above the box.

'What am I supposed to do with this now?' Skulpie says when he gets back to Spin Street and 'China' Berry who's the main man tells him to take it down to the basement room and he has no problem with that.

'You just better not forget about it,' he says. 'You'll know all about it if you forget about it and it starts to rot.'

'It's not going to rot,' Berry says. 'It won't be around long enough to rot because we've got other plans for it and they're none of your business. You just do what I tell you and then make yourself scarce.'

There are eight of them down in the basement and they say they've been sent but they don't know why.

'What's it for?' Jerome wants to know.

'Target practice,' Berry says. 'I told the boys you'd give them a little sample,' Berry says. 'I said, if they asked nicely, you'd show them your Walkman.'

'It's OK by me,' Jerome says.

'I asked if there were any volunteers for a try-out but I got no takers,' Berry says.

Then he does what he always does. He makes a cluck-cluck sound like a chicken squawking just to show what he thinks of them.

'Just to give us a little demonstration of how good you are at your work,' he says. 'None of these buggers was willing to take a chance on you getting it wrong.'

There are six of them and Berry and him and he knows them all.

Berry, de Waal, Junior, Esterhuyse, the Iron Man and little Robey, who's Berry's sidekick.

'Just take a look at yourselves,' Berry says. 'Put all of you together and you couldn't make one decent pair of balls out of the lot of you.'

Robey's standing there with a big smile on his face and everyone knows if he didn't have Berry to hide behind it wouldn't take five minutes before someone got hold of him and sorted him out.

Jerome is the centre of attention but he doesn't mind that. When it comes to his work he knows what he's doing. He doesn't need 'China' Berry to speak for him.

'Bring your baby over here,' Berry says. 'And someone set that thing up where it's supposed to be.'

Robey's always willing. He lifts the pig's head out of its box and it comes up with one eye open and one closed and a twist of the mouth that makes a small, knowing, pig grin as if the head still has a mind inside it and the mind knows what's going to happen to it and couldn't care less.

Jerome's been wiring a Walkman. It's delicate work and he's had to try it with different kinds of triggering devices. No good if it blows up before you're ready. No good if you have a couple of wipe-outs before you get where you really want to be. But that's Berry's job.

Berry has to do the set-up and the planning. Berry has to isolate the target and make sure there's one hit and a confirmed take-out and nothing goes wrong along the way. All Jerome has to do is provide the hardware.

That's how it works.

The pig's head is set up on a concrete slab in the far corner of the basement with the Walkman's earphones attached black on pink to its ears and the plastic-coated wires dangle down its cheeks and the compact plastic body of the Walkman lies on the grey concrete next to it.

There's a barricade of polythene-covered sandbags to absorb the blast. There's light from two spotlights on vertical dollies set up at a safe distance and it's like a TV film being made and the pig with its one eye half-open and a pig grin on its face is the star of the show.

They stand a safe distance away behind a special screen and Jerome is going to flick a switch to detonate and the pig's head and its winking eye and its grin are going to be blown to kingdom come right in front of them.

'Whenever you're ready,' Berry says and Jerome's finger is on the detonator and he can let it go just whenever he likes.

One thing you can say about Jerome. His hands are rock steady which is more than you can say for Berry, but Jerome only drinks Coke because he's a craftsman. He needs steady hands and he's not going to let anything get in the way of his work.

It takes the lightest touch of a fingertip. One quick click and it's done and there's a bang and a tremor that goes so hard through the room you'd think even the beams of light were breaking up into a million pieces.

Just the sound is enough to make you close your eyes and when you open them again the pig's head's gone and there's nothing left but the lights and the smell and a feeling each man feels of being shaken up and the red haze in the air.

Someone behind him says: 'Holy shit.'

'You want more?' says Berry and there's absolute silence.

But, silent or not, Jerome's earned his place. He can definitely count himself in as one of 'the boys' now.

'He's the jackal,' Berry says, pleased. 'Sly as any damn jackal you care to name but when he comes to the kill, "kaboom" and he's there.'

That's respect. When they smile Jerome smiles too. If 'The Jackal' is what they want, then 'The Jackal' will suit him just fine.

The black-backed jackal was the last animal created. He's a scavenger and vengeful and Man marked him chasing him away with the contents of a cooking pot, burning a black mark down his back and all other creatures shun him and leave him to kill and consort with carrion because that is his place.

But he's patient.

He sits outside the ring of fire and waits his moment. He'll sit there for a long time in that small place between day and night, between seeing and not seeing. In the line of Man's sight, bold to let Man see, so he'll never forget Jackal's there and when he's ready he'll strike and no-one will be able to stop him.

Jackal is sly and lazy. His heart is in killing but not in the hunt. That's why he likes to take sheep. A sheep doesn't have to be hunted down or tired out in a chase. To catch a sheep all Jackal has to do is wait till his moment comes and when it does he's ready. He already knows which sheep from the whole herd is his own and once he's decided he's deadly.

He sinks his teeth into the big neck artery and holds the sheep fast with his teeth and when it's bled to death Jackal takes his pick and eats only those things that please him most. The spleen, then the liver and then the hind legs.

Jackal is a neat eater and fussy. He'll take only the best and dine till he's satiated. What's left is for anyone to have. What's left is not his concern.

No other pack wants him and he has no territory. He moves from place to place, comfortable as a dog, looking at the world through soft dog eyes, but dogs have allegiances and a place in the world and dogs don't kill.

Jackal's man-mark on his back shows what he is. Carrion-intent, despised and rejected he's set loose to roam the world resentful and unwanted, howling with self-pity and taking vengeance where he can.

BEEKY

Her Brother's Book

Beeky is in her last year of school. For her end-of-year art project she's making a present for Conrad and it takes all her time and all her energy.

'A Book of Days' she calls it and every page is different.

Some pages have drawings on them, or little bits of poems scripted in flowing writing. She's made coloured drawings of the Cape mountain flowers which are her favourites which Conrad knows too and she knows them all by name.

There are yellow Golden Stars, Guernsey lilies, Salt and Pepper flowers, Painted Ladies, the Eight-Day Get-Well bush and bright orange Shy flowers that always hang their heads.

Into the book goes her life and his and their mother's, painted and pasted and carefully coloured into one life that belongs to all of them for him to take with him when he goes to the Army.

There's the black kitchen kitten with a triangle face and the smallest of smiles from behind a glass jar of springtime nasturtiums. There's a goose and her goslings and a blue pond beyond and the lemon tree in its tub by the wall in the garden and lemons hanging from it like lanterns. There's a slithering gecko that sleeps in the sun and over the page a double page of navy blue paper decorated with silver stars and she's checked and rechecked and every star in Conrad's book is in its right and proper place.

'It's your going-away present,' she says. 'From me to you. I wrote inside it. I want you to keep it with you.'

'What for?' he says.

'To write down your life,' she says. 'Your life without me. I've left you plenty of space to do it.'

She hates him going to the Army.

'They want you to be a killer,' she says. 'That's what the Army's about. They take you and change you and make you kill other men.'

'Not me,' he says. 'I'll end up in the Signal Corps or as a storeman somewhere.'

'You asked for active service,' Beeky says.

'Everyone does,' he says. 'But it's a big Army and a small war. Not everyone gets it. I wouldn't worry about it if I were you.'

'What if something happens to you?'

'Nothing will,' he says.

'If anything happens he'll be the one who's responsible.'

'It isn't about Pappa,' he says. 'It's about me.'

She shakes her head because she doesn't want to hear.

'If anything happens to you I'll hold it against him for ever and I'll never forgive him,' she says. 'It's people like him and his friends who cause all the trouble in the first place. Why should you be made to go out and kill people just because they tell you to? Tell them you won't.'

'I can't,' he says. 'Even if I wanted to I couldn't and I

don't want to. It's National Service. I have to go. I want to go. Can you just imagine Pappa if I didn't?'

'Tell him no,' Beeky says. 'Be a draft-dodger and proud of it. I'll hide you so they'll never find you. They could come looking for you and do anything they liked to me. I'd never give you away. Never.'

Beeky has come back from school against everything.

'Which is all the bloody thanks I get for trying to do the right thing,' his father says.

'They taught us to think,' says Beeky. 'Not like at this house. At school we could think what we liked and say what we thought and I did.'

Of all the things she's against, she's most against men like her father who look on and do nothing while people make laws that say human beings are somehow less than human. She thinks of her brother and how men like this will send boys like him out to kill those who have the courage to stand up and say it is not right, it is not so and it must be changed.

Even her brother is looking at her in a different way these days. He loves her as much as he always has and he fears for her. He says she's an ostrich anxious to fly, held back as ostrich must be for ever by the fire under her wings.

'You know what Pappa would say,' she says. 'Too much time with the Bushmen. You think they have the answer for everything.'

'They have the answer for this,' he says. 'You can't take on the whole world. Not when it's really just Pappa you're against.'

'What I'm against is you going away,' she says. 'If you have to go to the Army just so we can go on using "whites only" toilets I'd rather pee in the street.'

One thing Pappa has done by hating her the way he

does is make her free. There's no-one to disgrace and no-one to stop her. She can do as she pleases and she's happy among strangers. She goes to forbidden rallies and risks being taken or held for questioning by the police. She walks in protests and holds up banners to end the call-up. She talks to natives on the street and sits with coloureds on the bus.

She spat at a policeman and when she got into trouble and they told Pappa he shook his head and wrote a cheque for the Police Widows and Orphans Fund and said in a low man-to-man voice about the madness she caught from her mother.

'Be careful,' Conrad says. 'Don't look for trouble.'

'How much trouble can I get into in art school?' she says. 'Art all day, every day. It'll be like heaven to me. Nothing bad can happen to me there but what about you? I don't want you to look for trouble either. I don't want it but I can't do anything to stop it. You're going to the Army anyway.'

He sees fire in her. He wants her to be free but he's afraid for her at the same time.

Everyone knows the story of Ostrich. How when he lifted his wings fire was let loose on the world and because Man didn't know it or the way it was, it consumed everything in its path.

Before fire came, all in this world and other worlds and the cosmos were members of the same family but when fire came all natural things feared it. It frightened them away and Man, who embraced it, was left alone to enjoy what he'd found.

We say Man loves fire and he does but only because it's better than loneliness and the dark. Before fire there was nothing in the dark to be afraid of. Man wasn't alone. He knew all the creatures of creation and had nothing to fear.

After fire, he had glowing coals and heat and the sight and the sound and the smell of it and he was drawn to the fire and treasured it because it was all that was left to him. Without it he would be left alone in the dark.

In this calamity, when Man by his greed and foolishness was severed from creation, Ostrich who had fire in his keeping had his part to play and it's because of this we remember his story.

Ostrich has two wives. They sit on either side of his fire cooking spiny jelly melons, Ostrich's favourite food, which he will only eat cooked and Ostrich watches them and waits and his mouth waters at the savoury smell and all of his soul hungers after hot melon meat and Man stands beyond the fire where he can't be seen, but Man sees Ostrich.

He sees that he is greedy and Man is greedy too. Ostrich hungers for spiny jelly melon and Man hungers for fire which Ostrich has in his keeping, safe under his great wings, so that when the time comes and the Greater god calls for him he can give fire to fan into flame so the animals can be branded and sent out into the world, each one different and particular and none the same as his fellow.

In the great game of life there are other smaller games too and the contest between Ostrich and Man for the possession of fire is one of them and it proves that, of the two, Man is the more cunning.

'Look up,' Man calls to Ostrich. 'See what I see at the top of the tree.'

At the top of the tree are the best and tastiest fruits safe from smaller birds and animals who do not have Ostrich's long neck and sharp eyes.

It's a small thing for Ostrich to lift his eyes from fire and look up. It's a smaller thing, hungry as he is, to take his eyes away from fire completely and reach up his long neck for the fruit he sees there.

Foolish Ostrich to trust Man, for while his head is turned Man steals some fire from the place where his wives are cooking and runs away with it and takes it to his own two wives so he can have fire to cook his spiny jelly melon over.

And Man's wives are wily like their husband and lay a trap for Ostrich and the trap is a bed of Devil's Thorn to tear at Ostrich's feet and in between a path of wooden strips for Man to make his escape and so it was that Man ran free on his wooden path and has fire and Ostrich was ensnared on a bed of Devil's Thorn and hurt his feet so badly that to this day he has to run on his toes.

Beeky goes to the station to say goodbye to her brother.

'To embarrass you,' she says. 'If no-one else pitches up you can hug me and kiss me and say I'm your girlfriend. If twenty-five girlfriends arrive to give you a send-off you can tell I'm your sister.'

She's the only one who'll be there and the only one he'll miss and he's already in khaki and on the train, bent waist-high out of a window watching for her, willing her to come and to hurry because time is flying fast and he feels alone with so many people around him and when she comes she's late and running.

She's a student these days and dresses like a ragbag poor woman. She looks like a gypsy. Her bright blue skirt floats behind her like a puff of cloud. The shimmering sequins on her Indian silk top glitter like diamonds in the light.

All around them people are saying goodbye. There are girls in summer dresses and small-town mothers come to the station wearing church clothes and hats. There are shy country girls in flared skirts and blouses and street-smart city girls in too-tight denim jeans and stretch tops that are stretched to the limit but there's no-one like Beeky.

Sweethearts are kissing. Mothers are crying and fathers are standing back, the way men do at funerals.

'Everyone on board,' the sergeant major says but they aren't absolutely in the Army yet and nobody listens.

Rolls of toilet paper white-arc through the air and each open window is a Kodak snap of brown-clothed boys all teeth and shorn-off hair and faces shining in the light.

'On the War Path', 'Non-Stop to the Border', is chalked on the brown side of the railway carriage.

'Beeky!' Conrad calls.

She's running down the platform on sandalled feet just as the train groans into life and he's watching out for her with his eyes and all of his heart and an anxious constriction in his throat because although he knows her and how she's always late he's almost given her up.

'I've brought you flowers,' she says.

She has to shout above the hubbub so he can hear and point to the bouquet she has in her hand so he can understand.

It's a bright bunch and she holds it up high so he can see and they're Beeky's flowers, the simple mountain flowers she picks in the spring. Mother's Bonnets, Spider Orchids, Lady's Hands and Painted Ladies with sprigs of herbs stuck in between and tied together with a strip of grass.

'You're crazy,' he shouts.

There have been food parcels and roasted chickens and biltong and long strips of *boerewors* and fat pieces of sugar-preserve fruit and cold drinks and sides of ham but no-one else has brought flowers.

'You're embarrassed,' she shouts holding her flowers towards his window and laughing and some of the other windows laugh too and the air is filled with the sadness of parting and the excitement of beginnings.

'Here you are,' she says.

He stretches down and she reaches up to him and his face is close to hers and his hand closes over hers and the flowers are clasped between them and in the light starting tremble of the train they are in their boat bed again and safe.

'Take care,' she says.

She's stretching up and her face is close and his hand closes tighter and he feels her swimming towards him and he bends down lower so he can smell her breath.

'I love you, Con,' she says. 'I'll always love you. Always, for ever. Best of anyone.'

Then it's over. There's a terrible grind of steel on steel and she stands where she is splashed with the colour of her clothes, so different from anyone else's clothes and her hands quite still while everyone else is waving.

He stretches out and lobs the bouquet up in the air and the grass knot holding it together comes loose and it comes apart lightly like a bridal bouquet after the wedding is done and the flowers cascade down like a windburst of petals in an orchard.

Azure blue and dark red on pink, every shade of leaf, a burst of orange and soft deep mauve and she stands on the grey railway platform free-handed and waving and smiling while the flowers make kaleido-scope patterns all round her.

The Day the Lord Has Made

It takes a little while for everyone to settle down but soon Conrad does what the others do. He counts days and the days are full and everything everyone said about basic training is true.

You get used to it. They can ask anything they like of you and you do it and in the end it becomes tolerable.

He doesn't say this when he writes to Beeky because it will stir up all her old angers again and get her into even deeper trouble.

Instead, he tells her what will please her which is what he sees.

'There is Tamarisk and Ringwood, Buffalo Thorn, Wild Fig, Euphorbia, Sweet Thorn and Green Hair Fern and you would like the birds. There are so many of them.'

The bush people say not only birds can fly. Buck can fly too. So can any spirit taking animal form. When they dance the eland they put their arms back to make wings as a reminder that all spirits can fly and the spirit of man can fly too if only he can remember how.

Conrad tells Beeky about the starlings and the dusky sunbirds and the red-eyed bulbul and how the small pools where the last of the water is trapped echo to the call of the gallinule.

Every day the chaplain calls them for prayers and most of them go because it helps break the monotony of sitting around base camp listening to the same old stories, having the same old squabbles and telling the same jokes.

'Lord,' says the chaplain. 'Let today be the day You deliver the enemy into our hands.'

They've each been given a Bible. *The New Testament and the Psalms*. A new translation. Special issue for the Defence Force. It says so on the inside cover.

Their enemies carry Bibles too. They've seen them put out for inspection with the other possessions of the captured or killed.

You get used to being shouted at and punished for no good reason and pulled out of your bunk in the middle of the night to go on route marches.

You become accustomed to making your bunk and sleeping on the floor so it stays perfect for inspection and even so having it pulled apart by a red-faced sergeant major who's happy in his job and wants you to make it again anyway.

Once you get used to it you can live with anything. That was a lesson he learnt in the nights he lay in bed with his sister and held her close in his father's house and made her safe.

Custom reconciles people with conditions. He can become accustomed to this life but if he is to survive it and still remain himself he must search for something good to make it endurable.

There is no Beeky here. Here there is only the bush and it sings to him with its same siren song and anything is bearable if the bush is there to wrap around himself at night.

He is brown, earth brown, from hours in the sun. His wrist strapped by his watch is a bloodless white band. A stranger's skin. A white handcuff waiting for its mate. His bush mark suddenly made visible.

'This is party time,' the sergeant says. 'Enjoy it, girls, because this is as good as it gets.'

They rig up a kitchen, makeshift latrines and concrete showers with small tins tilted down on a string from tree branches. The food is good. When they're not on manoeuvre familiarizing themselves with the terrain they sleep under canvas at the base camp and the fires burn high outside and only the Ovambo sleep beyond the camp perimeters with their bodies at one with the ground and the night wrapped around them like a blanket and he knows why they do this and would like to lie with them but it isn't allowed.

There are letters from home and *Forces' Favourites* crackling over the radio and in the afternoons the officer's voice and the maps and the strategic plans and the terror stories of what the 'so-called freedom fighters' do if they get hold of you; how if you get hold of them first you knock the shit out of them and rattle information out of their guts, out of their bones, out of their heads, into their mouths and into our care because information is power.

Knowing what the enemy know and their not knowing what you know is what's going to win the day and all the while as they learn their new trade the day sings outside and the day is beautiful.

At night, before 'lights out', they're allowed to write home.

> Dear Beeky [he writes]
>
> Do you know the little klipspringers? They make themselves scarce when they see us coming but all the same, I saw some the other day. Did you know their thick bushy tails are not just there for decoration? They protect them from falls.
>
> I saw a rock kestrel today and a chacina baboon and there are plenty of rock rabbits around. They couldn't care less about us. They sit on their rocks and watch us go past. There's no doubt in their mind who the monkeys are around here and it's not them.

He doesn't mind the heat or the camelthorn trees. For those with eyes that see the camelthorn is a symbol of hope. It dries out in winter and you think it's dead but each spring it comes back to life.

It is camelthorn that begins to spike the landscape as they move further north following dry river courses to the granite flatlands, looking for they don't know what, finding springbok and gemsbok and oryx.

'No shooting,' the sergeant says. 'No bloody picking off animals just because you haven't got anything better to do. This isn't a picnic.'

He knows there are African adders and Egyptian cobras seeking shade in the rocks and lethally venomous Parabathus scorpions but this is his world. He's a city boy but he is not like other city boys and when they have Church parade and are told to pray he prays that someone will realize this and see that he gets sent to Special Services.

There are stories about it. The men in Special Services are shit-hot with balls of iron. They get dropped in the bush miles from anywhere and are left to do their job and find their own way back. If they don't make it no-one knows them. No-one takes responsibility for them. They must live off the land and their own resources. For the rest of the world, until they're heard from again, they cease to exist.

He doesn't mind. No matter what they ask of him this is the direction in which he scents the possibility of belonging to himself again and for this he thinks no price would be too high.

He and Jan Steynberg are the only two from the initial intake who have been selected for Special Services training.

'Now they're talking, man,' Jan Steynberg says. 'Now the fun begins.'

It's different here and they're treated differently. 'Mr Hartmann,' the commanding officer says. 'Mr Steynberg. Pleased to have you with us.'

Never depend on anyone else. The only person you can depend on here is yourself.

'If it's too tough for you boys you can always pack up and leave,' the sergeant major says. 'If you can't take the pace, the gate's always open.'

They are in khaki smocks and trousers now. 'Somewhere in the bush'. No-one outside is allowed to know where. They aren't allowed to know themselves.

You may not: Put dates on your letters. Complain about conditions. Give any information about the training you're receiving. Spread rumours about where you may be going. To any and all of the above questions the answer is: 'I don't know.'

They've forgotten what it is to sleep. Every night there's a code word and you lie awake waiting for it and sometimes it comes and sometimes it doesn't. Firefinch. Big Makulu. Bat Hawk.

His shoulders ache. His heart pumps like a piston gone mad. Air surges in and out of his lungs. They run with bags of cement and sweat pours into his eyes and an ambulance with the Red Cross on its side follows them.

'If you get tired, say so,' the training officer says. 'Just give the word and you're RTU, return to unit and it's all over.'

He's too tired to sleep. He's beyond sleep. Day and night are the same to him now. All that matters are the names of operations. Firefinch. Big Makulu. Bat Hawk. Whatever they say he's ready.

Red Eagle is the call and when it comes he reaches for his gun before the words reach his brain. He's on the floor running. Everyone is booted and running and ready and they're loaded into trucks and bumped along a road and at the end of the road is a landing strip and a plane waiting.

They do what they've done a hundred times before and a hundred times until they can do it in the dark, in their sleep, in the darkest hour of midnight with the world tearing apart around them or in absolute silence. Until they can do it perfectly without question.

The plane bumps through the thin light of morning and they bounce along in silence and the silence threads them together. Ten minutes, five minutes, stand up, hook up and below them the bush gives way to open ground and undulating land.

'Don't look so bloody miserable,' the officer in command says. 'Your training's over and there are some silly buggers out there who actually think you're soldiers now.'

He feels empty. He wants his sack of concrete and the training officer's voice spitting insults and orders and his own blood thumping in his ears. He wants the hot dark and permanent sleeplessness and the call in the night that might, or might not, come.

No-one looks up and there's the drone of the

engines and their pitch changing and the jolt of descent and the air warming as it floods the open hatch and apart from that absolute silence.

It's the end of summer. The light is leaving sooner, blazing away in a glory of copper sunsets. When the rains stop and winter comes the men they are seeking who are seeking them will come and they can expect their first engagement. Their instructors have told them this but if they hadn't the bush, all-knowing, would have whispered it to them anyway.

You can move in the winter.

'The sun shall not smite thee by day . . .' the chaplain says.

'*Ja*,' says Jan Steynberg standing next to him at church parade. 'The sun shall not smite us but it won't smite those other buggers either. They'll be moving soon.'

Here they don't have to wait for Sunday church parade to pray. It's the 'operational area' so they pray every day and more if they like.

'For practice,' Steynberg says. 'To keep our hand in. Believe me if the moment comes and things get tight, no matter what you think you believe now you'll want to scream out for the Father, Son and Holy Ghost and anyone else who can help you.'

He's bush-smart like they all are, counting days, saying he wants to get out and go home and find a girl who thinks the sun shines out of his arse and knows how to behave herself. Then maybe he'll even settle down.

'Grant us protection,' says the chaplain. 'Deliver the enemy into our hands.'

'Amen,' they say.

In winter the bush offers no shelter. There's nowhere for the prey to hide. That's why the hunters come. They walk in a line spread out with trackers in front, eyes always down, looking for the telltale glint of mine metal in the soft sand which is the new spoor-print of this land.

The first blooding has not yet come and they're ready except no-one is ever ready and when it comes, it comes quickly and it is terrible.

A house has been attacked by infiltrators. An old lady has been killed and a boy. The old woman has been shot, the boy's head beaten in with a rifle butt.

'Bloody barbarians,' the officer commanding says. 'Find them and take them out.'

They're supposed to know what to do. What they know is that they know nothing.

'Taking out gooks is like taking out vermin,' the OC says. 'Get out there and *klap* the shit out of them.'

They've heard it a hundred times but this is Conrad's first time and he doesn't know what to expect.

They're going in on the ground. As a team. They're swaying along towards the reported position in a Hippo armoured truck, sitting shoulder to shoulder, their rifles, dearer to them, they've been told, than their mothers and fathers, pointing upwards between their knees.

When they reach the place they're offloaded, black-faced and fearsome, their rifles held ready. The Ovambo trackers, light-footed, are in front, eyes to the ground for landmines and they keep in tyre tracks until the tracks run out and they're asking the bush to speak to them, to crackle its secrets, to give them these men who are not men as they are but fit only to feed carrion.

The winter sun pale in the sky lights the whole world and they are each of them alone, yet all together and by now they know the rhythm of the others. They know their strengths and weaknesses.

Each of them has his story to tell and each has given a small piece of his story to the others as if for a talisman, as if for safekeeping and all these stories link them together until all their lives are one life and all of them together are life itself.

This is the day the Lord has made. He has put each of us in the world for a purpose. Each of us has been blessed and although we know fear there is a terrible power surging inside us.

This is what is running through Conrad's head. A ceaseless tape with no 'stop' button, first in the chaplain's voice and then in his own.

Then it happens.

They're doing what their instructors told them to do.

'You take the initiative. You choose the time and the place. You decide when to attack and how.'

They know what the book says.

'They're assassins and cowards,' their instructors tell them. 'They'll run if they can and they'll keep running. Most of your job will be to find them and catch them. Find out what they know. Scare them shitless. Find out what they know. To win we have to know what they know. They're more afraid of you than you'll ever be of them. Remember that. Never forget it.'

It's not true.

They are led by the nose straight into an ambush and the ground and the air and the trees are shaking and the noise is terrible.

They have been silent, following their leader, using hand signals but after the hit that changes. Men are screaming like bells in different tones. Anger and fury, fear and defiance; a terrible shrill choir of death coming to look for us, perhaps coming with a slip of paper in his hand and my name on it and it is not like they told us it would be.

I who have stood alone in the face of thunder and looked at lightning think what a fool my father is because what he tried to teach me is something that can never be taught.

I stand alone at the mouth of hell and know that my father is not in overall command of this world. There is witness of a power greater than man which in the end will decide all and if I never knew this before I know it now.

Our tracker is gone.

'Blown away,' the regulars say. Disintegrated. No blood, no bone, no brains or pieces of limb splattering down to remind us there was once a man.

'Dead meat,' someone shouts.

Where once there was a man there is nothing.

'Oh, God, please help me now. God, Lord Jesus, Mary and Joseph and all the saints. Every angel, good or bad, it makes no difference; oh God! anybody out there, anyone who can help us now please get us out of this mess.'

He lies on the ground with his face in the sand. Automatic gunfire, rifle grenades, RPG7 missiles and mortars, he lies there and in the middle of the unthinkable with the green of AK bullets and the red of R1s flecking the sky over his head the impossible happens. A wonderful peace comes over him. In this place he does not belong to himself. His fate is not his to decide. He knows he's in the hands of whatever God happens to be in charge at that moment, this is where he draws his comfort from.

It won't last for ever. Nothing lasts for ever. He learnt that in another place at another time. The thuds in the night pass, so do the silences. Thunder and lightning pass and if you survive, you learn something.

'Up boys, up,' the lieutenant says and he talks soft because it's quiet. It's over. It's melted away as though it never was and they have taken a hard hit and the sergeant is calling for them, trying to get them together and formed up for pursuit.

'Anyone *klapped*?' he asks.

Anyone down? Anyone dead?

They make jokes before they go out.

'Soon sort it out,' they say. 'Won't take long. See you in a jiffy.'

A Jiffy is a body bag.

He's in one piece, uninjured but even so no longer as he was. Something in him has changed. He is a man, not a gun-happy fool and he has been misled. He has underestimated the enemy. He has thought too highly of himself and been punished for his mistake but he's learnt and it won't happen to him again.

'Hartmann. Where's Steynberg?'

The lieutenant's eyes are pale, sweat-streaked in his corked face.

'Where the hell is Steynberg?' he says.

We find him behind a tree where he's sought shelter. He's sitting propped up against a *kokerboom*, his gun lying at his side, his hand resting lightly on it, so much himself, so nonchalant, I want to talk to him. I think my nerve is going because I want to laugh. I want to crack a joke, one of the stupid jokes he likes so much, so I can laugh and get it all out of me without sounding like a maniac.

'Oh, fuck!' says the lieutenant. 'Fucking, shitting, hell!'

His lower body has been shot away. The sergeant

looks at him and looks at me and I am a soldier now and cannot look away.

There are no helicopters to transport him. We'll have to call for one and there isn't time. We can both see that.

We have medics but we're too far from base to give the medical help he needs. If we were closer to base, if there was a hospital nearby or proper help it would be different. This is what I think but I'm lying even as I think it. I can see he is beyond our help although in the big artery in his neck a pulse still flickers. I can look at him, I can look at what's left of him but I can't look at that.

'Oh, shit!' the sergeant says and then there's a small gurgle of sound and it's over.

It's the only sound I remember. One fatality and a few minor injuries. It will say in the report we got off lightly.

Dear Beeky [he writes]

It's wonderful here and strange. You know the *kokerbome*? Quiver trees the English call them. They grow very tall. The Ovambo say they can grow as high as seven metres. You'd think they'd be a good place to shelter but they don't grow close together like the pines at home in the Constantia Forest do. They spread out and stand not too far from each other but each alone and separate.

It's such a strange thing. The quiver trees bloom now, even though it's winter. The flowers are bright yellow. They burst out on top of the tree like candles on a Christmas tree. You can hardly believe they're real. You'd think someone had set them alight and they were burning yellow fire.

The land looks as if it's covered in rust. I think

as I'm writing to you how I should describe it and try to make myself see what you see and all I see are stars. Do you remember the stars I taught you, which I learned from 'Oom' Faan those winters at Liefdefontein?

Look south first for the Southern Cross, our Star of Africa, gatekeeper of the Great World. Do it and remember me and I'll do the same and if I can remember I'll give you a proper telescope when I get back, for your birthday, then maybe you'll return mine to me. Conrad.

Bush people believe death comes equally to all men. In the world of the spirit there is no good nor any bad but there is memory and the memory of those taken young is bitter. Their going makes them vengeful and they come back as dust devils angry and unwilling to go on alone, looking for the companionship of the band they have been taken from.

This is the time to be wary for they seek most of all the spirits of those who were their companions and will try to catch them and keep hold of them and stay with them a little way further along the journey because this is all they know.

For those taken young and unready there is still much to learn so they cling to those who still walk the earth because what they know is not enough to take them on.

Dear Beeky [Conrad writes]

I'm still around. I'm not allowed to say where but it doesn't matter. You drive the censor mad with your letters. Especially the drawings. I know you and can guess what you're doing but making fun of the powers that be doesn't go down very well here so in the end all I get are black blots.

I pretend they're the blacked-out face of the boy in the picture at home and try to imagine what he looked like and how terrible whatever it was that he did could really have been.

I pretend they're ink tests and read what I like into them so if you want to make me smile, your time isn't wasted. You'd be amazed what you can see in a single blot. Don't stop doing it. I'm sure you're giving the censors a good laugh even if they're not allowed to say so because believe it or not they have a sense of humour too and even after they've finished, there are still some things left to read and I like to read them.

I can't tell you much. It's beautiful country and you know that means a lot to me. The other day while we were hanging around waiting and doing nothing I saw the nests of carmine bee-eaters. They'd burrowed them right into the dry bank of a river. There were dozens of them pecking away, getting on with their lives like brilliant red and turquoise dots on brown. I thought how much you would have liked it.

Thank you for the star drawing. I saw the question mark of the Pleiades. Is the question for me? Is the answer that you still have the telescope you took off me and that it's still working?

It's beginning to get hot again. I always think it's strange when people talk about a place in the sun. Here all we want is the opposite. When we're out and take a break there's always a free-for-all and everyone tries to grab what shade there is. We must look like those sheep you see round Durbanville way and at Darling. All bunched together under one tree, sitting on top of each other, making each other even hotter while we look for shade!

Next time you pull yourself out of bed early enough look for the Morning Star. You're always chasing lost causes and looking for things to feel sorry about. Why don't you put the Morning Star on your list? Feel sorry for him. He may be the only star that prevents the triumph of day over night but he's also the only star always ahead of the sun so he never has his moment in the shade. This is something I learnt a long time ago from the bush people.

I'm fine and intend to stay that way. Your book is always with me. It's wherever my things are. I haven't written in it yet. I would rather write to you. Take care of yourself and keep the letters coming. Mail call is very important here. It looks bad if you don't get letters. Love, Conrad.

He's seen other things since Steynberg but it's Steynberg that's the most difficult. He wonders what will happen to the girl Steynberg was going to meet; the one who would know how to behave herself and think the sun shone out of his arse. She'll meet someone else and never know Steynberg existed.

Conrad isn't the only one who saw how it was that day. Others saw it too. They pretend it isn't important. They still make jokes about Jiffys but they all think the same thing.

It could have been me.

They don't talk about it. There's no rule but when they talk, all the talk is about invincibility and survival.

If you believe everything you hear there are miracles enough for everyone. AK bullets that whistle past your ear and don't hit you because they don't have your name on them. The print of an Army boot sole right next to an unexploded landmine. Your foot in the boot. Your foot still where it should be: in one piece, attached to your leg because you were two inches into the right place. Men who make a last-minute change for patrol duty and the change is with the one who doesn't come back.

We're the cream, the 'hawks', the ones who can go in anywhere and come back from anything still in one piece. We don't do the dirty work.

Extracting information is up to the police units and the home guard. *Koevoets*, crowbars, we call them. They can prise anything out of anyone. We don't ask how but even without knowing, we know.

There are regular letters from his father and because of who he is these days they come to him unopened and uncensored through the officers' mess, sent in the special bag flown in from Pretoria.

These letters are always half-thrown at him with a sideways look from the messenger. Being singled out in any way is not a good thing here.

From his father he hears what a good job they're doing. How they're keeping the country free from Communists and safe for God-fearing people to live decent Christian lives in.

His father says every day there's something or other about it in the newspapers and the loony-left propagandists have been put in their proper place and if they haven't learnt their lesson by now things will go harder for them and in this he includes his own daughter.

'I see now that there's nothing she won't do to embarrass me,' he writes. 'University is fine for her. It teaches her to make a bigger fool and public exhibition of herself than ever.'

Apart from that all the news is good and there are certain people who are going to make sure that's the way things stay, so morale at home as well as in the field is always what it should be.

He says how proud he is to have a part in all this and he, Conrad, is that part. Which he takes as a sign that despite being tried as sorely as he has been, in ways he won't mention, which Conrad is only too well aware of, in one way God has at least chosen to smile on him.

This is what he writes: 'I want you to know and always to remember how very proud I am of you.'

His father has something to be proud of too. His name has gone forward to be head of the newly formed Board of Censors.

'I don't want to be wise before the event but I allow myself to hope that despite your sister's best efforts to drag our name through the mud, there are people who know me too well to pay much attention and my chances are good. Some important people are backing me and much credit must go to your stepmother.'

He signs himself: '*Met liefde van Pappa.*'

JEROME

A White Man's Trade

'Just listen to this,' his mum says. 'It says your friend's father is going to be head of the Censor Board.'

'Going up in the world,' says Doris. 'She's his friend these days, is she?'

'You know what I mean,' his mum says.

'You never read it right,' Doris says. 'It never said he's got the job. What it says is, his name's been put forward.'

'He'll get it,' his mum says. 'No-one else will have a snowball's hope. Not with him knowing all the people he does.'

'I suppose he dropped Jerome's name,' Doris says. 'That would do the trick for him. The way you go on I'd be very surprised if it didn't.'

'Why's it in the paper?' Jerome says.

'I told you,' says his mum. 'It's because the Hartmanns are important people. What they do is news. That's what news is. It's about important people who do important things.'

'It's as if you left the door of your room unlocked for a change so your mother could get inside to clean it,'

Doris says. 'That would make such a change, it'd be important news too. I wouldn't be surprised if it didn't make the front page.'

She's bird-beaked, crêpe-necked, getting older and always trying to rile him but he won't let her and she has to be quick these days to slip in her one word or two before his mum stops her.

'There's a picture here,' his mum says, handing the paper all folded back to him. 'Have a look then show it to your Aunty Doris.'

It's a new picture taken at a party at their house.

'It's the Senator's birthday,' his mum says. 'It looks as if the whole world was there. Just as well no-one dropped a bomb on the place. They'd have wiped out half the Government.'

The crazy girl's there. Beatrice Marie, with a face like thunder but full of herself just the same and a woman his mum says is the new wife and the old man all the fuss is about.

'You can tell quality when you see it, can't you?' Doris says.

'And how would you do that, Aunty Doris?' Jerome wants to know.

'By looking,' Doris says, fixing her eyes on him and giving him that look she keeps just for him when he uses that tone of voice to her. 'Just the same way you can tell other things just by looking. Things that make you want to hold tight onto your handbag, especially if your widow's pension happens to be inside it.'

'They look nice-looking in this picture,' his mum says. 'Of course you can't always tell from a picture.'

'You can't always tell from real life either,' Doris says. 'Handsome is as handsome does. Nice-looking's fine as far as it goes but that's not very far. In some cases not even as far as here to the front door.'

His mum's got a way now, when Doris talks like this, of pretending she hasn't talked at all.

'Was she nice-looking?' his mum wants to know and she asks him direct and doesn't even look at Doris.

'Who?' he says.

'The Hartmann girl,' says his mum. 'Was she nice-looking up close and in the flesh?'

'He hasn't seen her in the flesh has he?' Doris says. 'And he'd be the one to know wouldn't he? We all know what a ladies' man our Jerome is.'

She always likes to have her dig because he hasn't got a girlfriend.

'Not interested,' he says.

'Plenty of them chasing after him,' his mum says. 'I've told him it's all right to take his time. He's just waiting for the right one to come along, aren't you lovey? Then, when he's ready and if he's got a fancy to, he'll let himself get caught.'

All the same it worries her.

'Was she nice-looking?' she says.

'Can't remember,' he says.

'Never mind,' says his mother. 'Why don't you take the paper and cut out the picture and save it for a keepsake. After all, you've been to their house and if anyone asks you, you can say you have, because it's the truth.'

'You do that, Jerome,' Doris says. 'Cut out the picture and show your mates at Spin Street and tell them, just in case they didn't know, what grand company you keep.'

He isn't interested in what Doris says. He takes the kitchen scissors anyway.

'That's right,' Doris says. 'You go ahead. And while you're at it, seeing you're such great friends, why don't you keep it by you and next time she asks you over for tea take it with you. Ask for her to sign it for you. I'm sure it'll be her pleasure.'

Sometimes they like to give him the details of a job he's been involved in but he doesn't want to hear.

'You did an ace job,' they say. 'You should have seen the mess.'

He isn't interested in the mess and names don't mean anything to him. He did a job on a car once that blew a man to pieces. They told him about that too. When the wife came, asking if she could take her husband away and bury him, they had to say she couldn't because there was nothing left to take.

Everyone knows these stories about his work and sometimes they tell them just to take the mickey and see if they can get a rise but they never can.

What he likes is to work. He isn't interested in what worked or how it worked or what went wrong before they could get it to work. That's their business. Not his.

He may not have his journeyman's papers but he is, after all, a white man doing a white man's trade. That's what his mum tells people and in so far as it goes, it's the truth and there's no denying it.

CONRAD

Blink

I've made a contact. He says he's eighteen but he looks younger. I think I take such an interest in him because it was me who found him.

It was nearly the other way around. They nearly caught us but in the end we were the ones who did the catching. We laid an ambush and they walked into it and it wasn't because they were brainless fish swimming straight into a net and couldn't see what might be coming, which is what our officers said.

They were unlucky, that's all. It could have been us.

It was the end of the second day and we were told we would be out for two days only. We had food for two days but two days was enough and in that time we found them.

Our trackers, 'as good as any dog', our sergeant said, sniffed them out and we hid in the bush melted down to invisibility by our stillness and our camouflage.

There were eight of them. Terrorist infiltrators, our instructors told us, who'd go as far as the cities and townships if we let them and get hold of the people there and poison their minds and threaten their lives.

Dog meat for men like us.

They move towards us single file, right in, among us, past us, towards our ambush. Their AKs slung over their backs on rifle straps, chatting and laughing. Oblivious.

One is killed. One 'floppy' and one we take and I'm the one who takes him and I take him running.

He's dumped his equipment and begun to run but I can run too and I run the way a man does who doesn't know who's behind him or on either side or with what guns because at a moment like this you don't believe in bullets with someone else's name on them, or the bootprint next the unexploded landmine or some other man getting tickets before you.

In moments like this you think you're going to die.

I take him in a flying tackle. A clean catch round the knees and he comes down hard, winded, his shirt flung free from his pants exposing his naked back and I'm panting like a dog on a hot afternoon.

He's thin and tall but much lighter than I am and he's panting too and we're both powdered with dust and we lie there entangled in each other unable to move. I for fear of losing him if I let him go, he afraid that if he gets away and begins to run he'll be taken down like a hare, only this time, the next time, it will be for once and for all and all around us men's voices are shouting.

The others get away and it's over and we break radio silence and before sundown helicopters come in for a pickup to take us back to base and this one and the 'floppy' too, in case someone recognizes him or there's anything of importance on him we've missed, we take back with us.

* * *

We call my catch 'Blink' which means shine because he has a gold tooth and despite his circumstances he doesn't mind flashing it in a smile.

Maybe to show he's not afraid. Maybe he thinks that because he's alive he has something to smile about.

All we want from him is information. Our CO is debriefing him and at supper time, over our mess tins, *varkpanne*, pig pans, across our grapevine, we hear he has very little to tell.

This is what he says and I believe him. I don't know why.

I'm not supposed to talk to him but it's easy enough. He's one, we are many. He doesn't have to be locked up and bolted in. Leg irons are enough to hold him and he sits to one side of the fire and he's given black rations the same as our own blacks, which is less than our own and different and he can keep to one side or hobble around the camp if he wants to. He isn't going anywhere.

After supper it's easy to break away and go over to him where he sits crouched to one side close to the fire and going towards him I think of the Liefdefontein dogs, the ones in the *kampong* and the way they would sidle to the fire and how no amount of shouting or abuse would keep them away.

Our CO says he isn't worth much, which in a way affects me. I came in full of myself as if I was bringing back a shark and it turns out to be a *klipvissie*, a little rock-pool fish. I don't really mind.

He's a lot like our Liefdefontein men. An ochre person, not any one thing but a little bit this and a little bit that. You can see Bushman blood and I have some of their language from my days on the farm and his English is good. I have a cigarette for him.

'Lucky Strike,' he says, turning it over and reading the brand.

I throw a box of matches in his direction and he lights up and takes a deep drag and throws the matches back.

'*Dankie, basie,*' he says and his gold tooth blinks. 'Little master' and it comes easy and light like a joke to his tongue and he takes another drag and with a clang of chain he squats where he is on his haunches in the Bushman style and settles from one foot to the other.

'What now?' he says.

I shrug. I don't know. Waiting for orders. Another debrief. A camp somewhere. None of his business so I have nothing to say.

We are together in silence. I stand and a short distance away he squats and the fire crackles and a sudden small movement catches my eye and his.

Between us from nowhere scurries a scorpion going towards the heart of the fire and automatically, without thinking I head it off with the toe of my boot, redirecting it towards darkness and safety and the bush boy sees and his eyes crinkle and he blinks his smile at me.

'Is it written on the wind, little master?' he asks and his gold tooth shines as if he knows something I don't but I won't be drawn. These people like riddles and I don't know what he means and he looks at me as if he thinks I should.

'You're a lucky bugger,' I say. 'One of your people got killed. Here you sit among us, while he's food for the vultures.'

He finds this funny. He puts his hand to his head and laughs. He laughs so much he's racked with an old smoker's rack of coughing from laughter.

It makes me angry.

'I don't know what's so funny,' I say. 'Your comrade is dead. By now his bones are picked clean.'

'Now you come. Now you go,' he says. As if it is of no great importance. 'But I have a question for you, little master. You who know so much. Who are these vultures and what are their names so that when I see them again I may know them?'

When I look for him again he's gone. They came and took him, someone says and when I ask who 'they' are they say Recces which could mean just about anyone.

It's because he said he knew nothing. Men who have no answers always have answers for the Recces.

I don't know why it worries me so much but it does.

When they come back they're in the makeshift mess drinking beer, ice-cold, straight from the bottle. They're still in their bush clothes with the smell of the bush and their own sweat still on them and there's a feeling between them. The feeling like electricity that moves between men who have just come in from outside and are still bound together by what they've done and not yet disbanded.

I have no right and it is not my place but I demand to know where they've taken him and all I get are looks and then someone flaps his arms like a bird and makes a sound like an owl.

I have asked but I don't want to know. Something inside me is breaking and splintering into a million pieces. I am disintegrating. I have seen men disintegrate. I know what it is and it is not like floating through the crack in the rock from one world into another more wonderful one.

It is much more terrible than that.

I am not all there any more. I want to be away. I want my mother. I want to go back to the good time.

I am with my mother at my father's house. The

house is called Drummer's Hill. We're sitting on a sofa covered in light. I am on one side of my mother and Beeky is on the other. My mother is wearing a dress with blue and red flowers on it. There's a picture book open on her lap. Open on a lap-field of flowers. *Favourite Nursery Rhymes*. She's reading to us.

' "The wise old owl sat in an oak, the more he saw the less he spoke . . ." '

'Are you listening?' she says. Her arm's around me drawing me close. I'm small. I can feel the fullness of her breast mother-soft against my cheek. 'You ought to listen because owls know everything, you know.'

My mother's hair is brown but in the sun it has little flecks of gold in it. Like Beeky. Not like me. I have black Hartmann hair.

' ". . . the less he spoke the more he heard. Oh, why don't we copy that wise old bird?" '

'Where did you take him?' I say.

'What's it to you?' one of the Permanent Force officers says.

'I want to know, that's all,' I say.

'If he wants to know tell him,' someone says.

So they do.

They've taken him up in a chopper, asked what he knows, tried to make him tell, asked him again and 'flared him out', kicked him out at 100 metres.

'Is that a good enough answer?' one of them asks. 'Are you happy now?'

I'm not happy. I feel the room closing in on me and my head throbs and I start to sweat, ice-cold sweat all over my body and the smell of beer and so many men together is sickening.

'We've got something to remember him by,' one of them says. 'Here.'

He puts his hand deep in his pocket and pulls some

small thing out. A pebble I think. Something small and hard like a pebble.

He throws it towards me. It arcs light through the air and I lift my hand to catch it and I catch it clean in my fist and I open my fist and look down and Blink's gold tooth lies in my palm glinting up at me.

I feel my entrails slithering around inside me. I want to be sick. I want to deliver them up onto the swept clean floor of the mess hall.

They don't know the bush people. Things are given to them that are not given to other men. They know things other men don't know. They can read eternity and no man leaves this world without passing on what he knows to some other man and I am the one who brought Blink in and we know each other and I am him and he is me.

'Load of bollocks,' my father would say.

It isn't so. What Blink said was so. The answer was in the air and he has given me the names of the vultures and mine is among them and it is the most terrible moment of my life.

I walk out blind and as I go I put the piece of gold into the extended palm of the man who gave it to me.

Dear Beeky,

This is your Christmas letter. If I could do letters the way you do there would be sleighs and bells and fat Father Christmases over the paper.

Nothing much is happening here. It's too hot. Men with families have preference for leave and this is fine with the rest of us . . . the old man said he could 'arrange things' so I could be 'home' for Christmas. I said 'no, thank you'. I don't mind staying here. We have our own Christmas tree, the Kalahari Christmas tree. It's called the Sickle Tree. Its flowers hang down like upended candles. If you hold them right side up – wrong side for the tree – they look like gold flames in mauve candle holders. So, don't think we're not having a proper Christmas here or going short of anything. We aren't. We even have turkey.

It's beautiful here. This is not the place where I can write the things I would like to put in the wonderful book you made for me but if I had a game book and remembered to fill it in, Pappa and 'Oom' Faan and the 'boys' would be green with envy. There are steenbok and klipspringer and wild cat and genet . . .

It seems amazing to him that this other world which is so different from their own goes on just as it always has while theirs falls quietly apart.

. . . there are caracal and jackal, bat-eared fox and aardwolf.

There are also ratels, honey badgers; of all the small animals they are the ones most feared and most admired.

The ratel, a carnivore which strikes at night and is so ferocious it will even attack a man. The name of an armoured vehicle. The emblem of the anti-terrorism unit.

Perhaps next time you can draw me some unicorns. The censor boys won't know what they are and will probably leave them alone. There are Arabian oryx here. You've never seen any buck so big and fat or so arrogant. Their horns are skinny as your legs so when they stand sideways it looks as if they have only one horn. 'Oom' Faan says this is where the unicorn legend comes from. I don't know. Love, Conrad.

I try very hard but I feel that world slipping away from me and I lick down the envelope and cannot remember my sister's face.

A LETTER FROM LUCIFER

BEEKY

Tea with the Queen of Sheba

There is a New Madam at their house these days. Their father's wife. Her name is Emmeline and Beeky has been sent for to get to know her better and told she must come to tea.

'She's asked me to the house because she doesn't want to be seen with me.' This is what she writes to her brother. 'But she doesn't want too much of me in the house either. Just enough so the world can see she's doing her wifely duty but nothing can change which side it is she's on.

'I was at his birthday party, not because he wanted me. "In case people talk," he said. I don't think it was his idea at all. I think it was hers. In any case, I'm invited to "know her better" so it's back to the house for me.

'Everything is censored nowadays,' she writes. 'I don't know how much of this will get to you but goodness knows, the missing bits will be in good company.

'I suppose there's a bright side to everything, if only you know where to look for it. Censoring is a good job for retired schoolteachers. Just imagine them tut-tutting their way through *Lady Chatterley's Lover*. You can forget about *Playboy*, by the way. If you or any of your Army friends are stashing them away you better warn them. It's the devil's work published by the Devil's Press and you can go to hell just for looking at it. Did you know that?'

Black Beauty has fallen to the oxymoronic. Little Noddy pays for his disrespect to Mr Plod the patient law-enforcer and is taken from the nursery library shelves.

Her brother's letters never arrive complete in one piece. She has 'activities' now, to end the draft and because of them any letters she receives must be checked and checked over.

Words are cut out, sometimes sentences and even whole paragraphs slashed out by the military censor but even after he's finished with them, they're thumbed through again.

She calls it desecration. Her father says it's a crucial matter of public safety. He's on record saying so because he wrote it in a formal letter to the Minister.

She's told her brother that Pappa is still desperately trying to play his cards right so he can be Head of the Censor Board. It's an important job. A prize and something worth having. The announcement hasn't been made yet but it's what's being whispered for him now.

'That's why she wants to have a look at me,' Beeky writes. 'People ask her, I suppose, about the peculiar daughter.'

Beeky walks light on the road home.

'I don't think of it as "going home",' she writes. 'But I don't mind going back to the house.'

The Old Madam smells her from a long way away.

Young-smell, free-smell, smell of the past, with a whiff of the future in it and it nudges at her and stirs the grey coals of memory. It shakes loose the heady odours of freedom and then adds a dash of the pain which is the price at which it comes.

As if she's forgotten.

The emerald-eyed cat peers out from a bright bed of pepper-leaved nasturtiums and the terracotta-tubbed lemon tree displaced by ground tilted by the river below stands slightly skew in its old place at the gate to the kitchen garden.

The goose tap-dances at the side of the pond and clacks at her goslings and the gecko sleeps on its rock in the sun.

It's her brother's life and her own Beeky walks through and she leaves footprints invisible across the land and they fall soft, far away, on the book she once made him in which to write his life down.

'I suppose you're feeling pleased with yourself,' her father says.

He asks to see her alone, in his study, before the new wife is sent for. It's a quiet room and cool. It smells of smoke and men and damp and age and the pin oaks outside the window and the mountain behind are majestic.

He tells her to sit, then remains standing so he can look down on her.

There's a new photograph of Conrad. One she hasn't seen before. In Army fatigues, with another soldier. They have their arms around each other's necks and brown bush-hats on their heads and they're smiling.

So Conrad has his place here now and one day others will come into this room and look at his picture and wonder.

She's always liked the traitor's picture best. The colonial boy who thumbed his nose at the old Queen and was shot, despatched quick-smart, for his trouble.

'Spook picture,' the servants say and sometimes, when someone tells them it's high time, they dab at it with a duster.

'The devil pulled his eyes out,' they say. 'Under the black there's just empty holes.'

The devil doesn't worry Beeky. What worries her is the way the long-dead boy makes her feel. It's the small shroud of sadness like an aura around him that gives a blood-pull at her heart and makes her feel funny. Odd. As if she was him and he was her. As if the owl called her name.

'You might have made some effort,' her father says. 'You could at least have worn something decent.'

'I don't have much call for decent things,' Beeky says.

The Master's Room, the servants call this place. Pappa's Room her mother used to say and we must be quiet when we go past, so as not to disturb him while he works.

'You won't like it,' Conrad said. 'There's the head of a dead gemsbok stuffed and stuck up on the wall. One Pappa shot himself.'

'What's this meant to be?' her father says looking at her shoulder. 'It looks bloody awful.'

'It's my same old mark,' she says. 'A friend put some paint around it, that's all.'

Her mark is a star in the centre of a painted arm-band. Blue and red body paint with the crimson birth-star nestled at its heart and some crimson flashes coming out of it etched with white.

'You find that amusing?'

She thinks, if she closes her eyes and wills it, a breeze will waft her mother in and she will cover it up softly and say what a small thing it is and how it's not so bad as it looks and will soon go away.

'Art students do things like that,' she says. 'It's meant to be a decoration.'

'Like a bloody savage,' he says. 'A savage making a public exhibition of itself demanding rights for other savages.'

She can feel her brother's gentle finger and the sweet strange smell of *sasa* on her face. So you look like a lynx, he says and the lynx is the most beautiful cat in Africa and walks alone and is afraid of nothing.

She wonders why her father hates her so.

'I can't stop what you do outside this house,' he says. 'But while you're here I don't want you to say or do anything that will embarrass me or my wife.'

'Like what, Pappa?' she says.

'No nonsense,' he says. 'No stories about the past. The past is dead and forgotten. No need to dig it up.'

She used to be able to smell her mother moving through the house on a quick soft drift of roses. Now all she smells is dust and there are Stargaze Lilies everywhere and they're flashy to look at and determined as far as scent is concerned and their smell blots out everything else.

'We won't have any politics either,' her father says. 'There's not much I can do about you making a fool and a spectacle of yourself outside but I won't have any of it in my house.'

To which she says nothing at all.

She's a tall girl. He'd forgotten. When she stands up she's almost as tall as he is and her hide-colour hair hangs loose and when she turns to look at him, her mother peers out, mocking him, safe and untouchable behind the locked gates which are her daughter's eyes.

*   *   *

There are scones for tea and Black Forest cake and silver cake forks crested with stunted foxes and the new wife is the one who raises the question of what she calls Beeky's 'activities'.

The new wife is wearing a mauve suit and a smart little chiffon blouse with a flounce down the front. Her hair is webbed with lacquer.

A lizard made of marcasite with glinting red eyes is anchored to her lapel.

'I'm interested in your views,' she says.

Each of them, unasked, has been given cake and the cake oozes liqueur-soaked cherries and clots of cherry-stained cream. These slices of cake rest uneasily on the plates that once belonged to her mother and the smell of cherries and alcohol and cream about to sour mixes uneasily with the heady odour of lilies.

'Your father thinks you're looking for trouble,' the new wife says. 'Things are going to get far tougher than they are now. The police have been on the sidelines till now but one of these days they'll intervene.'

'Then that will be that then, won't it?' Beeky says.

She's trapped in a glass bell jar. The cream on the cake is the colour of foam-flecked blood and her skin is being flayed with her father's distaste.

'You'll excuse Beatrice,' her father says. 'These days she finds her friends in the gutter as you see from her manners.'

'It's all right, Jack,' the new wife says. 'I know what young people are.'

'She works very hard at being different,' her father says. 'She'll do anything for attention. It's always been her way.'

'I don't do it to get any attention,' Beeky says.

'And I'm the bloody Queen of Sheba,' says her

father. 'If you don't want attention you've got a damn funny way of showing it.'

She's being picked clean by the new wife's eyes and the silver jackals prance and leer and she keeps her eyes down and away but she knows them.

To find the jackal you must look to the outside and it'll always be there waiting and watching ready to pounce the first moment it senses an opportunity to scavenge.

'You're a bloody Communist,' says her father. 'Do you really think your going around bleating about ending conscription is going to make a blind bit of difference?'

'If I didn't think so, I wouldn't do it,' Beeky says.

'People much smarter than you are use silly little fools like you for their own ends.'

'If you say so,' she says.

'What else are you then? You tell me. You're a pathetic little puppet parroting stupid party slogans using my name to get noticed. You think I'm a bloody fool? You think this is the first time this has happened to me? I've walked this road before, I can tell you. Without my name you're nothing. You're just another piece of student shit on the pavement.'

'Please, Jack . . .' the new wife says and she motions him to silence and turns her attention back to Beeky.

'Your father's name has been put forward as possible head of a Board of Censorship,' she says.

'I know,' Beeky says.

'He wants very badly to have it and everyone who knows him thinks he should.'

'Then I hope he gets it,' Beeky says.

'I hope so too,' says his wife. 'I don't know you, Beatrice, but I wouldn't like to think you'd knowingly do anything to damage his chances.'

'I'm far too small and unimportant to be able

to "damage his chances" even if I wanted to,' she says.

'You've no right, you know, to embarrass your father the way you do.'

The new wife is all devoted wife, with her fine bone china teacup aloft and her bosom straining at the buttons of her blouse. She sits, broad-beamed, on the Old Madam's Huguenot chair and the Old Madam doesn't like it.

'I have some advice for you, Beatrice,' the new wife says and the flounces on her blouse ripple approvingly. 'Stop this silliness before it gets out of hand and you get into real trouble. Think of other things. Nicer things. Boys for example and dresses and parties. The kind of things other girls your age think about. It'll make you feel better.'

'I don't want to feel better,' Beeky says. 'I want to feel what I do feel while I still can. While we're at least allowed to do that.'

Which is a sentiment even a blood-gone, grave-cold, heartless Old Madam can warm to.

BEEKY

The New Madam

The New Madam is making changes. She's getting rid of the past.

She's down in the River Room, nose twitching with damp and disdain but not half as disdainful as the Old Madam, billowing free all around her, flounced out by such impudence, in her cloak of ice air.

'That old gable-domed armoire will certainly have to go,' the New Madam says. 'One look's enough to know there's nothing there that's worth saving.'

It doesn't look good. It's mottled with age, its door's half unhinged. Its mirror weeps shards of silver but in its empty spaces lie huddled all the secrets of this house, quite safe from the New Madam who has neither the heart nor the inclination to truffle them out.

'I hope you're going to leave at least something of the old house I know,' today's Hartmann says and he tries to make light of it but doesn't succeed.

'An old house is fine, as far as it goes,' is the New Madam's view. 'And a museum's a fine thing too. To spend a morning in, to see what they've got, but a museum isn't a house. Nobody wants to live in one.'

He isn't sure.

'I don't know,' he says. 'This house has always been like this. It was the same in my mother's day, the same in my grandmother's.'

But the New One is troublesome and has ideas of her own.

'We have to think about ourselves,' she says.

Which, the Old Madam thinks, is probably what they'll put on her tombstone in the end.

'The present belongs to the living,' is the New Madam's view. 'Which is us. It's today that counts. The past's dead and gone. It has nothing to do with us.'

Which just goes to show how little she knows.

The Old Madam gives a tired grave sigh that goes straight to the neck hair, but she knows while she sighs it, it's a waste of old air. Some learn the hard way, to some it comes easy and then there are others who don't learn at all.

'I'm not sure I like it,' today's Hartmann says.

She's quite sure he won't but, like it or not, there are going to be changes. She's already begun.

The gemsbok head has gone. It was the first thing to go.

'Don't be silly, Jack,' the new wife says. 'You can't hole yourself up in here and not allow anyone in unless you give the say-so. That's nonsense.'

'Well, then, I'd like, at least, to have some say. After all, I'm paying for it.'

'You will, dear, you will,' she says.

But not all the say in the world can keep the gemsbok head where it was. It comes down in a cascade of plaster and a shower of dust. Glass-eyed and amazed, it rests sideways, leaning slightly drunken against the wall and after that, secure for so long but not one minute longer, it's the time for the past generations.

The painters are busy, the wall creaming up nicely lick after lick, and the ancestors are down already, stacked on the floor. One lot cheek by jowl, willy-nilly with the next, with no respect for the things that kept them in their places and held them together in the first place.

Company directors get precedence over politicians. Generals jostle with theologians and one academic, Afrikaans/Nederlands, is so distressed at dislodgement that his frame comes apart in the workman's brown hands.

The newspaper editor who comes after him, caught in fine light by an ambitious photographer, finds himself face to glass face with the traitorous boy whose story has changed generation to generation and never been properly unravelled.

Streets and airports, scholarships and buildings named after them. Made immortal in oil and brass and at least one equestrian bronze. It makes no difference now, as the past is rearranged and sometimes even vanishes under the command of this determined New Madam, quite fresh to the game, with only two native garden boys and a kitchen maid to help her.

Which just goes to show, as if we didn't know it already, that history is anything but even-handed.

'Cleaning,' she says. 'Just cleaning. Making this place less of a monument and more of a place two people like us can call home.'

All of Us Have Children

Beeky has a boyfriend. His name is Tom Webber. Her father and the new wife have heard all about him but not from her.

There was a 'yes, my friend, thank you, my friend' phone call. From someone well-placed. The new wife can hear what it's about from the 'yes, sir, no, sir, because I don't have any option, sir' tone of her husband's voice.

Which always means a fight afterwards, because he hates having to kowtow to anyone, no matter how important they might be.

'She's doing it to upset you, Jack,' the new wife says. 'It upsets me too, you know. Because everything that affects you, affects me too. There's no escaping that.'

She might have expected this from a ready-made child, not the kind bargained for.

'Girl's bloody mad,' says her father. 'Capable of doing just about anything.'

Her boyfriend's name has been in the newspaper along with her own. Put an end to conscription. Say no, we won't go. No-one to fight for their country any more. Everyone to stay home and watch the flowers grow. That is their end. There's no secret about that and it's also their beginning. It's how they met.

'I suppose he knows what he's got hold of,' her father says. 'She's not in her right mind. I've got a psychiatrist's report to prove it. She's a madwoman. I can't be held responsible for her. I certainly can't be held responsible for the company she keeps. That's what I told them.'

'Perhaps you ought to speak to her,' the new wife says.

'And what good would that do?' he wants to know. 'I could just as well talk to the wall. That's all the good it'll do me.'

'I don't want to interfere . . .' the new wife says.

'You have interfered,' he says. 'Ever since you came, you've done nothing but interfere. You've changed everything. You've pushed yourself into every part of my life. You're the one who said she should go out and find herself a boyfriend.'

'To take her mind off things,' the new wife says.

'If you'd asked me, I could have told you what you were dealing with. Except that would have been a waste of time too. You're just like her mother. No brains but you think you know everything.'

'I know enough to stay on the right side of the people who count,' the new wife says. 'Which is a lot more than you seem to be able to do.'

'If you knew what I know about my so-called daughter you'd know not to put any ideas in her head.'

'I said a boyfriend,' the new wife says. 'I didn't say an agitator.'

'Who did you think she was going to come up with?' Beeky's father wants to know. 'Judge Cloete's son, perhaps? One of the Wolhuters? What decent boy in his right mind would even think twice about a girl like her? Surely you could at least have thought that far ahead?'

'For myself I don't care who she mixes with,' the new wife says. 'But this kind of thing, this silly kind of association, won't do you any good in certain quarters and things that aren't good for you aren't good for me either. That's the only reason I mention it.'

'Do you think I don't know that?' Beeky's father says. 'Do you take me for a fool? Do you think I need you to tell me that all this nonsense isn't doing me any good in certain circles? And speaking about certain circles, what the hell would a two-bit little name-dropper like you know anyway?'

There's been a call from the Special Branch. To the house. Discreetly arranged through the Ministry. First a phone call from the Minister himself. Man to man.

'We all have children, Jack,' he says.

His voice is friendly but not as friendly as it's been in the past. 'The point is your girl's getting out of hand. This boy she's keeping company with is a stirrer. He needs to be put in his place and so does she.'

He wants to say, 'Leave it with me, I'll deal with it,' but he's said that before and nothing came of it and it won't wash twice.

'It doesn't look good, Jack,' the Minister says. 'A man in your position. A boy on the border and your girl trumpeting her mouth off telling whoever will listen to show the finger to the call-up. It doesn't look good at all.'

'It's student rubbish,' he says. 'You know how they

are at that age. Think they know everything. Nothing you can tell them.'

'It's a friendly warning, Jack,' the Minister says and he has to say 'thank you'.

'It's not the first time,' the Minister says. 'It's not the second and it's not going to happen again. It can't happen again. I'm sure you understand that.'

He has to say he appreciates it.

'We have to knock this thing out,' the Minister says. 'Pull it out at its root before it has any chance at all of taking hold. That's all I can tell you. You understand what I mean?'

He says he does.

'Then do it quick, Jack,' he says. 'Because when they clean this thing up it's going to be every man for himself and it's not going to make a bit of difference what your name is or who your father happens to be.'

The new wife is worried about the newspapers.

'We can do without it,' she says. 'Your family's your affair but I don't need my name dragged in. I have a family too you know and I've pulled my weight in this marriage. If I was quite honest and less polite I'd tell you I think I deserved better.'

She has a tight-lipped way of looking at him these days that he doesn't like. As if having a lunatic daughter has left some kind of mark on him. As if it's his fault. As if he's God Almighty and can tell Beeky to stop her nonsense and somehow, Christ knows how, she will.

As if his purse-lipped wife doesn't know just as well as he does that his daughter will go on doing exactly as she pleases and if it upsets him, so much the better, and there's not a thing in this world he can do about it.

* * *

A student's job these days is to sign up for lost causes. This is what Beeky's father says. When he was at university, when her brother was, they understood what privilege and responsibility were. They went to university to work and repaid their parents with excellence.

These days campuses are packed full of loafers with nothing better to do than round up hopeless causes to protest about and what Beeky has chosen is 'End Conscription'.

'A bloody disgrace,' her father says. 'Parading along Rondebosch Main Road on Saturday morning with a bunch of lunatic leftists pushing leaflets at people telling them to say no to the call-up.'

What, he asks, will it seem like to her brother should he be unfortunate enough to hear about it? Her brother who is at that moment slogging his guts out on the border with men just the same as he is. Men who know what duty is and don't try and slime out of it.

She knows what her brother will say. He will say what he always says, which is that she must do what her heart tells her is right. But she doesn't tell her father this.

He thinks when the police got hold of her and broke up their protest they should have taken her off somewhere, knocked the nonsense out of her and some sense into her head, because what would she know about duty or service or the honour of defending one's country anyway?

These are men's things and nothing to do with a girl.

He's ashamed of her.

He told the new wife that Beeky is pathetic. Like a mongrel dog who'll attach itself to anyone who'll have it and do anything they ask, just so long as she keeps her place by their fire.

She could have chosen anything, he says. God knows she's perverse enough and do-gooders find plenty of causes if they go around looking hard enough for them.

But 'anything' isn't good enough for her. 'Anything' would have been shameful but standing on street corners like Salvation Army Sally in full public view, telling people not to let their husbands and sons and brothers go on call-up, is the last straw.

It's the final insult to himself and her brother and to everything they stand for and not only them but their forebears as well.

She might just as well have come right up to them and spat in all their faces, the living and the dead, because that's what she's doing anyway and she's doing it to spite them.

She resists authority. She won't listen. She resents him and she's always been jealous of Conrad because Conrad is the worthwhile one. Conrad is the only true child of this house. He, thank God, is everything she's not and precisely because of it a blessing on the family and a credit to their name.

Her father has made a point of reminding her of this. Who he, Jack Hartmann, is, who her brother is and what he's doing, how she measures up when he looks at her and her goings-on and which of the two of his children he's the most proud of and why.

She tells him she's proud of Conrad too and all the same, despite everything, she knows he doesn't mind what she's doing.

'How do you know that?' her father snaps back. 'Do you read minds these days as well as all your other stupid tricks?'

'I just know,' she says.

'Then you know a lot more than I do,' her father says. 'And let me tell you something else. I take great exception to you speaking for your brother. I think I know what my own son would say if he knew what I know. He'd say you were a bloody disgrace and everyone we know would agree with him, because that's exactly what you are.'

He's very angry. More angry than she's seen him for a long time. The new wife is on her feet with her hand on his arm but he throws it off and shakes her away. This is old business, unfinished business, private business, not a thing you can clean up or paint over or rearrange and it has nothing to do with her.

'Don't you ever again speak your brother's name to me in this regard,' her father says and his voice is a hiss. 'I won't have it. Am I quite clear? Do you understand me?'

She looks at him and says nothing.

'You may not have the brains to see it but you're playing with fire. I know things you don't. I'm welcome in places that wouldn't let you in at the back door never mind at the front and I tell you one thing. When you get into trouble, as you almost certainly will, you'll be on your own and I won't lift a finger to help you.'

These are not the things she writes to her brother about. When she writes to him these days, her letters are full of a man she's met and the man's name is Tom Webber.

'Boys,' the new wife said. She ought to be interested in boys. She isn't interested in boys at all but men interest her and this one particular man interests her most of all.

Everyone who's interested in Army or call-up or all the arguing that goes on around it on campus finds themselves with Tom Webber in the end.

'He's just the sort of man you would have imagined

for me,' she writes. 'And I know that you'll like him and have great talks with him when you meet.'

Webber is solid and private. He's a postgraduate engineering student. A head-down get-on-with the job kind of person and a slow speaker.

No-one expected it but when all the talking was done, he was the one who sent his call-up papers back to the Department of Defence with a polite letter saying he wouldn't be going anywhere and why he wouldn't go and how it's up to them now to decide what to do with him, because he's made up his mind and isn't going to change it.

'Which has made him quite famous on campus,' Beeky writes. 'People here have a lot to say about what's going on but no-one does very much about it. When the time actually comes what they do is report for duty just as they're told.'

'Your brother's more famous than I'll ever be,' Webber says. 'He's a hero, isn't he? At least that's what most people would say. Anyway, he's doing the right thing.'

'You're doing the right thing,' Beeky says. 'It's funny, isn't it, but Con wouldn't mind a bit what you're doing. He'd understand absolutely. He'd respect you for it. I know he would.'

'I'm not so sure,' Webber says. 'Sometimes I'm not even sure I respect myself.'

His head, when he bends down, has a full fall of dark hair that brushes his eyebrows. He has neat big hands and he uses them thoughtfully so they seem to enfold anything he touches.

'Why do you look at me like that?' he says.

'Because I want to,' she says and she gives him a slow, sweet smile and he smiles back because that is how things are between them these days.

'You know, I tell Con everything about us,' she says,

but she says it to tease him and won't say exactly how much 'everything' is.

'Is he going to come after me with a shotgun?' Webber wants to know.

'He'll think you must have the heart of a tiger and the soul of a saint,' Beeky says. 'If medals meant anything you'd probably get one. Just for putting up with me. He'd give it to you himself.'

'I doubt that very much,' Webber says.

'I mean it,' Beeky says. 'He knows better than anyone that I'm quite capable of getting into trouble without any outside assistance. I've been doing it all my life.'

She's greedy for Webber. For the solidness of him, because he's a big man and strong.

She's hungry for the way his eyes crinkle up when he smiles; for the slow way he says things and most especially for the way he always has time for her and is soft with her and careful and the dark brown tone of his voice.

'I'm with you because you're a celebrity, you know,' she says. 'My father will tell you. He'll say I'm a chaser after causes. I'll snap up any cause that comes my way and you're my cause now and I'm your girl.'

'Are you?' he says.

'Of course I am,' she says. 'If it were the other way around it would be the same. If I were a man I'd do what you're doing and be famous for it, just like you are.'

He wouldn't mind being famous if being famous brought Beeky to him.

When other people pull his leg about all the attention he's been getting, he tells them it isn't his letter to the Department of Defence that should single him out. His actual claim to fame, he says, is that he comes from Jan Fourie's Kraal and Jan Fourie's Kraal is probably the smallest and least known town in the country.

When Beeky asks him he says he has a love-hate relationship with it.

What he hates is its small-mindedness. The way the churches are full every Sunday and before Sunday's even over the congregation are already out again breaking every commandment ever written and even finding a few new things to do that no-one ever bothered to write down to warn them against.

'What do you love about it then?' she wants to know and it isn't a question he'd usually discuss but because she's the way she is and he feels about her the way he does he tells her.

'The thing about small towns is that you're part of them whether you like it or not,' he says. 'You're part of them and they're part of you. I don't always like it very much but those are my people and even when I'm liking them least they're still the people I know best.'

He and Beeky are both out of favour. She with her father and Webber with a whole town. She because there's an article about her and her views on conscription in the newspaper.

He, because he's refused the call-up and in a small town like his, news like that spreads faster than a veld fire and is just about as welcome.

He says at first, before he thought about it, he actually considered going.

'You know what it's like,' he says. 'There's nothing else much to do. On days like Republic Day the whole family sits in front of the television watching the parades in the big cities and to people like us it looks marvellous.'

She doesn't know what it's like.

'When it's something special like five or ten years of

Republic someone somewhere remembers us and sends an air-force jet flying over really low just for our benefit and the whole town goes out to have a look.

'We stand in the streets, on our stoeps, outside our houses just looking up with our mouths open at the idea that something so wonderful could happen to us and it's a funny feeling. It makes you feel proud to be part of it.'

She doesn't know about that either. All she knows is how it is at their house.

At their house, in these days of the new wife, there is a big party on Republic Day just in case there's any possibility of uncertainty about exactly where her father's sympathies lie. Never mind those of his dutiful wife.

There's an ox braai. A whole ox splayed out on a spit and it braais all day with two staff just to keep separate fires going, so there are always hot coals to put under it and to keep basting it with a mop dipped in a bucket of herbs and salt and sunflower oil.

There's lamb too and liver in caul fat and 'puff adders', intestine stuffed with minced liver and yards of sausage, and every kind of salad and maids running backwards and forwards, taking plates away and bringing back clean ones.

The flag flutters on the flagpole in the garden and it's the one day her father stands down in his own house and lets someone else speak. Because on that day, among all the influential people who were pleased to accept their invitation, there is always someone far more important than himself to 'take the word' as they say.

He does it for another reason too. Whoever speaks, out of courtesy to his house and himself, there'll always be something to say about the Hartmanns.

The blood of those gone before sails on in their veins generation to generation. All that once was, is in them now and this day is as good a day as any to mention it and this year it's something he needs to hear.

Then it's like church. Despite the glasses in their hands and no church hats but party dresses instead everyone listens with their heads bent and when the words are over and the toast is given, all hell breaks loose.

There's laughing and coughing and applause and arms around each other and remarks thrown backwards and forwards and sometimes women cry because they simply can't help themselves.

She doesn't know how it is in small, halfway off the map towns. She never thought about it before she met her Tommy. Now she knows him she's suddenly become very interested.

'Would I like it?' she says.

He says small towns aren't for everyone so he doesn't know and his mind is not on small towns, his own or any other. His mind is on other things.

He hasn't got over the wonder of touching her yet. These days she owns his hands. They move towards her whether he wants them to or not.

'Is it true what they say about Sunday afternoons in all those little *dorpies* all over the country?' she says. 'All that stuff about what people actually do when they tell their children they're going to lie down for their afternoon "rest"?'

Perhaps it's true. He hopes it's true. He would lie down with her anywhere, anyhow, any time of day just for the joy of it.

He hasn't become accustomed to the taste of her yet. Or the beautiful sweet-pea, redhead smell that rises up from her skin or the soft down on her upper lip or the whispering flutter of her eyelashes when he comes close to kiss her and she closes her eyes.

'In small towns they spend a lot of time minding each other's business,' he says. 'They talk a lot.'

'Would we give them something to talk about?' she wants to know and her breath mingles with his and her body inside its Indian cotton dress is sliding towards his like a magnet.

'I would hope so,' he says and if there was breath left for words he'd tell her that his hope is a fervent one.

Beads and Feathers

He says he isn't interested but Jerome's mum has cut out Beeky's father's picture anyway.

'At the opening of Parliament if you don't mind,' she says, with a nod to Doris. 'And his new wife with him. Just look. She's hanging onto him as if she won't let him go in a hurry.'

'The opening of Parliament's not so grand,' Doris says. 'Anyone can go. All you have to do is send a letter to your MP and tell him you want to go and they send you an invitation. After all, it's our tax money that's paying for it.'

'I don't suppose they can expect fancy wine and fish eggs then,' his dad says. 'Not with the kind of money people like us get paid. They'd go broke if they depended on us to pick up the bill.'

'The Hartmanns aren't people like us,' says his mum. 'And they certainly aren't the kind of people who'd have to write anywhere to ask for an invitation. They'd be top of the list, first-name terms, you can be sure of that.'

To Jerome she says, 'Why don't you keep the picture

anyway, lovey? Put it in the book with the others?'

'Because I don't want to,' he says.

His mum's funny the way she talks to him, as if he was still a 'special' but he doesn't mind. She's got her ways but he doesn't mind that either. It makes her happy if things go on just like they always have and that's all right too. It suits him. It's nice to do his work at Spin Street and be someone the boys look up to and then come home to his mum and to count for something there too.

'Cut it out anyway,' his mum says.

His father opens his mouth and closes it again and Doris gets a shut-up look and his mother has the last word. 'You cut it out and keep it with the others,' she says. 'After all, you know the family.'

Which is meant for Doris and as much as his mum knows, because he knows a lot more than 'the family'.

There are some things Jerome doesn't tell his mum. One of them is exactly how much he knows about Beeky Hartmann.

He's been to her room. Not just staring from the outside. Right inside it; that's where he's been.

It wasn't difficult. No 'Special' school bus this time and no grand house or iron gates. No guard dogs pushing their noses out for a look, or coon boys too big for their boots or high and mighty girls handing out favours to people as if they were animals let out of a zoo.

Things are different now and her name and her picture and all that it says in the newspaper about her are in the files down at Spin Street. So he can look at her any time he likes and if there's something he wants to know about her, all he has to do is ask.

She's his now. It's as if she came to him. As if, even though she doesn't know it, she's the one who's come to his house looking for favours and he's the one who can give or hold back, just as the mood takes him.

Over Easter long weekend all the students are away. The campus is deserted. You can go where you like, do what you like and take all the time in the world about doing it.

There's no-one to stop you and her room is easy enough to find. It even has her name on a little card in a brass frame on the door, almost as if it's an invitation and you feel so free and easy it's as if you could make yourself at home and it wouldn't matter, even if you didn't bother to close the door behind you.

There isn't a drawer or cupboard he hasn't opened. He's touched all her dresses as if they were shop dresses hanging on a rail wanting to be touched and held out to be looked at. As if they were lonely dresses, hoping someone would like them and buy them and take them away.

He's taken her jerseys out and put them side by side on her bed and looked at them and touched them and wool's nice and better than summer things because you can still smell the person on wool. Their scent clings, almost as if they were flesh and blood inside the jersey and standing right in front of you.

She has lots of letters and he's taken them out and put them on top of the desk and picked up a picture in a frame of two kids on a beach and looked at it, but not for very long, because it's only kids and nothing to see and that's not what interests him.

He's had all her highbrow books down from their shelves and fanned them open one by one to see what secrets she might be hiding inside them and then put them back again so neatly that no-one would ever be any the wiser.

He sits on her bed and the springs are old and they

creak in the middle but he sits there like a king with no noddy-head teacher to tell him what he can and can't do, because the world has changed and he's changed with it. Now he can do what he likes and no-one can stop him.

She's not neat the way he is. His mum would say that's what people like the Hartmanns are like. They don't know how to fend for themselves any more. It comes from having servants running round after them all their lives and being allowed to leave anything they like lying around and always being sure there'll be someone coming up behind them to tidy their mess.

He doesn't mind. It's a good thing. People who aren't neat aren't the kind of people who notice the small thing out of place that tells them they've had an uninvited visitor and that suits him.

He likes the idea of being in her room with all her things around him and her not ever knowing he's been there.

He's washed his hands at her hand basin and dried them on her towel. He's looked at his face in the same mirror above the basin where she must have looked at herself a hundred times over.

On the shelf underneath the mirror next to some bottles of make-up and a toothbrush is a black plastic hairbrush with hard white-tipped bristles and caught in the bristles are strands of her strange-coloured hair.

He saw a red horse once with a coat that colour and a thick mane stretching along its spine, stiff and upright close to the hide, then flopping over and hanging down free below. Firecracker hair. Some men like redhead women because they smell different. They make a joke of it and say it just goes to show all cats aren't grey in the dark. You can always smell a redhead.

He takes a few strands of her hair for a keepsake. It looks soft when you look at it in photographs or see it hanging down her back but when you hold it to a light and pull both ends it holds fast for a long time before it breaks, like fine silk that's always much stronger than you imagine it will be and the colour is different too close up. There's more gold in it than you'd reckon on.

He stays a long time. Long enough to be comfortable. Long enough so his smell lingers.

It's like Osram's shop and Nick's. It's like having all the world spread out in front of you and you can take what you like and keep it and that's where the joke will be.

You wouldn't even have to be there to see why it's funny.

You could laugh just imagining the person wondering what's happened to something; what they've done with it and where they could have put it and how they might have lost it somewhere without noticing.

She'll never miss the hair. So where would be the fun in that? So, he takes an earring instead. A strange thing. One of two made out of beads and feathers and the feathers are sprayed with tiny white spots and soft, as if they were pulled from some baby bird who didn't know enough to look after itself.

One he takes. One he leaves behind and it lies on the desk exactly where she left it.

They're all very busy with the crackdown so the Captain's going to give her boyfriend to Berry.

Berry says what about the girl? Two for the price of one, it's all the same to him but the Captain says to leave the girl out of it and when he asks why he's told 'no questions asked'. Which means someone is looking out for her.

Berry doesn't like it that it's only one. Even with the girl thrown in it wouldn't be a big enough job for someone with his experience but he's getting it anyway and the Captain's told him he has to play it straight.

'It's no big deal. Just a kid stepping out of line.'

'Bloody chicken,' Berry says. 'Scared shitless. That's his trouble.'

'Give him a good kick up the jack to put him in his place; and that's all you have to do.'

'I'll make sure he gets the message,' says Berry.

He's got that look on his face to show he knows he's being given an amateur's job and he doesn't like it. The one thing you don't do with a pro with a proven record, is treat him as if he was an amateur.

'You tell him if he doesn't keep his ideas to himself from now on, if he puts one foot out of line and we catch him, before he knows what hit him he'll be praying to God to send him to the Army because from that moment on, from where he's standing, the Army's going to start looking like a Sunday school picnic.'

'I'll tell him,' Berry says.

This is how it happens.

The car is always an ordinary car. A Cortina cruising by or a Ford Escort and it pulls to a halt and someone gets out. A man. Just an ordinary-looking man. He comes up to you and asks if you'd like to go for a little ride and if you know what's good for you, you go quietly and sometimes the pick up man goes with you and sometimes he disappears.

There's no fuss and it's all over so quickly no-one else on the street even has time to notice.

There are usually two of them. The driver and the one who sits in front with him who's going to do the talking and you in the back and all the doors locked on automatic lock.

'So you don't get any ideas about looking for trouble,' the front one says.

Webber's not a hero. He never thought he would be. Now he knows for sure. He can smell fear on himself, seeping out of his pores sharp-sweet, like tomcat spray floating sickly through the car.

The one in front, the one doing the talking is soft-spoken and regretful.

'You better be nice to me,' he says. 'I'm a very busy man and I'm going out of my way to give you some free friendly advice.'

Webber makes himself look him straight in the face. Not insolently, because you'd be a fool not to know that with people like this it doesn't pay to be insolent. Just a look straight into the eyes, man to man, to show you can act as a man is supposed to act no matter how you feel inside.

Sometimes it's a drive a few times around the block. They say what they have to say and when it's finished they take you back where they found you and drop you off.

They talk quietly and they're very polite. All you have to do is listen. Not every time is like this time. Often they don't even turn around to look at you. They know what you look like. They have a photograph of you on a file. They have photographs taken on campus and at rallies.

You know why you're there and what you've done to upset them. You've brought this little visit on yourself because you couldn't stop yourself shooting your mouth off. That's what they tell you.

They say they have a job to do just like everyone else and you're where you are because you're not making their job any easier, which isn't something they like.

Everything's nice and friendly and easy.

'We're all grown-up people here,' the front one says. 'You can make a mistake but you don't have to be a bloody fool.'

All you have to do is listen.

'You didn't think it through properly. That's all. Now you have. You thought about it again and now you know you were wrong and it won't happen again and if anyone should ask you, maybe that's what you should say.'

Pay attention to what they say and everything's sorted. You take a drive back. Everyone goes their own way and gets on with their lives. No-one wants any trouble and no-one's going to get any and as for this little talk, it never happened.

'Just remember,' the front one says. 'This is the first time. I'm sure you understand.'

It's a joke. It's the joke about the old farmer and his young wife and the donkey who baulks at pulling their cart. The first time it refuses the old man gets out of the cart and flicks the animal lightly with a whip and says: 'That's the first time.'

The same happens the second time.

The third time the old farmer gets down from the cart, stands in front of the donkey and instead of remonstrating with it, he takes out a gun and shoots it dead.

'That's the third time,' he says.

His young wife, distressed, takes her husband to task.

'What did you do that for?' she says and the old man looks at his young wife and he's not about to allow her to question what he's done.

'That's the first time,' he says.

It's an old joke and when they tell it they laugh and

some part of him wants to laugh too. With relief at such banality.

There was an inter-school debate once. In the town hall in Mossel Bay. A long drive through an area where aloe-spiked semi-desert gives way to farmland and hills that roll down to the sea.

'Should good citizens obey bad laws?' That's what the debate was about.

He didn't speak. He went to listen.

They went in the school bus and by the time they arrived there was a big crowd of kids. Kids from all the outlying towns; all bussed in for the great inter-school debate except there was a change of plan.

'A programme change,' the teacher in charge says. 'A snap debate instead of what we've been preparing for.

' "Which is superior: the Communist education system or our own?" That'll be interesting don't you think? It's something we've discussed.'

It wasn't what he came for. It wasn't what he wanted to hear.

'The other would have been better,' he says.

'The other was the wrong choice,' says the teacher in charge. '"Should good people obey bad laws?" I don't know whose idea that was because it's pointless really. It would have been a very short evening. Hardly worth such a long ride.'

That's that. Except he doesn't agree. Perhaps the others thought it was pointless too. Perhaps he was the only one who didn't, but even so he doesn't agree. He didn't agree then and he doesn't agree now.

He wanted answers then and didn't get them, so he went the long road home through the dark feeling empty. Empty and waiting for answers which have come to him now and make him feel emptier still.

After the warning he stays away from rallies. When he sees Beeky he takes her somewhere quiet. 'To be alone together,' he says and it's true but it isn't altogether true. There's more to it than that.

He avoids people who ask him how it's going and what he thinks about things these days. He keeps away from any place where he can be singled out or even noticed because anywhere there's a group together, there's someone whose job it is to notice and report back.

Beeky doesn't understand. She wants to know why.

'Exams are coming up,' he says. 'I'll still need my degree when all this is over. It'll come in handy when I'm looking for a job.'

'It means a lot to people if you show up,' she says. 'You're famous, remember? People expect to see you around. They like to know you haven't changed. It makes them feel better.'

'Later,' he says, not looking at her. 'When exams are over. Not now.'

'It's too bad,' Beeky says. 'But I'm going to go on with it anyway. I'm not going to stop just because you have.'

'I haven't asked you to,' he says.

But he wants to.

He has a funny feeling. He has a feeling something is coming and when it comes it's going to be something bad.

CONRAD

The Music of Life

My sister sends me a newspaper picture of our father and our stepmother taken at the State President's garden party.

'Look at the old fool,' she writes. 'Older but no wiser.'

There is a dotted newspaper picture and black-inked in, a moustache and a pair of devil's horns springing from the crown of our father's fedora. On either side of his hat, firmly attached, Beeky has swiped in a pair of pointy ears.

The new wife has a smile as wide as the Blaaukrantz bridge. It spans her face. A stream of black-ink hearts spring from her left breast and float across the page like bubbles.

Above them on top of a fully blacked-in cloud, tight as Hottentot hair, a malevolent cupid lies, its mouth snarled upwards, the bow in its arrow pointed precisely in the direction of their father's jugular vein where it lies embedded in the folds of his fleshy neck against the starched white collar of his shirt.

'Happy landings!' That's what Beeky has written in

her generous, lopsided scribble and it seems to me a message in a bottle, come from some other world a long way away and I am uncertain now because I no longer know which world it is I might claim as my own.

The aporosaura lizard is a foot dancer. It can also swim through sand. It stands four-footed on a rock and when the rock heats up it leaps from foot to foot, two feet at a time in the air and two feet down. Two up, two down unswerving in his ungainly life-preserving dance.

You can spend a lot of time watching him and his dance doesn't vary. Always two feet in one world and two in the other. It's so natural to him he doesn't even know he's doing it.

He's a stick leader now. In charge of a stick of four and leader because Janneman is *klapped*.

Everyone thought if anyone had someone looking out for him, and a charmed life, Janneman had. It was impossible to believe that anything would ever touch him and then he was there and then he was gone, taken by a clean shot through the head.

They are doing vertical envelopments. Spotting gooks on the ground and dropping people in to take them out.

'You handle it,' Janneman says.

Handling is controlling from above and he says no. Janneman's too old for jumping out of helicopters. 'You call the shots and we'll do the hard work.'

'No,' says Janneman.

He needs experience and Janneman says what he himself needs is exercise. He needs to get out on the ground and stretch his muscles.

The pilot says he can see gooks and he's got a grid

reference and the gooks sure as hell can see them from miles away and must be getting ready for them and Janneman is shouting 'contact' 'scramble' and showing thumbs down for a jump-out and the Alouette is going down chop-chopping the top leaves from the marula tree on its way.

'Stand by for deployment.'

'Roger. Copy that.'

When they hit the ground they'll be silent. No talkback from them.

He can see them going down, falling like acorns. He can see them through the noise and the dust. Hitting the ground running while the gunship protects them. Looking for cover in a featureless landscape and the pilot going round and round in circles, making loops around the contact zone and he doesn't know how he does it because for that moment he's a sitting duck with nothing between him and eternity but a sheet of perspex and he knows it.

Then he's in control, talking hard, which will come to them as whispers through their headphones. The voice of God and they're running blind and their lives are in his hands. They're running on faith and experience and dozens of reruns of other engagements and what worked then and what went wrong and endless, never-ending debriefings.

He can see the gooks and his team can see nothing and they're tuned up with waiting and silence and they've no-one to direct them but him and God and if God's on the stands sitting this one out, then he's all there is. Their lives in his hands.

'Stopper,' he says. 'Four gooks 100/400 waiting to run into you. Go to the left and behind. Ammo up.'

His throat's dry. His ears are ringing. He knows what they feel and he feels it too. The blood rush. The killing rush. Pumped. Pumped up. His whole body on fire with adrenalin. The helicopter rocking and his head on automatic.

'Take under instruction,' he says.

The instruction is his. He's sweating like a pig. They tell you the Army swallows up weak guys. They sit out their service and keep their heads down so no-one ever knows exactly when they would have broken and how much it is they wouldn't have been able to do.

Not Special Services. Special Services are performers. Tightrope walkers. Fire dancers and one step wrong and you die or one of your people dies because of you and no-one ever says anything about it once it's over and no-one is to blame but everyone knows.

He doesn't want it to happen to him.

'Not on my watch. Please, God. Let it not happen but if it does, let it be someone else and not me. Let it be some other time and not now. Not while I'm in charge.'

'Contact. Ten, maybe five seconds. Get in, take them out. Make a clean sweep. Then we're out of here.'

It's done and they're out. Only Janneman *klapped*. A clean shot. No-one's fault. No-one to blame. It happens.

This is the music of his life now. The chop of helicopters and the dull thud of mortars. The popping rounds of rifle shots and the green and red tracers marking the air with phosphorescent arcs of fire and when they're back in camp and it's quiet someone plays a mouth organ and it makes no difference what tune it is he plays. It's still the mournful music of man he hears.

He longs for a different kind of quiet. A quiet he knew when he was different. A quiet which curled and wrapped itself around the delicate notes of the five-string //gwashi or the tender flute call of a simple mouthbow or the silvery tinkle of a duet of thumb pianos with a wonderful sound that falls like water in wild places.

Something goes wrong in an 'encounter'. They are converging on a farmhouse which is not much more than a labourer's hut. Square, mud walls, corrugated iron for a roof with blue paint peeling away from it. One window has a piece of cracked glass left in it.

Half a dozen or so insurgents come on them from behind. They are not the first group here. Others have passed through safely so they feel safe and then it happens and they don't expect it.

The noise is terrible. Most people would find it unbearable but they are tuned into a different frequency now. No-one is dying and it's over quickly and the enemy are on the run and orders are being shouted at them. They will have to pursue them.

He can feel blood pumping through the artery in his neck. His throat is dry and burning and full of dust. His rifle is in his hands. He is outside himself and it is from outside himself that he sees them.

Two children. Girls. He doesn't know where they came from but suddenly they're there. Skirted. Poor-looking. Brown and neat. Bare feet. The way children like this are.

'Get them out of here,' someone screams but it's too late.

An AK bullet whines past and one of the children is lifted up bodily into the air like a rag doll and she comes down skirt billowing in slow motion. Or so it seems to him. A blue and yellow parasol drifting down. The colours are bright against the sky and she drifts down light in the air and his eyes follow slow as she is slow and he is at Liefdefontein again and the dog-boy is throwing bottles up for target practice and his rifle is hard against his shoulder and he's bringing them down with one shot.

She lands heavy for such a small person with a hard thud on the ground and for a moment there's the silence of truce because they are, after all, men and it has come to this.

Then it starts again.

She isn't dead. The bullet has entered her chest and they seal the hole with plastic to stabilize internal pressure. They put up intravenous lines. They do what they can. As soon as they can they radio for help. Her sister is screaming, dehumanized, crazed, screaming like a wild creature, far beyond their help and they don't even try to comfort her.

The radio crackles and fades, crackles and fades.

'Is anyone there, for God's sake? Jesus Christ, why don't they give us equipment that works?'

They will send out choppers to take VIPs game-watching but they won't send them for a civilian casualty. That's the rule and they wait and a Bedford comes and the child is evacuated first to the base military hospital and then to Windhoek.

That's what they tell us. That it's all under control and she'll be fine. I don't know if it's true.

I dream about it. I see her falling over and over, skirt billowing, skinny legs, wizened feet from too much barefoot walking, rag-doll arms, head and the blue and yellow parachute/parasol skirt filled with air and Blink's single tooth shining a single, upended finger at me.

'It's in the air, little master. It's in the air.'

I think there's something wrong with me. Bush-happy they call it and that's one name for it. What I think is that I have lost myself. I think perhaps I am going mad.

* * *

When I was a boy, in the season of lightning, when I was sent up a tree a baboon and came down a man something changed in me and Bastiaan, my 'boy' given to me by my father to teach me the ways of the bush, saw it.

After that day of the rain I kept to myself. I hung around the farmyard or sat alone on the old cane chair in the corner of the stoep. I avoided the men and my father in particular.

They were not in good humour. They were the way white men are who set out to hunt and find the hunting is bad. They passed the time drinking and playing cards. There was the roar of engines and wheel-spinning drives out into the bush and the cursing that goes with coming back empty-handed.

It was not as it had been the first time. Time seemed to go slowly. I was ashamed of myself because of what had happened and filled with remorse. I wished I could have my chance again and do things differently in a way that would make my father proud.

I took to walking and Bastiaan walked with me and because I was all confusion it was he who chose the direction and set the pace. We walked in silence, sometimes for many miles. He in front and I behind as was our way and every now and then he stopped and waited for me and if there was something of interest to show, he showed it. But the flowering of the bush after rain is a short thing and soon everything was back to itself again and to my mind there was nothing much to see.

There was Bushman grass which is tall and golden and very delicate when it bends graceful and submissive as a dancer before even the slightest breeze.

There were mixed thickets and in them trumpet thorn and the poison grub commophorbia on which the Diamphidia beetle feeds, beneath which the Bushmen dig for the beetle's grubs which they use to poison their arrows.

I knew their arrows. Bastiaan showed me and they are very fragile and made in a special way of four parts. So, once struck, an animal will not be able to dislodge them. It will rub its rump against a tree and try to rub the arrowhead loose but all this will do is embed the arrowhead more deeply so no matter how hard it tries to dislodge it, the arrowhead will stay and the poison, inevitably, will take its course.

It was a time of silence and dancing grass and the mild days of winter when the air is very clear and all the smells of the living bush which are the sweetest smells in the world are caught up in it.

Sometimes our walks would take us many miles from the house and keep us away for several days. Then, we would snare what we could, to eat. Birds or a hare and if we were lucky, a guineafowl.

Bastiaan would make a noose snare from the bark fibre of the acacia tree and tie it around a small stockade of twigs stuck in the ground into which he would put sweet gum as a bait or the small bulbs that he knew the guineafowl relish.

At night we would sleep on the ground and Bastiaan who carried his fire sticks with him would make fire.

To do this he had to take the fire sticks from their quiver and one would be quite smooth and the other have a notch cut in it and the notched one had to be held to the ground and the smooth stick fitted securely into it.

Then he would begin rolling the sticks between the palms of his hands pressing down as he did so to increase the friction.

It's not an easy thing to do. The muscles of his face

pulled tight with effort and all his concentration was on it and he was breathing hard.

In the beginning I doubted his ability. It seemed impossible to me that a man could make fire this way but in the end I saw it was possible and I believed.

In a short time the softer wood of the notched stick begins to powder at the point of contact. The powder turns to black and starts to smoulder. When this happens Bastiaan tips in some tinder and blows on it hard until it flares.

We cook on his fire and eat. We sit by it and sometimes he will take his pipe out of his pouch and fill it with tobacco and reach with his hand to the edge of the fire for a lighted coal and take it with his bare hand and light his pipe with it and then throw it back.

We were in harmony then and when the time came to sleep I would lie by the fire with my pack under my head and look at Bastiaan crouched by the coals, highlighted in fireglow. I would hear the faraway rattle of a leopard cough and the sounds of the bush would enfold me and I would know peace.

Since that time I have learnt something. I know things now I did not know then.

A new fire for a Bushman signifies a new start. A Bushman band dogged by misfortune will move elsewhere and kindle a new fire in the hope that it will usher in a better time, with the possibility of good fortune in it for them.

I think Bastiaan saw my need and my need was great and he hoped this might prove true for me also.

It was on one of these walks that we came upon a veld fire.

Bastiaan wakened me to it in the early morning and I stood up to see an enormous red light blazing many miles away in the still-dark sky.

We stood and watched it and it was like standing at the open door of a giant furnace and I imagined how terrible the heat would be if we had been closer.

Men should fear fire when it comes like this but I did not and nor did Bastiaan. He stood beside me watching the great drama unfold and I did what it was he had tried so hard to teach me to do. I saw it with his eyes.

With his eyes I saw this was nothing to be afraid of at all. It was merely the whim of the Greater god who had chosen this moment to show us the smallest part of his might and it was nothing to fear, for it was just one of the many of his wonders and the most natural thing in the world.

Before dawn the wind lifted and the fire blew back on itself and Bastiaan told me that in this way it would blow itself out.

The sky turned grey and then rosy and bushes and trees emerged from the darkness taking on shape and form and finally outline. The Morning Star faded and hundreds of miles away on the horizon the great sun rose up trailing dawn in its spoor and the new day rode in behind it.

We came upon the devastation in the early afternoon. The ground was still warm beneath our feet. Around us were the smouldering trunks of fallen trees, some with their top leaves still green. The air was thick with the smell of wood burning.

Bastiaan walked ahead of me and I behind through the strange landscape. Warm dust, fine as talcum powder, rose up with each footfall and dying trees and the succulents and vines that mark the water routes, murmured and sighed as they gave up their being in that strange air.

No animal, no bird, no snake, no lizard, no living thing was there. All had gone or were burned. There were tracks of fleeing animals half-filled with ash and Bastiaan pointed them out to me.

Soon, he said, the first birds would come back to eat dead insects. Birds were the first to sense fire and flee and the first to return and later we saw a pair of secretary birds and later still a swarm of vultures hovering hot-foot above the ground with their great bony wings flapping, seeking whatever it was that could be scavenged.

When we got back to the house it was almost night. We were dusted in ash, so we came out of the bush and up to the house like phantoms rising up from the dead and my father came out to greet me.

He said he'd been worried. The fire had come close to the house before the wind turned and no-one seemed to know where we were.

He said he was pleased to see me and relieved. The others said so too and they took me into the house and made a great deal of me and my experience and I liked my father again, although I knew it would never be the same between us.

But that was a long time ago and I have seen other things since then.

I know how it is with the land after fire. It remakes itself. Land needs fire. Fire helps it clear itself of dead vegetation that threatens to smother everything and leaves the way free for new growth.

After the first rains the Camelthorn will bloom again, in its burst of wonderful yellow blossom. There will be Mopane and Monkey Orange and Red Syringa.

It is not like that with the human heart and I am become that devastated landscape and what I possessed, that I might call life, has left me or been taken from me and my skin is all that remains and I drape it over myself to hide my emptiness.

BEEKY

Special Delivery

The candlelight rally is Beeky's idea. She wants a spectacle everyone will see and she's fired up with the idea and can't understand why he refuses to be part of it.

She goes on at him to be there and be one of the speakers. When he says he can't she gets angry.

'You draw people,' she says. 'If you come, other people will too.'

She can be cold, Beeky, when she's angry. Her eyes can melt but they can freeze too and he doesn't like her like this. Everything's spoiling around them and he doesn't like that either.

'I used to admire you,' she says. 'I'm not sure I do any more. You've changed. You say it's exams. I don't believe you. I think it's something else.'

'Think what you like,' he says.

He won't talk about the ride. If he talked about it, eventually they'd hear and they don't like that. You don't talk about the ride. The ride never happened.

'I hate it when it's like this,' he says.

'Then do something about it,' says Beeky. 'Stand

up and be counted. You've done it before. What's changed? You're always saying somewhere in all this mess you have to find a way through and it has to be something that lets you live with yourself afterwards.'

He looks at her and looks for a very long time.

'What is it?' she says.

'Nothing,' he says. 'You shouldn't quote people to themselves, that's all. I did say that but it doesn't make good hearing now and coming from you, the way I feel about you, I'm not even sure it's fair.'

They can hardly believe their luck and how things have changed, because first he seems to disappear right off campus, right inside himself as if he's thinking something out and not even Beeky sees him or knows where he is.

Then he comes back and the first thing he does is go to the rally organizers and say he's changed his mind. If they want him to speak, he will. If they want to and it'll help bring up numbers, they can even pass the word that he'll be there.

It's only after he says it and it's all arranged that he tells Beeky about his ride with the Special Branch.

'Why didn't you tell me before?' she says.

'Because it wouldn't have made any difference.'

'It does make a difference,' she says. 'If they gave you a warning, you're in danger and we need to know. If the others knew, they wouldn't expect you to expose yourself like this.'

'You wanted me to stand up and be counted. I'm doing that. I'll go on doing it. I'll do anything I need to do and go on doing it until it's over or someone who counts actually listens and something gets done about it.'

Something has happened. He was never like this before and she isn't ready for the change in him.

While she's looking for words and not finding them he's looking at her and his hands which are not his own any more reach out and touch her.

He takes her two hands in both of his and holds them by the wrists and her hands in his are warm but the day has a chill on it. There's a bite in the air, breath curls on the cold and needs soft words to warm it.

'I'm sorry,' he says. 'I don't want you to be afraid. I'm afraid too. I know men aren't supposed to admit it but it's true.'

'If you don't want to do it you can say so,' she says. 'It's not too late to pull out.'

'Why should I want to do that?' he says.

She would like him to draw her close but he holds her with his eyes and his eyes are lover's eyes and soft and she feels a terrible fear beating in her throat like wings.

'If you do this, they'll come for you,' she says. 'What happened makes it different.'

'I know,' he says. 'It makes it different but it doesn't make me wrong. It makes me more right than ever.'

There's a road that runs through the heart of the campus. It's called Circle Drive. It makes a break in the sandstone steps and the dark spires of yew that lead up to the Great Hall and the mountain behind.

At the base of the steps sits Rhodes in bronze, chin on fist, mottled green and pitted, sightless with age he dreams his dream of rock and heath and Empire, out beyond the sports field the vision goes and across a float of blue mountains all of a continent dreams its own dreams beyond.

There's a small group. Not as many as they hoped but a group just the same. Clumps of people not quite sure what's expected of them and no-one quite sure what to tell them to do.

Beeky has a cardboard box filled with candles. She pushes them into people's hands. A student named Frank who's supposed to be helping is unsure. His candle box is on the top step and when a new person arrives he stands a little away disassociating himself from it, as if he isn't quite certain who it belongs to.

'Help yourself,' Beeky says.

Some are brazening it out. As if coming to an illegal rally is an obligatory rite that must be observed. Some are embarrassed, more anxious to go than to stay.

There's no sign of Tom. People say he won't come. Beeky knows he will and fear flutters inside her and it's butterfly soft and holds back her breathing.

She's apprehensive and afraid and filled with a terrible feeling of foreboding that makes her want to turn around and run away and run as far and as fast as she can; but she can't do that and she knows he'll come.

The first grassy hint of autumn is in the air. The sun goes down early. There's an informal early training session on the rugby field, a brilliant wash from the floodlights over grass that's oil-baize green and the smell of damp ground.

Frank has given up on his candle box.

'He's not coming,' he says to Beeky. 'I knew from the way he's been acting lately that his heart isn't in it. I had the idea when it came to the crunch and he really had to put himself on the line he'd probably chicken out.'

She hates the I-told-you-so satisfaction in his voice.

'If he wants to make an entrance he better get a move on,' Frank says. 'Otherwise by the time he pitches up everyone will have pushed off.'

'Perhaps that's what he wants,' someone says. 'Perhaps that's what this is all about.'

It's not safe to be there. No-one knows whom to trust any more. If Tom is a police informer with his message as bait it's those who have come and are willing to listen who are at risk. They're the ones whose names will be taken. If he's a police informer playing a clever game he's in no danger. Nothing will happen to him.

When he comes, he comes down the main steps and he's not alone. There's a man with him. It's no-one they know but they think maybe he's brought someone else with him. Someone important who has something to say.

They're walking fast, as if they know they're late and keeping people waiting. As if the man's the reason they're late and Webber's been delayed because of waiting for him but all the same he was someone worth waiting for.

They reach the main road and stop in case of traffic and in the half-light it looks as if the man is a close friend, but older. It looks as if he has Webber by the arm but lightly, in a friendly way although it's hard to be sure.

It's as if the man is holding him back. 'Watch out for cars.' 'Look left, look right, look left again.' 'Be careful when you cross the road.'

That's the way it looks but there's hardly any traffic at this time of evening because most of the students have gone home and cars are few and far between.

Then they hear it. There's a terrible sound of a car going along The Circle too fast. A student car with a souped-up exhaust. That's what it sounds like.

They can hear the clatter of wheels hitting speed

bumps much too fast and the protesting trumpet of the exhaust and everyone looks up.

Beeky is at the top of the steps with her candle box still in her hands and she looks up too but it isn't the car that interests her.

She looks up for Tom and the car comes over the speed bumps like a fury with its headlights cutting the night and Tom with a short, sharp shove is right in front of it and there's a terrible thump and him flying up rag bag and boneless through the air.

She sees it all. She sees the man. She sees the bundle flying over the bonnet coming down with an awful thud and the crack of head hard against the pavement and a terrible assault of sound and smell and feeling.

The image is engraved on her eyes making her blind to everything else and in her blindness, stories crash in the air and collide.

There are shards of bottle glass falling down as her brother's bullets hit their mark and Blink tumbling from the sky and a little girl made out of blue and yellow who floats in the air and two skinny legs pointing out from a parasol.

When she blinks again they're gone, the way dreams are gone in the morning and the man's gone too, as if he went on his way with them and perhaps he was there and perhaps he was never there at all.

There are lights on and faces at the windows in the student residences. Light falls on the garden of late-blooming plumbago, the last of the frangipani and the swathes of red and orange cotoneaster that colour the campus.

Everyone out on the road crowds forward to see what's going on and they all seem frozen but Beeky's box is down in a tumble of candles and she's running, freezing cold and running down the steps as fast as she can. Running to Tom and when she reaches him he's very still and seems crumpled up all in the wrong directions. There's blood on the ground and the car is right alongside her slowed down as if it's stopping, like cars are supposed to after an accident. Except it isn't.

The men in the car are wearing woollen caps pulled down low. Beeky can see them. The driver has his hand on the hooter. To warn Tom? To stop him? To wake up the world? The noise is terrible. It bangs from the night like a drum.

The man at the passenger side has his window down and Beeky can see him too, through the deafening hooting, in the car sliding slowly away.

'We've got something for you,' he says. 'Special delivery.'

He reaches down to his lap and throws something out and in a heart-stopping flurry of white it comes out alive. It squawks with terror and it's hard to believe what it is.

A live chicken, terrified by its sudden release, is frantically clucking its fears at the night and the noise is magnified and made horrible by the roar of the car as it speeds away.

No-one knows what to do. Beeky wants to shout out but she can't. The lights from the residence rooms shine down. The rugby players pound their way up from the training field in a tap-dancing clatter of boots.

'What's happening?' they say. 'Someone get help. This poor guy needs help.'

The campus security are on their two-way radios calling back to their home base and asking for help and Tom with one shoe thrown loose is lying still in the gutter, his head on the pavement, his socked foot in the road.

On the pavement the chicken, beady-eyed with affront, puffed large in feathery indignation, blinks in the light of a street lamp and settles its wings.

The night has gone sour around them and campus security are organizing everything now. Some of the girls are crying. They tell them, it's over, there's nothing to see, nothing more to be done till the ambulance comes.

They say, take it easy, break it up. Go back to residences or digs or wherever it is they've come from.

'What's going on?' someone wants to know.

'It's hit and run,' someone else says. 'Hit and run and the bastards have driven away. Has anyone taken a number?'

But there was no number to take.

Beeky's crying. She thinks she's crying. Something sad and terrible is clawing its way out of her throat and it hurts very much so you'd think when it came out it would be a cry all the world would hear but the sound when it comes isn't like that at all.

One of the security men is kneeling next to Webber. He's taken his hand. His head is bowed down. He wears gold braided epaulettes with the name of his company on them and when he looks up for his colleague you can read in his face what he sees.

'No-one must touch him,' he says. 'We've sent for an ambulance. It'll be here any minute. They'll sort it out.'

'Can't someone find a blanket?' someone else says. 'Shouldn't we cover him? Isn't it about shock or something? It's so terribly cold.'

There's blood. He's marked with it, blooded on his face and his head but it's hard to know where it comes from.

'It's going to be all right,' Beeky says whisper-soft, mother-soft and one of the security men moves forward to tell her to get up from the ground, not to touch him but the other one stops him and says it's all right.

She thinks it will be all right now because it's just the two of them. She thinks they're alone. If there was anyone else in the world surely she'd see them? She won't let anyone hurt him. She won't let anyone touch him. She won't let anyone near him. She won't let anyone hurt him. Not ever again.

'Don't be frightened, Tommy,' she says. 'Don't be frightened. It's only me. I'm with you now.'

She thinks that even in that terrible place where he is, he can feel her and knows who she is and she kneels beside him, this broken, hurt creature who is a man whose touch she knows, whose mouth she's kissed, whose hands have touched her, whose beautiful body has loved her own, and smells Death on the air dancing close by, coming closer and she knows where it comes from because she's felt it before.

JEROME

A Letter from Lucifer

All of them who know Berry know how it is with him and the Captain makes it worse and takes him off ops. Because of the student not going to make it.

'What got into you?' the Captain wants to know.

'My job got into me,' Berry says. 'I was only doing my job.'

'Your job was to talk sense into him. Not put together a whole bloody circus.'

'I did talk to him,' Berry says. 'We had a little talk.'

'It must have been some little talk,' the Captain says.

It's no use asking Robey about the talk because this time he wasn't there for it. This time, he was just Berry's driver. He doesn't look at Berry. His job is to drive and to wait in the car while Berry does his business so they can get away nice and clean and quick. What Berry does when he's out of the car is his own affair but when he gets back in it's over and he's ready to ride. He's the boss, just like he always is. If he says to Robey to give the kid a good sideswipe, then that's what he does and he knows exactly what 'good' means. It means good enough to satisfy Berry.

'You must have been driving like hell,' the Captain says and it's his turn now.

'He was standing right there in the road,' says Robey. 'I couldn't have missed him even if I tried. Berry said bump him. That's all and that's all I did.'

'Kids who play in the road get hurt,' says Berry, as if there's nothing more to say, and he stares the Captain down and the Captain is the first one to look away.

'Whose bloody idea was the chicken?' the Captain wants to know and you can see at the corner of his mouth Robey knows all about the chicken and whose idea it was and his mouth wants to smile.

'You said for them to get the message,' Berry says. 'I don't think you'll be having any more trouble in that area. I think they've got the message now.'

Robey says it isn't right to suspend Berry just because he likes his job and is good at it. Berry doesn't like people who get between him and his work and being suspended makes him crazy.

'You better look out for him when he's like this,' Robey says. 'The Captain too. Berry doesn't like a half job. When a thing isn't finished right he won't leave it alone till it's done.'

Berry wanted the girl too but there was no instruction to do it and it wasn't the time.

'They're kids with a cause,' the Captain says. 'The word from upstairs is lean on them and make them aware, make sure they get the message. That's it. End of story.'

Berry doesn't agree.

He made a joke with Robey about it. About the two of them, the boy and the girl, being a twin-pack and him having plenty of time to sort them both out one at a time to suit himself and never mind what the word is from upstairs.

Right's right. Doesn't matter who you are. If you want to stir, it doesn't matter how many strings you can pull, there'll always be someone there to bounce you back into place. Captain or no Captain. One way or the other. One day or the next.

The Captain's an 'orders' man. He does things by the book but Robey could tell you, if you asked him, Berry's got a book too and it isn't anything like the Captain's.

He tells Robey it's his job and he'll finish it his way, no overtime required. Just out of doing things properly, the way they should be done, the way he always does.

It's supposed to be all for one and one for all. If you think someone's out of control, you can turn on them if you like and say they've stepped over the line.

They all think it about someone sometime or the other but they won't say so out loud and no-one will say so about Berry. Berry's the Captain's problem and until he sorts it out Berry can do what he likes, just as he always does.

If he asks for something, even though he's officially suspended, they'll still do it. No questions asked.

Sometimes he asks Jerome for favours and Jerome is the same as anyone else. He'll do Berry a favour without asking anything. Like whose authority he's asking on, or what he needs something for.

He never asks questions like that. All he asks is what he always asks. What exactly is it that's wanted? How soon is it needed? How will it be used?

That's all he needs to know. It's all he ever needs to know but when Berry comes for his favour this time, Jerome does something he doesn't usually do.

'Is it for the girlfriend?' he says. 'The girlfriend of that student who had the little accident?'

'What you don't know can't worry you,' Berry says but Jerome knows it's for her.

Letter bombs are difficult to do. Parcel bombs are easier and bombs put into a magazine are easiest of all.

No matter how good you are or how many times you do it things can always go wrong with a letter bomb.

'I don't know,' Jerome says.

'Come on,' says Berry. 'You can do it. You've done it before. You're a bloody past master at it.'

'It's not me I'm worrying about,' Jerome says.

They use letter bombs but other ways are safer and more certain. The trouble with a letter bomb is it being so delicate. Delicate mechanisms are temperamental. You can never be sure what'll happen once it's set up and goes on its way.

'You can do anything,' Berry says, sweet-talking him for the favour and for him to keep his mouth shut about it.

'I've seen how you fine-tune the watch, for example, which now runs like clockwork and it's a truly marvellous thing to see. I reckon if you can do that you can do just about anything. You ask Robey if that isn't what I said about you.'

It's her watch. That's what he's talking about although he doesn't know it and Jerome likes to have secrets too. He likes it that Berry doesn't know whose watch it is or where the watch came from.

He likes the watch. He's got used to it. Sometimes he times himself by the fine gold hair of the second hand that sweeps across its face swiping away at time.

'Do you have a problem with this?' Berry says.

'No,' says Jerome. 'Just give me something to attach it to and I'll do it.'

'Good boy,' Berry says. 'You do a good job on this and I'll owe you one.'

He can smell drink on Berry. Jerome doesn't like drink. He doesn't have any time for it. If Berry doesn't watch out the drink will get him. He'll start losing it and making mistakes. But that's his business. It's got nothing to do with Jerome.

'You needn't mention this to anyone,' Berry says. 'It's between us.'

Jerome doesn't say anything. He doesn't have to. Both of them know he isn't going to say anything; he isn't going to say anything at all.

It's Berry who gets hold of the letter. You have to work on a letter from someone whose handwriting they recognize, otherwise they might become suspicious.

You have to get it unopened on its way through the postal service. Which is easy to do. It's so easy, it's like an open invitation and you'd think someday someone would wake up and make it much harder.

It's not possible to keep a letter's destination secret from the bomb-maker. A letter has a name on it and address. That isn't going to change, so there's no mistake.

Jerome may not be able to read books or whole newspapers but he can see for himself who his little present is meant for. All he has to do is glance at it and he doesn't even stop working while he looks. He only wishes, when the time comes, that she'd remember him the same way he's remembered her and know he was the one.

It's his day today even though she doesn't know it. He's the one dishing out surprises. He's the one who'll decide who lives and who dies and he's not two-bit like she is with her stupid watch.

He's not a 'special' dumbo kid any more. These days he plays with the big kids and the device slides into the envelope as easy as you like and it's a good job, a real pro job, because when you play with the big kids, the one thing you learn very quickly is that you're playing for keeps.

It's quiet at Spin Street in the evenings, when a job's done and everyone's gone home. Quiet as an empty church except, every now and then, the clang of the lift gate clattering closed and the lift whining up and stopping and then whining down again.

Jerome has the earring that he took from Beeky's room and he's found out a strange thing about it. If you hold it in tweezers and lift it above a candle flame it will dance for you.

The heat from the candle makes it twirl. Jerome found that out for himself. It swirls around and dances up and down like a kid's toy and if you watch it too long it gets hold of you, so you feel half hypnotized but you can't take your eyes off it.

If you hold it just where a warm current of air hits it it'll probably dance its life away for you. Like the coons in the township, death-dancing in their necklaces of fire.

The bull roarer, the !goin !goin is also a thing that will dance in the air. A simple aerofoil made of a length of cord whirled around the head to make a noise like the buzzing of a swarm of bees.

//Gauwa, the lesser god, comes down from the two great trees in the western sky where he lives and turns himself into a giant and becomes the bull roarer wishing the bees away out of their hives and himself safe from them so he can make mischief and take their honey which is not rightfully his and //Gauwa is pleased with himself for using his power in the way that he has and satisfied with what he has done.

BEEKY

A Letter from Lucifer

Beeky's sick. She can't stop vomiting. She's retched herself into a headache. Every bone in her body aches. She's cried so much her eyes are swollen closed and her chest hurts.

She sits at the end of her bed with her arms wrapped around herself rocking backwards and forwards trying to be warm. She's wearing two jerseys. She has a blanket wrapped round her shoulders and she's cold as ice. More than anything else she wishes the impossible will happen.

She wishes someone would knock at the door and say it's all a terrible mistake.

She wishes she'd go out of her room and along the corridor and smell perfume and hairspray and hear girls laughing. She wishes that down the staircase in the hall Tommy will be waiting for her. To take her out for coffee or a walk or a movie or some place they can be alone.

She wishes he was in this world and they alone in it and she could taste his mouth and feel his skin and lie with her head against the soft hair of his chest and feel his beating heart and hear the rumble of his voice tender in half-light.

But he isn't here.

It was too bad, the doctors said. The injuries were multiple and severe the way they often are in accidents like that. Too much broken and damaged ever to put it right again and he was strong but not strong enough to pull through. For that he would have to have been superhuman.

Love is stronger than Death. The Bible says so. It isn't true. At least she's learnt that much; which the Old Madam might have told her, if there'd only been time.

The only people who come are matron and house mother. They say stupid things. They keep saying she's sick. They say she's in shock and they've sent for her father to take her home and she shakes her head no. She wants to be alone. She wants to be warm. She wants to be safe. She wants Tommy to hold her. She wants her brother.

The house mother says her father is worried about her. She's been through a terrible ordeal and he's sending straight away to fetch her because he wants her at home.

She shows no because she's too tired to do anything else. She's too tired to speak. She turns her face to the wall. She wants the soft sweet waft of roses that is her mother and wonders how it is no-one here knows she has no home to go to.

'You need someone to help you,' house mother says. 'You need care. I've spoken to your father and to your stepmother. They're very concerned about you. They feel as I do. That you need to be at home where you can be properly taken care of.'

A car is coming for her. Josias will be at the wheel

and the new wife, all madam, will be in the back seat. She's promised the moon for Beeky. She says she understands. A girl who's been through such a trauma needs special care.

She says what's happened is a terrible thing. An accident. People drive recklessly. Road-accident statistics are appalling. No-one is to blame but Beeky is a highly strung girl and needs special care. She needs counselling and rest and a proper environment to recover in. She will probably require medication and round-the-clock looking after and there'll be no problem with any of it. Beeky will have it all.

'It's not as if I want you to go,' house mother says. 'I can see you're resistant but please try to understand. We aren't able to give you the care you need and your family are. This is what's best for you now.'

Not everyone likes residence rooms but Beeky likes hers. The windows are old. They have criss-crosses of wood and small panes of glass bubbled with age. Ivy creeps in at the window. A small splayed gecko has made his home on the wall just outside, stuck fast, secure, defying gravity.

The other students have been kind. In such a very short time there are flowers in a jar and offers of help and a 'sorry' note with a round sun face radiating beams drawn on it. Thinking of you.

But Tommy is gone and her father is coming to fetch her and the world is changed again and can never be the same.

Such stupid things come into her mind.

There are reference books from the library on her table. *Dutch Painting. Painting in Florence and Siena after the Black Death. Neo-Classicism.* Someone will have to return them for her.

There's a photograph of herself and her brother

taken at the seaside in that other life they once shared and her mother is in her head standing behind a box Brownie saying: 'Smile you two. Smile for the camera. Say macaroni.'

The autumn sun is warm. If you lie out it caresses you but doesn't burn. It's like being ironed by the sure strokes of Nanny's nice warm iron and it's lovely to lie with your eyes closed smelling the grass with the light dappling the inside of your eyelids and the warmth of it soaking down into your bones.

She thinks she will never be warm again.

Her case is packed and she's ready to go. Her room is neat.

'People are amazing creatures,' house mother says. 'Bad things happen and we think we'll never get over them but life goes on and we do. I like to think it's because there's more to us than we know.'

House mother has a sweet smile. She wants to be helpful. She's trying to be nice.

'I've got something for you,' she says.

It's a letter. House mother takes it out of her pocket and holds it up and she can see by the look of it it's from her brother and everyone knows how much she loves his letters.

'Something nice before you leave,' house mother says. 'Maybe something to make you feel a little bit better.'

It's Army issue envelope and a special printed stamp and it's been opened and thumbed and restuck just like it always is and when she opens it, inside at the top of the page it will say 'somewhere on the border'.

Her name is on it in her brother's writing. It's a good letter. Nice and fat. She turns it over in her hand and thinks about him thinking about her and not knowing what's happened.

'I'll leave you to read in peace, shall I?' house mother says. 'Leave your room exactly as it is. Don't take any of your work things with you. When you're better you'll come back and start all over again and everything will still be here just as it is now. Waiting for you.'

She has a gentle way and sounds sure. Beeky knows she's meant to be comforted. She knows she's meant to say something but she doesn't know what to say.

She feels terrible and inside the terribleness is an awful feeling that despite what house mother says when she leaves she won't be coming back. Not to this room, not to this place, not anywhere else, not ever.

The Old Madam

Time is out of joint. It dislodges with such force the Old Madam is thrown out of her icy rejected cupboard and tumbles unfolding in the cold, damp air.

The River god anticipating the first rains rumbles under the floorboards sucking at the house foundations and the Old Madam is tilted free of time. Something is drawing her. She feels the irresistible urge of blood calling blood and a great wind coming from a far place and with it the moment she will have to move on.

Her time has come and she is about to be shaken out of the story.

Now she's gone. She's memory. All that remains is a portrait in oils, some letters and the grove of *naartjies* and bitter oranges she planted in the deep black loam brought down by the river that feeds the pool.

There's her name in the family Bible and the names of her two sons, long dead, and the servants' stories of an Old Madam who blows through the house on a grave wind and shakes down mirrors; who cracks down acorns so they sound like rifle shots and dances with blazing hair in the crackles of the fire.

That's all that's left of the Old Madam and she goes on her way drawn up on the force of a wind too strong to resist and a ghost girl soars past with hair flying like flames and the girl and the wind blow through the house and pull her outwards and upwards setting her free.

While we're locked in our dream someone else is dreaming too and what they're dreaming is us and sometimes we enter each other's dreams and go on together and Beeky is flying free, a pilgrim in a world of wonders lit by the light of a thousand suns and the light is pleasant and cool as the ocean floor and she's rising up like fire flame with her hair rising above her and the Old Madam is young again borne upwards on the great tidal wave of energy that is the past and the future coming into one and on the edge of oblivion, her younger son is waiting and when she flies past he reaches out and when he opens his hand to catch hold of her the last of his anger flows from his palm in small burning coals and his agony ceases and the coals fall through the cosmos too tiny to see and sizzle to the ground and take root and bloom the small speckled flowers of fire which people call Mother's Love.

CONRAD

The Famous Mint Sauce and Banana Ice Cream

Our time here is almost over and we have all been looking forward to 'klaaring out', to going home. You have to watch out for this. It makes you careless. Ekhard got it in the spine and we're so close to the end we're looking for omens now and all the omens are bad.

Ekhard has been looking forward to going home just like the rest of us. He had his plans. Nothing ambitious. Just small-town plans. How he's going to the caravan park at Midmar Dam where they go for Christmas and never mind it not being Christmas. He can't wait for Christmas because 'klaaring out' is like Christmas anyhow and never mind if it's almost winter Midmar Dam is where he's going.

When he gets there he's going to sit on his jack and do nothing but drink beer and make braai and enjoy himself. He's going to look at his wife's legs and if he never sees another stretch of bush or a marula or a shepherd's tree or another black face in his life, friend or enemy, dead or alive, that will suit him just fine too.

I tell him he'll make it but I can't look in his eyes when I say so. I tell him he's going to be all right. I know because the medics say so.

He's going out on a MedEvac. He's secured to a stretcher under a standard-issue blanket and his head's kept straight between thick polystyrene plastic buffer boards.

I think what the old hands say is true. You do get careless when the end's in sight. Safer to think one day at a time until they tell you your time's up. Dangerous to dream.

'Klaaring out' isn't an excuse-me dance. No-one gives you notice. When you go, you go the same way you came and for me it's no different.

I'm lying on my bunk in the red world between sleeping and waking and the code is Sparrowhawk and it comes in the dark hour before dawn. The officer of the day gives the alert and we know what to do. There are eight of us not four and we're ready to go and outside is the damp early morning air that always reminds me of Liefdefontein and the long-ago hunt.

There's no helicopter. We're loaded onto a lorry and someone is shouting. The lorry feels unstable and we sit there quiet, fully kitted, swaying inside and the lorry goes down a safe road to a supply base not far from the main camp.

When we come to a halt and climb out there's a supply shuttle, a veteran Shackleton standing on the runway like a sky elephant, and ground personnel and we look out of place here, black-faced bush men dumped in a modern world behind security wire and fuel tanks and overalled ground personnel and it's as if we're invisible and they take no notice of us.

'What's going on?' someone says.

No-one knows.

'What the hell's going on?' I say.

I want to shout. I'm meant to be shouting but my voice is thick with sleep and sand and it comes out a whisper.

Suddenly I'm tired. I'm more tired than I've ever been in my life. My eyes are boiling with tiredness. There's a feeling of silver foil slithering inside the back of my skull. It makes my head ache and my teeth stand on edge. It puts an iodine taste in my mouth.

I'm so tired, I'm beyond tired. I don't want to think any more. I want someone, anyone to think for me. He can make any decision he likes. He can order me to do anything. I'll do anything anyone tells me and do the best I can just as long as after I've done it, I can lie down and sleep.

I want to lie down on the ground and sleep for ever and never wake up.

'You'll be debriefed at Hoedspruit,' someone with a few pips and a clipboard says. 'Our orders are to collect you, take you back and drop you.'

'And then?'

'Then they'll debrief you, take your kit back and send you home,' he says. 'How the hell should I know? That's how it usually works.'

Which is how I move out of one life and into another.

My father tells me my sister is dead and there's nothing he or anyone else can do about it and he's sorry but this must be my homecoming.

It was no good sending for me. I was out on operations and wouldn't have been able to come in time. There was nothing to do about it. It's nobody's fault and he's sorry.

He didn't want some Army chaplain to tell me. He wanted to tell me himself.

He must give it to me 'straight' he says. It's the best way. I must forgive him. I know him by now. It's the only way he knows how to do things.

My father's house is dark. I'd forgotten. It seems small and I long for light and air.

Josias is old. Old and still offering to carry bags. Even the bag with my kit in it which is like my own body to me and has my sister's book inside it, which she gave to me to write all of my life in. In which I have written not one word.

I tell him to leave it.

I don't want anyone to touch me or anything that's mine. I don't want to see tired old black men carrying bundles too heavy for them and Josias sees in my face that I have changed and he does what I say.

'I'm sorry, Conrad,' my father says. 'It's a pretty bloody terrible show for a homecoming but there was no way of letting you know.'

We are in his study and Josias's tray is set out on the side table just like it always is, any hour of the day or night and my father pours a drink and puts it in my hand.

I don't want it.

My body's sweating. Red-hot with thick bush sweat. My body's in one place while I'm still in another.

I stink. I must stink. We all stink when we come out of the bush. We can't wash the smell of it off us. I don't know how long it takes before we smell like men again. No-one has ever been able to tell me.

I'm sure my father can smell me 'pongo' right across the room. I want the walls to fall down. A mortar would do it. I want the walls to fall down so I can breathe. I want Janneman to be here and make this thing go away and put everything right.

Janneman will know what to do. He won't mind my father trying to put his arm around his shoulder and all the shit about the brave boys in the bush doing their bit.

Janneman would listen to all the crap pouring out of my father's mouth and still keep a smile on his face.

I want my mother.

'Eva has cooked leg of mutton.' That's what the new wife says when I arrive and she comes down the steps to greet me at the car. 'With her famous mint sauce and after that banana ice cream. I hope that'll be all right?'

They are cruel people here. This is what she says by way of greeting knowing that as soon as we are alone together my father is going to tell me my sister is dead and the manner of it.

The new wife's face is a powdered moon with burnt-out holes for eyes. She must be dying because her mouth is stained with blood. That's not a good sign. It's never a good sign.

This is a bad house. In this house there are the terrible thuds in the night and the silences in between. You have to keep on saying it'll be all right. That's what I promised Beeky. I gave her my word but it wasn't true. It was a lie. It wasn't going to be all right at all.

The blood mouth is the giveaway. When you see that you know it'll soon be over. The eyes are still looking at you and sometimes the mouth even smiles and words come out of it but it makes no difference. It's dead meat talking and that's all it is.

'I did all I could to get you here,' my father says. 'Believe me, if there'd been a way in this world to have got you here, I would have but there was nothing they could do about it.'

I bend down my head and stare into the glass.

'They knew all about it already of course. It was in every bloody newspaper you can think of.'

I don't know why he's telling me these things that have nothing at all to do with me.

Sickness and disharmony are inside me, hooked into my soul like a devil thorn with no way to get them out and my father lets me sit like this and I know what he thinks.

He thinks I need time. He thinks if he's quiet, if he offers me a small parcel of time, I will be able to lock this thing up inside it and take it away from here and at some other time, without embarrassment to him or to myself, take it out and look at it again and perhaps find some way to begin to understand.

Before he says what has to be said he closes the door so we won't be disturbed.

My father is at Josias's tray pouring himself something, syphoning soda into it.

'I thought I'd better do it this way,' he says. 'Get it over with as quickly as possible. Funerals are performances these days. They're like bioscope. Damn freak show. I wouldn't allow it. I wouldn't have liked to expose you to it.'

In the bush you learn to be still. You can be still for a very long time. Sometimes your life depends on how good you are at being absolutely motionless.

You don't need words either. If there are others with you, hands do perfectly well for what needs to be shown. Even in wartime the bush has a music of its own and men's voices have no place in it.

I sit in the leather chair where I have sat before and I am without my uniform in light stranger's clothes that once were mine. I hold the glass in my hands and my hands at least are still my own, bush brown from the sun and that's all of the bushmark left on me that the eye can see and I feel naked.

We have been here like this before, my father and me. He stands facing me with the small of his back against the mahogany rim of his desk and tells me the manner of my sister leaving this world.

He's careful. He wants me to know it all and the things that led up to it. Not just how it happened but why and he says what he has to say in his own way and I am accustomed to instruction and hear it all without moving.

'I tell you something, Con,' my father says. 'It was a pro job. The investigating officer told me so himself. She was small fry. Not important enough for something like this but it happened anyway. That's the SB for you. One half doesn't seem to know what the other half's doing.'

Outside the window, in one of the pin oaks in the park, a pair of squirrels are having a game chasing each other up and down the rugged bark of a tree. Scurrying from branch to branch, shaking leaves loose.

The ground is carpeted with leaves. I know this house and I know this place. Outside you will be able to smell full autumn coming and it will sweep in grandly, at its own pace, as the tides of the sea do.

At this time of year there's an aroma that comes from the orchards. A smell of orange and pear and quince and apricot and under your feet the fragrance of herbs. Acrid, pungent, peculiar. Buchu, wild geranium and sunshine. The smell of the Cape and my home and my childhood. The smell of my sister that carries her laughter in its heart.

Soon the gardeners will have their time cut out raking and burning leaves. The head gardener, the one who came right into the kitchen on the day my mother died, will tell them what to do and how to do it.

There will be bonfires and smoke curling up and on these pyres dying vegetation and worm casts and the last of the softness of spring and summer before the cold rains of winter proper arrive.

'Conrad?' my father says. 'Are you all right?'

I want a compass in my hand and the feel of clothes my body knows and the sound of men's voice that ring to a tune I understand.

I want the shouting and the red burning world of half-sleep. I am come new from another world to a place I no longer know and I don't belong here and my heart is running sick with longing for the place I am from.

'Conrad?' my father says.

I look up and he blurs in front of me and behind him hanging from the wall are the old pictures he likes so well.

Our history. New-framed and gleaming but the pictures are the same.

The tightly posed shots of important men doing important work with their names and titles printed neatly beneath them, so long after they're gone their names will not be forgotten.

The hazy photographs of old hunting parties and men and dead animals and the small crinkled faces of the trackers tagged onto the end of the picture.

The snapshot of myself and Steynberg, two men I no longer know and down the wall our Hartmann ancestor, the wild colonial boy who followed his Boer blood and betrayed his masters.

I had not wished to see it but I see it now. Our history is no more than fables agreed upon and we deceive ourselves and let men die to give life-breath to it.

My father follows my gaze and says that boy should be my inspiration. Like him I should always remain true to my blood. Be unquestioning. Fight a good fight, run a straight race, finish the course and keep the faith.

'You think I should have waited for you before we had the funeral? If I could, I would,' he says.

I say nothing. Things are different and funerals are nothing to me.

'I had to make decisions,' my father says.

I nod to show I understand and he straightens his back and I can see he feels better. It is as if it's over and done with and will never be spoken of again and I can see his relief is incalculable and we are man to man again. Two men talking about things in an offhand way. The way men do.

'You know what I can never work out,' he says. 'All her life in everything she did, right to the end, your sister opposed me. If I spoke out for something, she was against it. Everything I stood for, she rejected. Can you understand it? I certainly can't.'

SEASON OF THE SUN

CONRAD

Season of the Sun

My father thinks there's something wrong with me. The border 'war' is done. I have done my 'duty'. The Army is behind me and I am doing what my father says. Which is getting on with my life.

I have a job, which isn't the kind of job my father either expected or wished. I got it through one of my old commanding officers who remembered what he called my 'affinity with the local people' and my knowledge of their language and their ways.

'We're going to be active in your part of the world,' he says. 'Moving them off the land. We've got a place, don't worry. It was an old Army base camp we have no other use for any more. It isn't very much but they can't stay where they are. They'll die. Someone has to explain this to them.'

I am to be the one doing the explaining. A liaison officer attached to the Army. A civilian. No rank, no uniform, no gun.

'It's a mess out there,' he says. 'There's always such a bloody mess when a war ends.'

The Government in Namibia has changed. The

Government here is changing and it occurs to me that if I had come just a few years later and my sister after me the world would not have been as we knew it and our lives would have been very different.

I think my old officer expects me to say something but he has my combat record in front of him and in the face of it, I have nothing to say.

'Those who were on our side in Namibia had to refugee after the change of Government and when they came over our own people didn't like it. Wasn't enough room for all of them, they said. Couldn't sort it out. So they've all been put under our protection and in the end, they all have to go.'

He says there's dissension among our people and those from the north. To make it worse there's illness and drought and the orders are they're all to be moved to a new place where things can be properly controlled and a settlement's to be made for them there.

I tell him Bushmen are nomadic by nature and by inclination and I don't believe they'll go.

'Used to be perhaps,' he says. 'But the war's changed that too. Those who took tracker jobs are sell-outs to the new order. Their own people don't want them because they've gone half white and we don't want them because there's too much bush in them. Poor little buggers. It's a big bloody mess.'

He snaps his file closed and tells me the bush people can't live off the land any more. They've gone too soft for that and it's difficult to know what exactly it is we're supposed to do with them but we're going to have to try.

I can hear the tablets are cast for the bush people and the brown hyena has fallen upside down. It is the season of the sun and the season of the sun is a death thing.

* * *

I am back at my father's farm and it's as good a base as any. The house still stands, large and square under sloping corrugated iron with the stoep running round three sides, two rainwater-storage barrels on top of the roof and the empty animal water troughs to the side.

The camelthorn tree that shouldn't be there is still there, lifeless against the sky and I see that it is like all of life here with the heart and soul seared out of it.

The house has been closed for a long time but it still stands and everything in it. Many people have passed this way in the refugee migrations from the north and no-one has touched anything.

I think it's because this is a death place and a place of bad fortune and their blood warns them they must walk around it and away or be destined to take up its ill fortune and carry it along with them.

All that is left of the *kampong* is rubbish and rubble and scorched black patches of earth where fires once burned. The people have moved on.

Things are not well with the land which is the way it is when Rain withholds his favours. There is drought. Everything is scorched and the land is leached of life. The water courses have all dried up. There's nothing left, not even in the deepest most secret places.

There are no *bi* bulbs to dig up for the treasure of moisture in their roots. The caches of water for bad times hidden in ostrich-egg shells are used up and the air shimmers, playing tricks with the eye, making mirages of trees floating and great, long-gone herds drifting across the plains.

The game has gone in search of greener pastures. The night creatures stay hidden against the burning furnace that is the day.

The people who have already gone, have gone in the

way they always go. If you look to the land to find trace of them it is as if they were never there at all.

The branches and bark and desert grasses that make their shelters soon return to the earth and decompose. Animals roam through the places where once fires burned and stories were told and dances danced.

The wind comes and everything is blown clean and the bush and scrub cover the land's face and every now and then a drunken dust devil, which is the soul of the unquiet dead, makes its way across the emptiness looking for that which is gone and will never be found again.

The old hunters of my father's day who used to give seasonal work no longer have the stamina for the chase, or the hands to hold a gun steady, or the clear eye of youth which can cause an eland to fall.

All they have now are stories and they're old men's stories and tired and they are far on their journey and travelling further. The land has outlasted them and they have moved on.

This is the way with the great herds too and the smaller creatures and even the majestic cats who walk alone and unafraid through the vastness of the African night.

It is the way with the bush people too. When the bad seasons come and the land can no longer support them, they must get their band together and break down their *scherms* and move on to some other place.

Some go to farms and to masters. Some to the Army as trackers. Some attach themselves to white people in settlements and on smallholdings, exchanging their labour for nothing more than a promise of food every day and not even that can be depended upon.

When their leather clothes fall apart they must beg cast-offs and you see them, in these places they've come to, small people in ragged white-men's clothes, each day more estranged from their own people and customs.

Sometimes they're accused of stealing. Of killing a giraffe or taking cattle. Then you see them on prison work details sent out as convict labour to white settlements.

For those who do not know such things it's strange to see convicts who are neither chained nor locked up nor guarded. It's strange to an onlooker who does not know, how it is that they make no attempt to escape and their overseers who shout commands and the occasional insult are desultory and unarmed, defenceless against them.

It does not happen like this in that other world but this land is large and has rejected them. They could break away and run. They could run for many days to the very edge of their strength. They may run as far and as fast as they like. There is nowhere for them to go.

A young Bushman named Tsoe has attached himself to me. He came as Bastiaan did. Sitting at the perimeter of the farmstead at the edge of light where the bush licks at the yard.

I know he's there. I wait for him to show himself and when he does, he comes timidly because those who remain in the bush are afraid of white people. They fear they will be taken away. They think white people are sorcerers and have magic in them strong enough to take a man from his place.

It is because Bushmen do not know how to argue that they go. They strive for harmony and are always anxious to agree. If they are asked to go anywhere, as a courtesy they will go, even though they know the price they will pay for it.

Tsoe is handsome. His skin is pale gold, not yet

darkened and weathered by the sun. His face is oval, with slightly pointed chin and high cheekbones. His eyes are large and wide, slightly slanted. They are the colour of amber. The translucent colour of the bush honey his people love so much.

Tsoe comes and goes as he pleases. He attaches himself to the place but he lives outside it and for a long time he doesn't address himself to me. If his hunting is good he brings me gifts but it is not easy to find anything in this bad season and I put out food for him. Maize meal and cooked samp and *marog*, the sharp bitter spinach that grows in the vegetable patch.

On the day he snares a small hare he comes to show it to me and he says that he will skin it and make fire so he can cook it and we can eat it together.

This is the day he talks to me for the first time and I go and sit with him and let him see something of myself.

I tell him it is easier for two men to make fire than one. I can see he doubts me but is too polite to show it. I crouch opposite him and when he brings out the fire sticks I make fire with him as Bastiaan taught me.

Two men rotating the hard pointed stick in the cleft of its soft wood partner make more friction than one man can and ultimately heat and a spark and in this way, we make our fire and share what he has brought and afterwards I offer him tobacco.

I know he has a pipe. I've seen it. It's made from the shin bone of a small buck.

He lights his pipe with a hot coal from the fire taken bare-handed and thrown back immediately the pipe flares to life and we sit beside each other warmed by the coals with night wrapped around us and I dream myself as I once was and wonder at this stranger who has taken my place and lives in my skin.

* * *

I don't know what will become of me now but I've assigned myself a new task. I take pen and paper and an oil lamp and set them up on a table under the corrugated overhang of the stoep. I bring out a straight-backed chair good for sitting on and in the evenings, when the day's proceedings are complete, with the flicker from the oil lamp dancing over the page, I sit there and write.

I write down what fragments I can as I remember them. I write with great honesty such detail as I recall because these stories are not mine alone and must be passed on.

I am no scholar. In that regard others, more able, have walked this path before me but piece by piece I finish them in the best way I can and send them to my 'Oom' Faan who understands such things and ask him what my best course will be now.

I work at my task and Tsoe's eyes are upon me. I don't know what he makes of this. Tsoe doesn't know writing but he knows electricity. He knows we can fill our house with light whenever we wish but on hot nights electric light only makes more heat and it's better this way. To sit out with only the soft light from the lamp spilling out across the table and onto the pages is to invite stories in.

Tsoe is interested in this new thing and comes up close to see what I'm doing and he looks at it and shakes his head because he doesn't understand. Bushmen know about drawing but writing is strange to them.

Bushmen are great artists. Their work is delicate and beautiful and in some of the elongated figures there is a feeling of El Greco. The colours they use, near purple to brown, yellow, black and white, remain fresh from the moment of painting to the instant of sight.

Long ago the artists who made the first pictures carried their pigments in little horns secured to their belt, each one containing a different colour.

Various oxides of iron such as haematite or red ochre and limonite or yellow ochre account for the red and the yellow. For white, kaolin and the sticky juice of the plant *Asclepia gibba*. Manganese oxide or charcoal from the fire accounts for the black.

For every colour there was a different brush and brushes were made of bird feathers inserted in reeds.

For mixing red colours eland blood was used and as a mixing medium ostrich-egg yolk, and egg yolk was the mixing medium used by painters in tempera before oil paint came into general use in Europe.

Tsoe doesn't know this but he knows about pictures. He's seen them and knows the stories they tell.

I tell him about writing, which in its way is the same as a picture. It catches the story of a people and puts it down, not on rock but on paper.

It uses different signs which make pictures in the minds of those who have learned how to see. I tell him that in this way too, the stories of a people can be passed on and other people can come to know them.

I tell him how the going of his people grieves me. That I am writing down their stories as they were given to me so other people might one day know them and remember.

It's not the proper way. It's not how it ought to be done but I am doing it anyway, in the only way I know.

Bushmen are great storytellers and to properly understand a story one must hear it told with all its great drama and nothing left out and everything faithfully recounted.

A story properly told must fill the air with music in

the way the *t'kna* does. It must be full of resonance and open minor chords. It must be rich in timbre and at its heart there must be rhythm and truth.

Tsoe asks how these stories came to me. He knows of Bastiaan and my time with him and I tell him it was he who told me. He asks how Bastiaan came to know them and I say they came to him on the wind from a far-off place and floated into his ear.

He tells me he sees that my head is not always bent to my work. Sometimes I gaze out into the darkness and will sit there for a very long time looking out.

I tell him that is the way of it also. You must be still and wait and listen and if you listen well enough, the stories will come to you and when that happens, that is the moment to capture a story's essence, which is its soul, so you can pass it on to other men before you let it go. For stories have their journey too and we cannot detain them for long.

I tell Tsoe that any man's death diminishes us but the death of a storyteller is the worst death of all. The death of a storyteller sends a long, sad note ringing out over all of the world.

Of all the children of man the storytellers are the most loved, the strangest and the furtherest from the reach of other men.

When a storyteller dies he does not die alone. His stories untold, who live with him, must die with him also because that is their destiny.

The storytellers of his people carried inside them the Moon and the Hare, Mantis and the Antbear girl. If he had not told it, with the storyteller would die the story of the Morning Star and Lightning's Gift to Rain, the Wives of the Water, the lion's roar, the pipe of the night plover and even the self-pitying cry of the hyena who cries out for shame for itself.

All these are his and when the storyteller of a

people dies their stories die with him save those he has spoken and given life with his breath. These alone live on and are not buried with his body.

All things that are needed in this world may be broken over his *scherm* and the bush may reclaim them but these stories remain, sometimes resting in silence, until they once more find voice and come back to shake us and remind us and awaken the living.

The Bushmen have a rich language. It's beautiful to the ear and those who have studied it say it is denser and more compacted in meaning than any other tongue.

It carries inside it the secrets of the land. It is in this way such things that need to be known are passed from one generation to another, so those yet to come may know the way of it and live and not perish in this unrelenting place where !Goa has placed them.

When a Bushman speaks of himself he says he is the least. Every creature in creation, in this world which we know and all the other worlds which not every man can enter, takes precedence over him. His word for himself in his own language is as if to say: 'It is only me.'

I tell Tsoe it is this and many things other than this that people have a need to know now. The writing down of the stories, the small parcels I hand to the truck man, the officer in charge, so that he may send them to my uncle who will pass them on, are only the smallest part of the stories of his people.

I tell him, in this moment of his people leaving, what it is which troubles me. I tell him I fear others, who should know, may not be told that once they were here.

'The stars will know,' he says.

It is the stars who know the time at which we die.

When someone dies a star falls down in sadness and in sympathy and that's how we know they're gone.

He asks me if I have lost someone. I tell him I have. I have lost many who were dear to me and others I did not know but their loss is mine also and I must take it to myself.

I tell him I have lost my blood sister who was a part of myself and her life as precious to me as my own and how I grieve for her going.

'Did the stars tell you?' he says.

I tell him I saw no sign of it in the stars and he shakes his head.

'Then she will come to you,' he says.

I shake my head no. I say I do not think so.

'She will come,' he says. 'She will not go without taking her leave.'

My writing down of stories is not a thing my father considers a suitable job for a man. It's certainly not what he considers a suitable job for a Hartmann.

My father writes to me. We are in the laundry business now and all our laundry is dirty. This is what he says about the Truth Commission.

'They had the nerve to ask Koot to go,' he writes. 'Bloody cheek. Of course he said he wouldn't. That's the way things are now. We're supposed to stand up, cap in hand, and say how sorry we are. What it is we're supposed to be so sorry for I really don't know.'

My father is my father. He won't change. 'Oom' Faan knew it. Bastiaan knew it too in that first season. I see it now and I see something else also. Something I feared but did not know in that time of lightning when my father sent a boy up a tree a baboon and he came down a man.

I know now that my father is in me and I am in him

and although we both must fight for mastery one over the other, I am not my father.

He says the man responsible for sending the letter bomb to Beeky has been identified. He has been invited to go and have a look at him when he gives his evidence at the Truth and Reconciliation Commission.

It's suggested that if he admits to what he did and is sorry for it and seeks forgiveness, my father might like to be there in order to give it to him.

It is a 'free-for-all' my father says and I may also go if I'm inclined to. My 'Oom' Faan says it is something I should consider but I don't think I can do it, although not for the reason he thinks.

It isn't everyone who can look at the face of a killer without shrinking.

When someone dies violently, in the moment of death the image of the killer is engraved on the eyes of the dying. This is what people say. I don't know. I think perhaps the living carry that image with them also.

I am afraid to go. I keep away because I think if I see this man who took my sister's life and look him full in the face, what shall I see if not myself? For I too am a life-taker.

This is what I fear. It is what I turn from most of all.

These days people from all over the country are coming together in front of the Truth Commissioners. In school and church halls. In community centres. In any one of the places where people used to gather in that other time when things were different.

To talk to each other. To bring out into the open what my father calls the 'dirty laundry'. To see it for what it is and deal with it the best way they can.

'Caliban's kingdom now,' my father says. 'Anything goes these days. Everything decent gone down the drain. Expect the worst and you won't be disappointed.'

He thinks what is done is done and should be put behind us. Time will see to that. We don't need any bloody Truth Commission to help us do it. That is his view.

No use raking over old coals. The dead aren't going to rise up out of them. They have gone untimely and there's nothing we can do to bring them back and I wonder again at this strange land in which we live where we can neither live nor die in peace and the unquiet dead are all around us.

JEROME

The Solitary Song of a Yellow Bird

Their unit is disbanded. One minute there, the next not. The Captain says not to worry. The SAP is big enough to soak them all up. They'll get other jobs. They can take transfers and if they're offered early pension his advice is to grab the money while the grabbing's good.

'Buy a new car or something with it and then go out and look for other work.'

But you can see he's not happy about it.

'We did a good job and they know it,' he says. 'But the big boys haven't got the balls for it any more. They're too busy falling over themselves to hand the country over to the coons.'

Jerome doesn't care. As far as he's concerned they can do what they like with the country. Makes no odds to him. There's always a job for a man who's good with electrics. He can find a place on the railways or with Telkom. Someone will put in a good word for him and the job will be his and that'll be the end of the story.

After that, if people start digging around and asking questions, he'll be just another man doing another job, complaining about pay, saying what an arsehole the boss is and the blacks are such bloody fools anyway. Wherever they look all they'll find are men with no past and if they should ask no-one will remember anything.

That's what the Captain says. That's how it's meant to be, so that's how he thought it would be.

When they set up the Truth thing he still wasn't worried.

Doris says they'll be lucky to get to the bottom of anything and: 'If they do and they find the truth, I hope they bring some of it to this house. It seems to be in short supply around here.'

He told them he left Spin Street. He said, out of the blue, he got a better offer at Telkom. Working on phones.

'A step up in the world,' is what his mother says.

Doris gives him one of her looks, just like she always does and just like he always does, because he knows it gets on her tits, he gives her one of his specially nice smiles. The kind he'd give her if he really liked the old bitch.

The boys don't see each other any more, although sometimes you get a bit of news.

Like the time the Captain sent the word around about the Truth Commission.

If they want to they all have a chance to go in front of the Commission and get things off their chests and say whatever it was they want to say, but the word comes around the Captain says no.

No-one sees any of the big brass stepping forward. No sign of the ones who gave the orders and took them for shit and thought being boss kept their hands nice and clean and made them nice and sweet and clean as ice cream.

What's good enough for them's good enough for the rest. So no-one says anything. No-one's going to offer to carry the can and no-one's going to shop his mate either.

The Captain took early pension. He bought himself a nice little smallholding with peach trees on it and apricots and he's going to go in for dry fruit for export, because sending stuff out of the country is where the money is now.

Berry got a golden handshake and a testimonial. The last they heard he got a job in the Transvaal as head of security on a mine and his backside in butter.

Of all of them, it sounds as if Berry landed on his feet and did best of all and it was like the Captain said. As long as they keep their mouths shut nothing will happen and they'll all be OK.

It's hard to think of Berry without Robey because Robey was always there, but when it was over Berry was finished with Robey. When he went to the Transvaal he went by himself.

If you think about it now, it was as if Berry was some kind of king and all Robey was there for was to sing his praises. In Robey's eyes, everything Berry did was right.

So, it comes as a big surprise when it's in the newspaper that an ex-policeman is accused of crimes and is called to come in front of the Commission and Berry is the policeman and the person who put him away is Robey.

No-one thought Robey would be the one to tell. Berry can look as cocksure of himself as he likes, Robey telling will mean his fancy job down the drain. Berry won't like that. He'll find a way to sort Robey out for that and Robey must know it.

It's all in the paper what Robey had to say.

Jerome's mother sits with her tea in front of her and

reads it out to him. How Berry was Robey's hero and all his hopes were pinned on him. That he was almost like a god to him and as far as Robey was concerned, he practically walked on water.

'Isn't that a man you used to work with?' his mother says and Jerome says 'yes' without looking up and goes on with what he's doing.

As if it's the last thing in the world that he's interested in. As if it has nothing to do with him. Which it hasn't. He just did what they told him and the rest wasn't his business.

'It says it was him responsible for that student boy dying that time and the Hartmann girl. You remember when that happened, don't you, lovey?'

'Who says he did it?' Jerome wants to know. 'It may be what's in the newspaper but you can't believe everything you read in the newspaper. You said so yourself.'

'Even so, it was such a shame,' his mum says. 'A girl like that, from a family like that. She could have had anything in the world she wanted.'

'Well she can't any more, can she?' Jerome says. 'Because now she's dead.'

'No,' says his mum. 'I suppose she can't.'

His mother says it's in the paper that Robey's standing in front of everyone crying his eyes out, saying he can't live with himself if he can't get what he knows off his chest and all he wants is to tell the truth.

'It says here he can't sleep at night because of what he's done,' his mother says.

'Plenty of people sleeping very nicely and a very long sleep because of what he's done,' Doris says. 'It's because of him and people like him the country's in the mess it's in today and so many people are dead. For my part I think they should all swing and it wouldn't worry me at all.'

There's a photo of Berry in the paper and two lawyers who are speaking for him and Berry looks the same as he always does. Like butter wouldn't melt in his mouth. As if he's not a man who's ever even heard of the word sorry, never mind has any intention of using it.

'Isn't it just like the newspapers?' his mum says. 'We don't need to know all the details, thank you very much. Makes a person feel quite sick. And the families don't need it either. I'm sure the poor Hartmann family have had enough of it by now. You know what I mean. It's not very nice for them, is it?'

'If you don't like it you shouldn't read it,' Jerome says. 'No-one's making you.'

'You know me,' says his mum. 'I may be one of the living dead stuck in a place like this but I like to keep up to date with what's going on in the world.'

If she wants to keep up to date he could tell her a few things she won't find in the newspaper but he looks at her and he thinks, right deep down, she's just the same as everyone else. Just because you keep your mouth shut no-one thinks you might have a few stories of your own to pass on and maybe it's better that way.

CONRAD

Ochre Dust

The Army has begun its job. They've started rounding people up. It's easy. Because of the drought the Government has declared the area a disaster zone. They send in water trucks and people walk many miles, on bare feet on hot ground, carrying buckets and plastic bottles and even sheets of plastic and canvas to carry their water ration away in.

But the water-bearers from the Government come with a message.

The delivery of water is too costly. The water has to be carried from far away over long distances and men are needed and trucks and even so, there are too many in the wasteland and it will not be possible to bring water for all.

The rains will not come. Not today or tomorrow. Not the day after. Not soon. They are certain of this. They say so because there are men of great learning who have told them this is the way it will be.

The people know these things are possible. They have heard of it. They have known old people who were fully grown before they ever saw rain or walked in a river or saw children splash in mud.

It is possible. If Sun seeks vengeance and Rain holds back his horsemen this drought can go on for a very long time.

If the Government says they must move to where water is then they must prepare themselves and I see they know something the young officer in charge and his men do not know. But I have eyes and I know.

They take nothing with them. Neither bows nor arrows nor string for snaring. The take no knobkerries or pouches or fly whisks. The things they need in this world they have discarded. They have been broken and left behind as it is when someone dies and his *scherm* is broken down and his possessions strewn over the grave.

The officer in charge has made my father's house the gathering point and I have agreed to it. It's as good a place as any and people know where it is. The Army trucks roll into the yard and those who are ready to go wait in small clusters by the side of the house and at the yard's edge, and I stand on the stoep and watch the convoys being loaded.

It's very hot. The sun bakes down in trembling waves through the corrugated iron overhang and there's a smell of burning dust from the dry over-heated wooden pillars that support the roof.

I am a brown man now. Brown from too much time in the sun but I am not one of the brown men they have come for and the soldiers on convoy duty are polite to me and treat me with respect.

The Army is the Army and cannot change.

'Women and children in the front trucks,' shouts the officer in charge.

A small barefoot tracker in a faded brown felt hat translates and shoos at them with a show of waving hands and, small and ragged, one or two with their karosses about them but most with only their leather aprons, they go.

Army trucks are not made for such small people. They are much too high and someone has to bring an empty box to use as a step.

'Hurry it up,' the officer in charge says.

To me he says: 'No good them having long faces about it. Doesn't make sense. They can't stay here. They'll die.'

The young soldiers on this detail sometimes ask why Bushmen go so docilely. I tell them it's because they are different from us. It's not in their nature to resist. They would much rather run and hide and wait until the danger has passed than defend themselves by force.

I can see they find this hard to believe.

I tell them Bushmen have no concept of bravery, nor do they measure the significance of creatures by their ability to overcome or destroy those weaker than themselves. The creatures they admire are resourceful rather than brave.

This the young soldiers believe because they've been told that supremacy and bravery is the white man's preserve and other men are incapable of it. So they believe what I tell them but they don't understand.

'Settle down,' the officer in charge shouts and when they're all in the back of the truck the flap is folded up with a clang, the bolt shot into place and they're secured.

They sit side by side, with children on the shoulder and on the lap looking straight in front of them. Old ones who have seen too much and young ones who know nothing and cannot know what lies ahead.

I know what they know. Like the old ones I know what it is they're leaving. Like the old ones

I know they will never return here, or walk this land again, or know its secret places, or show them to their children and those coming after.

The truck engines beat into life. The Army detail in charge of this transportation swings up inside the open flapping doors of the cabs and the doors bang behind them.

Everything that moves makes dust now. The trucks pull away in a crimson pall of dust that hangs heavy on the air and that is how I see these people go. In a cloud of fire dust that reduces them to the very faintest outlines, with a sound like the terrible rumble of thunder I once feared so much, and the dust gets in everywhere.

It dusts my face ochre as a death mask in an ancient Egyptian tomb painting. It wafts into my eyes and eyelashes and hair and when I look again, even before the dust has settled, they're gone, disappeared from sight and gone for ever as if they'd never been.

The last of the people are gone. My job, I suppose, is complete. It is just Tsoe and me left now. And the great anvil that is the flatland and the burning hammer that is the sun and the profound silence that seeps into my father's house, in which I try to finish my task and write down such stories as I know, before the wind blows them away.

Tsoe has given consideration to the things I told him and my enterprise, which keeps me busy and away from the city, has captured his interest and his imagination.

'It will be as if they still lived,' he says. 'It will be as if their footprints are still in the sand.'

I say nothing but I do not think so and he stands for a long time and quietly watches me and then, while

I'm still bent to my work, he asks me another question.

'Have you no story of your own?' he asks. 'Is that why you catch these stories that are given to you by others and put them down?'

He hunches over on the bleached boards of the stoep and shows, in mime, myself with my head down bent to my work, writing with my pen and I look at him and turn away and he straightens himself up at once, concerned he has offended me.

It is not so. I turn away from what he asks out of shame and because what he says hurts me and I cannot show him my face.

'Every man has a story,' I say but I will not look at him when I say it and he says nothing and asks nothing more.

CONRAD

I, and Not Another

I have decided to go before the Truth Commission. My father is beside himself with anger. Until I have 'come to my senses' he will not have me in his house.

'I can't believe it,' he says. 'When Faan came to this house, to this room and told me what you proposed to do, I couldn't believe what I was hearing.'

I can see, even now, he wants me to tell him some terrible mistake has been made. He wants me to say it isn't too late for me to change my mind but it is and I have nothing to say to him. So I keep silent but he does not.

'Why tell Faan?' he wants to know. 'That was the first embarrassment; the first insult. Why send him? Why not come to me yourself? Why not tell me man to man?'

He looks at me hard-eyed, expecting, I think, an answer. Knowing I have nothing to say that he would wish to hear.

'I'll tell you why,' he says. 'You went to Faan because you didn't have the balls to face me yourself. You knew I'd put a stop to it. I could if I wanted to, you know. I still have some connections that count.'

As if it would make any difference. I am beyond my father's 'connections' now. I am beyond any 'connection' that can't show me a path back to that man I once was.

Because of what I have done.

I have been a party to atrocities committed as part of special forces operations and I have asked for and been granted leave to appear before the Truth and Reconciliation Commission so I may stand up and speak about it.

I can speak for no other man but I can speak for myself and I must.

This is what has turned my father white-faced with fury. It's the reason I'm back in this place, in his house, under the lash of his tongue which in these new days has lost its power to hurt me.

'At first, when Faan came to me, I thought it was about that business with Beatrice,' my father says. 'If you'd wanted to have your say about that it would have been a waste of time but that, at least, I could have understood.'

I am silent in the face of my sister's name spoken in this room in this way but the reason for my silence eludes my father. He does not even begin to understand.

'I would have expected anything from her,' he says. 'I expected other things from you. I didn't expect this.'

Nothing has changed. Josias's silver tray, decanters half-filled, glasses sparkling, ice that never seems to melt; all this is on the side table just as it always is.

I could close my eyes and still see it all clearly, slightly readjusted by the new wife but unchanging all the same. Everything unchanged except me. I am different.

'Don't you think this family has had enough of the spotlight?' my father wants to know. 'This so-called "Commission" is a bloody sideshow, you know. It's like a soap opera. It's on television. Can you believe that? Half the bloody country sitting with their eyes glued to it just in case they miss something.

'Do you think they even begin to know what it's all about? Of course they don't. Bloody fools. Put anything on the box and shove them in front of it and they believe it. Is that what you want? Do you want to spill your guts out on TV and make a public spectacle of yourself and fools of the rest of us?'

There is no Beeky. There is no soft sweet trail of roses that mark the path my mother once walked. I am a man. My father is a man. The full force of his anger is directed against me and I detach myself in that way I have learned to do. I stand outside myself and this is what I see.

I know now what the bush people say is true. I am a man and the least and 'only me'. I am answerable to myself and I must do what I know is right.

'I think it's a bit bloody late in the day for you to wake up and discover that a soldier's job involves killing people. That's all it was. A job. A duty. No more and no less. No need for a sob story,' my father says.

Behind him, from the wall of pictures, Steynberg smiles and it seems as if he's smiling directly at me and I can see I have been deceived. I had thought him a man, fit to be a soldier. I see now he was only a boy with all a boy's sweetness still in his smile.

My father's face, livid, disbelieving and uncomprehending, comes between Steynberg and me but his power over me is vanished. It is gone for ever.

* * *

I have forgotten how it is in the city. I cannot sleep here. There are too many lights. They blot out the stars.

On such nights no man in the bush would venture out. If it should happen, as it sometimes does, that the heavenly compass of stars refuses to show itself, a man would be lost indeed and totally without direction.

While my uncle's house sleeps I sit on the stoep enfolded in darkness and my head and my heart are filled with the things that have happened to me, and my uncle, sleepless as I am, comes out in his dressing gown, pipe in hand and sits next to me as he used to in the old hunting days.

He says he will go to the Commission with me. He wants to go. He says it will honour him if he can sit beside me when I'm called, to be there on his own behalf and on behalf of our family to show his support and bear witness to what I have to say.

'It isn't right for you to do this alone,' he says. 'We're all responsible for these terrible things that have happened. When the time comes for shouldering that responsibility none of us can turn away. We must all bear the burden.'

My uncle's support has not made him popular with my father and his friends.

'Let the others turn their backs and go by on the other side of the road,' my uncle says. 'Let this old man do the right thing for once. Allow me the privilege of walking beside you.'

I tell him I would prefer to go alone.

I tell him I have not feared the sword. I should like not to fear the Judgement when it comes. It is I and none other who have done the things I have done. It is I and I alone who must take responsibility for them.

My uncle is my uncle. Our ghosts are the same

ghosts, known and loved by us both. They are with us when I say this and the sweetness of their presence is too much for me. I am unmanned too easily these days and I turn my face away and we have stood at this place before, he and I, but this time it is different.

I feel his hand clasp my shoulder and I wonder at the distance a man such as he has travelled, who once could not touch a boy to comfort him but now can take a man by the shoulder and offer in the warmth of his grasp both compassion and consolation.

The Coming of Rain

It is Tsoe who tells of the coming of rain. The humidity is high and the heat unbearable. The air is sulphurous with a hot choking wave that obscures the sun.

I know how it is. In times like this there are days like this and hopes build up but they are often false alarms but Tsoe is quite certain and I believe him.

The wind picks up and changes and everything is as it was before but by mid-afternoon the clouds to the north start to build up. White at first but growing in size and number and darkening and burgeoning upwards like mighty citadels of the air.

The light is peculiar. It has the opaque luminosity that presages the coming of some natural phenomenon and a distant rumble of thunder from hundreds of miles away heralds its arrival.

When the rains come after prolonged drought this is the way it is.

The first drops are heavy and full. They fall singly and dust rises up around them in small puffs. Then the heavens open and the rain falls down in torrents.

In a few minutes there are pools everywhere. Little rivers begin running again and feed their larger sisters and these larger sisters feed the pans and make small lakes and the dunes wet with rain are deep-etched against the pale light and the strong clear colour of brick.

It doesn't last long. In less than half an hour the force of the storm is spent. The clouds move away to the south-east. The sun shines again and the ground steams and the steam sighing up scents the air with the smell of wet earth which, in these dry lands, is the most beautiful perfume in all of the world.

Trees and shrubs are washed clean of their dust coats. Dragonflies come and tadpole shrimps. The birds come back. Starlings, weavers, lovebirds and flycatchers. There are doves again and they coo to each other.

Frogs appear from nowhere. Small sand and rain frogs and bullfrogs, all of them croaking together in their discordant evening symphony.

It is beautiful when water stands in huge lakes on the drylands. The sun sinking in the sky comes to see it and casts its reflection on the mirror of this water in this strange place and in the moment before it sinks all of its great solitude is reflected in this water and there are no eyes to see it but our own.

That night I sit on the stoep and Tsoe stands at the side of the stoep rail. All around us, in darkness, the land is renewing itself.

We'll walk tomorrow and in the days after and while we walk, the world will be transforming itself into a paradise of unexpected beauty.

The animals will come back. The springbok and eland, the wildebeest and the gemsbok and the duiker.

The flowers will come too. Shyly at first and then in

a glory of colour. Purple cat's-tails, pink and white three thorn and there will be the occasional flash of white and red carpet flowers.

The house stands open. Every door and window, open as wide as it can go, to the coolness carried in on the damp air and we are privileged, Tsoe and I, to see this rebirth and this is what is in my heart as I sit on the stoep steps and look out at the night.

In my father's house at Drummer's Hill the house servants say that this time after rain, when every door and window is open to the night, is the time for ghosts because there's nothing to contain them and every chance for them to fly free.

But these are old stories and we never believed them and my ghosts are hooked like Devil's Thorn inside me and although I have been drawn by the light, Devil's Thorn can never come out and I must take them with me wherever I go.

I think of Beeky. I would like to have held my sister and kept her safe but she's gone from me now and I wish, in that other place where she is, she will never be contained and always fly free.

'Listen,' Tsoe says.

He stands in front of me amber, glowing with light from the house and the house, like the rest of the world, is in celebration of rain and all its lights are burning.

The stoep is washed with light. It etches out the wooden balustrades and the old cane chair where I like to sit and the *riempiebank*, the wooden bench with cow-hide strips for seats and a back that stands against the wall.

The house is so radiant, anyone seeing it from afar must think it's a beacon to guide men on, along their way on this strange and special night.

'Listen,' Tsoe says.

It's the darkness he's looking at and I turn my head towards it and there's a strange and sudden sound. A great flap of wings and a rush of air and before I have time to be alarmed I see it.

A spotted eagle owl. A big bird and alone. In a swoop of wings it drops down and comes to rest in the yard in front of us and we are above as if on a platform and it is below settling down, looking up.

There's a small flap and its wings fold back and it stands still where it is and fixes us with its strange yellow gaze.

Tsoe takes hold of me. He folds his hand around my upper arm and his face turned away towards the bird is full of wonder.

'She is come,' he says. 'It is done. She will not come again.'

This owl is a big bird and young, feathered with finely barred pale grey plumage. It stands tall for a bird, quite certain of itself, its eyes still upon us, its iris-yellow bill cocked to one side, its yellowish claws on the ground.

We look at it. It regards us and for a full moment we three creatures of this world and another are held together in the timelessness from which we all come, to which we all go and then, with a turn and a mighty sweep of wings, it is gone.

Bushmen say when someone dies the heart cries out in anguish as the feeling strings are cut and this is why our pain is so acute in the face of such loss.

Since the coming of the bird I am different.

The wind has turned and brought those that are gone closer to me and I can look at them now with tenderness and contain my pain and something in me has changed.

When Tsoe sees me at my table I have a book new

to him and I beckon him closer because I want him to see it.

He knows me now and knows about writing and I put the book in his hands and ask him to hold it and look at it. I show what it is and we look at the pages together and I tell him about it and I know now that it isn't death that ties my sister and me together; it is life.

I tell Tsoe this is the book my sister made for me before she went on her journey. When he sees it, I tell him that in it he sees all her life's leavings and that other, the emptiness unwritten beside it, is mine.

Since the coming of the bird the wind has turned and something in me has turned also and I am changed.

I look out at the flatland and it shimmers with sunlight and in that mirage floating before me is all of my life and a story untold. Drifting inside it is my sister and the house at Drummer's Hill and Steynberg and Josias's tray and my mother with her grave box of memories and her bright scarf of clouds.

Men's voices call me and the rumble of thunder. The umbrella girl's falling and the small pulse point beating before Steynberg died. Bastiaan's with me, with smoke all around him, firesmoke and pipe smoke and the clouds tall as mountains and the coming of rain.

When I was a boy in my first season my father sent for an old Bushman tracker and gave him a job which was to be my 'boy' and teach me the ways of the bush and he became my teacher and in our days together, in a great gift of stories, he told me of his people and gave me more than I knew.

Each man is different. Each man is unique. Each man has a story which is no less than his life and he must live it and grow it and seek out its heart because when we are gone and our voices are silent, it will be all that is left to speak what we were.

When I didn't understand, Bastiaan told me again the high art of the storyteller and !Goa's great gift to the one chosen to keep safe all stories and pass them on one to another and hold them in readiness till the world needs them again.

He told me then, in those days when I did not know, that a story once told and told truly is the ostrich-feather wand before the wind that marks the parting of ways before we move on.

I have told this to Tsoe and he holds it inside himself now and it's his story too and I have told him much else beside.

Tsoe asks what will happen when my work is ended and my story told. He asks if the offering of my life to these pages will mean the end of it and the end of my days in this place and I have thought about it and know the answer, which once I did not know.

I tell him in the bush way, which is the way we both know, that when my work is done and my life truly told, my life will be ended but one life is all life so, in that same moment, my life will also begin again.

THE END

FRIEDA AND MIN

Pamela Jooste

FROM THE PRIZE-WINNING AUTHOR OF *DANCE WITH A POOR MAN'S DAUGHTER*

'ONE OF THE NEW BREED OF WOMEN WRITERS IN SOUTH AFRICA WHO ARE TELLING OUR STORY WITH SUCH POWER AND TALENT'
Cape Times

When Frieda first met Min, with her golden hair and ivory bones, what struck her most was that Min was wearing a pair of African sandals, the sort made out of old car tyres. She was a silent, unhappy girl, dumped on Frieda's exuberant family in Johannesburg for the summer of 1964 so that her mother could go off with her new husband. In a way, Min and Frieda were both outsiders – Min, raised in the bush by her idealistic doctor father, and Frieda, daughter of a poor Jewish saxophone player, who lived almost on top of a native neighbourhood. The two girls, thrown together – the 'white kaffir' and the poor Jewish girl – formed a strange but loyal friendship, a friendship that was to last through the terrible years of oppression and betrayal during the time of South Africa under Apartheid.

'A NOVEL THAT EVERYONE SHOULD READ . . . HAS THAT RARE ABILITY TO BE BOTH MOVING AND FUNNY . . . DESERVES ALL THE PRAISE THAT IT WILL SURELY GET'
Pamela Weaver, *Examiner*

'HAS A GOOD STORY TO TELL AND SHE TELLS IT WELL . . . HAS LOST NONE OF THE QUALITIES THAT MADE *DANCE WITH A POOR MAN'S DAUGHTER* SO CREDIBLE'
Isobel Shepherd-Smith, *The Times*

0 552 99758 7

BLACK SWAN

DANCE WITH A POOR MAN'S DAUGHTER

Pamela Jooste

'IMMENSELY MOVING AND READABLE'
Isobel Shepherd-Smith, *The Times*

'My name is Lily Daniels and I live in the Valley, in an old house at the top of a hill with a loquat tree in the garden. We are all women in our house. My grandmother, my Aunt Stella with her hopalong leg, and me. The men in our family are not worth much. They are the cross we have to bear. Some of us, like my mother, don't live here any more. People say she went on the Kimberley train to try for white and I mustn't blame her because she could get away with it even if we didn't believe she would.'

Through the sharp yet loving eyes of eleven-year-old Lily we see the whole exotic, vivid, vigorous culture of the Cape Coloured community at the time when apartheid threatened its destruction. As Lily's beautiful but angry mother returns to Cape Town, determined to fight for justice for her family, so the story of Lily's past – and future – erupts. *Dance with a Poor Man's Daughter* is a powerful and moving tribute to a richly individual people.

'HIGHLY READABLE, SENSITIVE AND INTENSELY MOVING . . . A FINE ACHIEVEMENT'
Mail and Guardian, South Africa

'TOUGH, SMART AND VULNERABLE . . . EMBLEMATIC OF AN ENTIRE PEOPLE'
Independent

'I COULD HARDLY PUT THIS BOOK DOWN'
Cape Times

WINNER OF THE COMMONWEALTH BEST FIRST BOOK AWARD FOR THE AFRICAN REGION

WINNER OF THE SANLAM LITERARY AWARD

WINNER OF THE BOOK DATA'S SOUTH AFRICAN BOOKSELLERS' CHOICE AWARD

0 552 99757 9

BLACK SWAN